THE TASTE BENEATH

DANIEL MUNRO

For Stanley Frederick Brown.
Forever in our hearts, forever giving us strength.

And

For Alfie.
The real Ironman.

AUGUST 2030, SIX WINTERS AFTER THE FAST WAR ENDED

From the lookout point where he hid with an L96 sniper rifle, a bag of beetroot, and three litres of grape water, he watched the enemy dance around the top of Maidhill. They weren't even trying to hide themselves in the treeline. The hyena-like laugh howled louder, like they were ridiculing the last attempt at killing them off.

Ryan moved his eye away from the scope when a sharp gust of wind punched him in the face. After taking his finger off the trigger, he reached into the bag and pulled out the last bottle. He hadn't even noticed it had been hours since he drank anything—the activity in the distance had kept him eagle-eyed on his duty.

Within the safety of the vineyard's walls, the post-war survival had offered everything possible to test Ryan's humanity and resolve. As the world decayed into an unnerving silence, the life he lived revolved around a strict moral compass. That's how he kept his family and community alive. Though the last fight was over seven months ago, it still ate at his sanity, pushing him down a one-way rabbit hole.

Now the enemy was back and as suicidally aggressive as before.

How much more of himself would Ryan have to sacrifice to keep everyone alive? He already felt like he was becoming a monster; maybe the threat across the road had more in common with him than he'd ever want to admit.

He'd have to spill more blood.

For the first time since the end of The Fast War, the thought of killing didn't bother him.

Not one bit.

1

---

utumn 2029, ten months earlier:

A pair of pounding footsteps and high-pitched giggling prepared Ryan for what was about to happen. He laughed in the mirror while brushing his teeth, dipping his toothbrush in the bowl of homemade toothpaste. His dark-blond dreadlocks hung over his shoulders, and bags had formed under his bright green eyes—the noticeable sign he'd done his best to stay awake for tonight's shift.

The door handle rattled impatiently.

"Daddy, let me in!" Maisie laughed from the other side.

"Daddy's not here," he shouted back. "Please leave a message!"

"I'll tell mummy I saw you smoking!"

Ryan's faced dropped.

Spitting out the remaining toothpaste and gulping a mouthful of water, he leaned to the right and unlocked the door. The handle slowly twisted, creaking the door inwards. Maisie was revealed like a prize on a game show. She stood straight, wearing blue baggy jeans, a pink T-shirt, and had ice-blonde pigtails. Her broad smile displayed a mischievous pride as she'd just outwitted her adoptive father.

"When did you see me smoking?" Ryan put his hands on his hips,

"I didn't," she chuckled. "I just wanted you to let me in."

Ryan burst into laughter and opened his arms. Maisie obliged by jumping into them.

"Why are you not dressed yet?" the six-year-old asked.

Ryan looked down at his white vest and black jogging bottoms.

"I am!" he protested.

"You haven't got your socks on."

"That's because Daddy's feet get sweaty, and then they start to smell, like you, smelly bum!" He tickled her, bringing another roar of laughter between the two.

Gently lowering her to the floor, he grabbed fresh pair of white socks and sat on the chair next to the sink.

"How come you sleep here on work nights?" she quizzed.

"I've said before, when I work nights, I have to stay here because of something dangerous."

"Is it a gun?"

"Maybe."

"Do you have it here?"

"Is this another day of non-stop questions?" He rolled the first sock over his left foot.

"Is that a problem?" She smirked.

Ryan could only admire the wittiness she acquired from her birth mother, his former next-door neighbour. "Yes, it's here, but it stays hidden at all times." That was a lie, he slept with it next to him. Whereas now, or whenever Maisie would be around, he hid it behind one of the ceiling tiles.

His night-shift bedroom was one of the smallest in the building. On the left was a double mattress with a dirty clothes basket at the foot of it. A built-in shower stood in the opposite corner, a chair and sink on the right-side wall.

"How can you sleep with your smelly shoes next to your head?" She scrunched her face as she passed him a pair of red running trainers.

"I sleep in a room next to you five nights a week," Ryan said with a grin. "Anyway, I've got a present for you."

"A cat?" Her eyes lit up.

"No, we have enough of them trying to set the traps off already," Ryan huffed. He turned to the back of the chair, reaching inside the front pocket of his dirty hoodie, then extending his arm out to her.

"A red ball?" she frowned.

"It's not a ball."

"What is it?"

"A tomato."

"Tomato?" She took it from his hand.

"Yes, it's a form of fruit."

"Fruit?" Maisie's face expressed confusion; Ryan forgot that she had never heard the term. The only fruit they grew were the vines for grape water and the wild berries they'd foraged. Other than that, she had only ever consumed the vegetables, grains, and eggs they produced onsite.

"I'll explain on the way down to see Cooper, he's gonna show us what his new rice-growing project." He tied the last trainer and stood.

"Cooper said he'll show me how to feed the chickens tomorrow," she smiled.

"I thought you were learning that next spring at school?" Ryan pulled the door open, holding Maisie's right hand as they stepped into the long, thin corridor.

"Cooper says we should learn as much about the animals and plants as we can." She jumped beside him.

Wise idea, Ryan thought, closing the door behind him and locking it in its thin balsa wood frame.

They descended the staircase to ground level, exiting into the empty cafeteria and turning left out the first exit. Ryan heard the basement generators beneath as they approached the southeast corner of the building, the wine estate's own cinema, previously used as the introduction for guest tours of the site. A large, square room with blacked-out walls; it held enough seating space for two hundred moveable chairs.

"Okay, no touching when we get inside. We don't know what equipment he's using in there," Ryan instructed as they reached the white double doors.

"Okay Daddy." Maisie held both arms out. Ryan picked her up and creaked the door handle, pulling it towards him.

A wave of hot air hit as they were greeted by an array of bright lights suspended ten feet above the ground and twenty feet from the ceiling. Sheets of plastic hung down, creating a makeshift room underneath the light display. The cinema-screen wall on the opposite side was no longer visible, and the carpet had been completely removed, exposing the concrete underneath.

"Cooper?" Ryan called out.

A silhouette moved behind the plastic sheeting. "Come on in," a thick, Texan accent replied. "It's safe."

"I've got Maisie with me."

"Thank you for my 'motato," she shouted.

"Tomato," Ryan corrected.

As they approached the sheeting, he pulled a strip to the side. Cooper stood in the centre of rows and rows of soil patches, all individually lined with a wooden border. The American stood at six-foot four inches, had shaved red hair and chin stubble. Ryan wasn't surprised to see him donning his favourite grey overalls and brown work boots.

"Welcome to Uncle Ben's," Cooper joked.

Ryan gazed at the lights above. There was protective netting between them and the floor.

At the end of each row, a hose slowly trickled water into the soil. Ryan saw they all fed out into the water purifying room next door. There was a mild roar, like that of a stove's burner, coming from outside of the plastic sheets.

"What's that's sound?" he asked.

"Patio heater. Has to be turned on for two hours of the day. The lights create heat, but not enough." Cooper pointed to the left side of the theatre. "I thought it was best to leave the heater by the fire exit, worst-case scenarios and all."

"Yeah, good idea mate." Ryan looked back to the hoses. "And the water?"

"Syphoned from the shower supply, only need ten litres a day once I've filled these up."

"Good stuff,"

"Well, can I cook, or can't I?" Cooper jumped over the rows of soil towards the pair.

"You can do more than that my friend, a hell of a lot more." Ryan kissed Maisie on the cheek with excitement and shook Cooper's hand. "How long before first harvest is ready?"

"Estimate five months until we start harvesting and hold it. We still have enough rice in storage for two winters." Cooper smiled with pride.

"What is all that for?" Maisie pointed at the soil.

"Rice, we're starting to grow our own rice now."

Cooper started to explain to Maisie about how he found rice seeds on his last excursion on an abandoned farm on the outskirts of Brighton, forty miles south.

"How much will one harvest produce?" Ryan lowered Maisie to the ground.

"Judging by the books, just under a ton." Cooper put his hands on his hips. "I'll set up a point in the corner of the room. We can thresh the rice there, out of the way and all."

"That's more than enough for all of us," Ryan gasped. They were well ahead of the day when they depleted all their salvaged rice.

"I've had to power up the third generator just to keep these lights on. We have enough oil for it until next summer, but I think we should start thinking about growing more corn or spreading out our search to places we haven't been yet," Cooper informed him.

"Okay, one thing at a time. Let's just celebrate what you've done here first." Ryan put his hand on Cooper's shoulder. "Maisie, shall we go tell Mummy the good news?"

"Yeah!" She jumped in excitement. "I can show her my 'motato."

Ryan shook Cooper's hand again, thanked him once more, and exited through the gap in the plastic sheet with Maisie following. He pushed the doors open and let his daughter through, making sure they closed behind them.

They turned right into the reception, which was full of rye corn in large bread trays, and stepped out the main entrance of the winery building.

The sun was roasting; not a cloud in sight.

They held hands as they crossed over the footbridge and onto the gravel car park, heading onto the main driveway that ran through the middle of the vast, protected land that they called home. In two minutes, they reached the correct part of the vegetable patch on their left.

"Okay, let's try to find Mummy in all this." Ryan eyeballed the vast wall of corn in front of them.

"Don't need to," said a familiar voice from the inside. Cassy appeared with both arms cradling a huge bunch of sweetcorn cobs.

At four-foot-seven, most of the vegetation they grew was taller than her. Dropping the bunches into a wheelbarrow and huffing at Ryan, she looked exhausted, although still beautiful to him. She had tied her long, dark hair back, the fringe cut perfectly above her large brown eyes, and her button nose was covered in a layer of sweat. She rubbed her hands over her black dungarees and smudged her white T-shirt.

"Busy?" Ryan knew that would wind her up.

Before she had a chance to reply, Maisie ran towards her with open arms.

"Careful sweetie, my hands are dirty." She tried to back away. That didn't deter Maisie from wrapping her arms around her adoptive mum's waist. Cassy shot Ryan an unimpressed look.

"It'll wash out, it's fine," he said, shrugging.

"Sure." She glared at him.

"We come bringing good news." He kissed her on the cheek. "Cooper can start growing rice now. I've seen the setup—it's ready to roll."

The scowl from her face faded, replaced with her gorgeous smile.

"That's great news," she laughed and kissed Ryan on the lips, one of his dreadlocks getting caught in her mouth. She turned her attention to Maisie. "What have you got there?"

"A 'motato," she replied.

"Tomato, Maisie," Cassy chuckled. "Can you help me wheel these in?" She pointed to several wheelbarrows on the driveway, all over-flowing with sweetcorn.

"Of course, my lady," Ryan said, trying to impersonate a posh accent. "On a serious note, I'll wash her clothes tomorrow when I do my lot."

"Thank you." Cassy smiled and kissed him again. "Who have you got on night shift with you tonight?"

"Er... three outside and one in the second reception." Ryan tried to remember the rota.

"Well, it's nearly midday. I think you should go to bed, make sure you've got enough energy for tomorrow's laundry day." She winked at him.

Ryan grabbed the handles of the nearest wheelbarrow. "I see, get me to do your dirty work, and then tell me to get lost."

"Pretty much," she kissed him one more time. "Sleep well baby, I'll see you tomorrow."

———

On multiple occasions throughout his life, Ryan had heard the phrase: *you don't really miss something until it's gone.*

As he looked out towards what should have been a brightly lit, dual carriageway shining light over the grounds, he realised he missed the illumination. He even missed the sound of commuters making their way home from work, lorry drivers heading north towards the M25, joining the inevitable rush hour that would bring the motorway to a standstill in the late afternoon or morning's early hours.

That was life then—life across most of the developed world.

Now, the lonely silence of the night was only periodically broken by the two idiot cows trundling around their paddock, followed by the occasional gust of wind.

The winery's guttering spotlights only shone to about ten metres effectively. Darkness engulfed the four-hundred metres of vegetable patches, animal enclosures and grapevines that circled the building out to their protective border.

From a distance, a person wouldn't be able to see the trench that circled the building like a dried-out moat, letting night shifts' patrol outside at night without having to venture into the dark.

Ryan stubbed his cigarette against the trench wall and flicked the safety on his handgun, doing his usual admiring gaze at it before tucking it down the back of his joggers.

He hadn't known anything about firearms before the war.

From the day the bombs went off, they salvaged over five-hundred and fifty guns from fallen policemen and the enemy of The Fast War.

There was the inevitable trial-and-error with learning about how to maintain different weapons, store them safely, identify ammunition types, and most importantly, how to use them correctly.

Ryan had no idea about the history of the Glock.17, apart from that it packed a hell of a kick, and since being in his possession, he'd had to kill more than enough people with it.

"Mikey wants to see you," Cooper's voice caught him off guard.

"Jesus," Ryan put his hand on his chest. "Scared the living piss out of me."

"Sorry," the American chuckled before turning serious. The guttering spotlights glowed on his orange hair. "But it's urgent."

"Did he say what?"

"Yes, but he wants to tell you in person."

"Can you take over from my lookout point?"

"Sure."

"Thank you."

It was rare Mikey would pull Ryan off his duty at night shift.

They had been best friends since secondary school, which felt like another lifetime ago now. They sought out shelter at the vineyard as The Fast War tore across the continent, helping to secure it as a safety point for other survivors and establish the community through the years of relentless survival.

Given Mikey's experience as a fully trained paramedic and Ryan's ability to make the tough decisions that the world kept offering, they were elected as two of the three joint leaders.

Ryan walked clockwise around the trench, ducked under the entrance's footbridge, and turned right, facing the wooden door that led to the winery's basement. Three slow, hard knocks signalled the eyepiece to slide open, revealing Mikey's tired, brown eyes. The red, bloodshot veins nearly dominated the white sclera.

Two loud clangs followed. Mikey slowly pulled the door open for Ryan to step inside. The room which had been dubbed as the second reception looked like an entrance to an underground cave. The support beams and dangling lightbulbs gave the room a feeling that you stepped onto the set of a wild, adventure movie.

"You wanted to see me?" Ryan closed the door behind him and reached for the bolts.

"Don't lock it," Mikey yawned, stretching his arms. He wore his favourite white T-shirt, blue joggers and white gym shoes. Even on a night shift, he still maintained his young, Italian looks. Clean shaved, olive skin, and jet-black, side-parted hair; his appearance had never changed since they first met. "Cooper knows to lock it behind him if the outside team has to come in."

"Where are we going?"

"Cafeteria. All my notes are up there."

Mikey opened the door into the winery's basement; Ryan hated this room. The only source of light came from the stairwell fifty metres to the front and left, which was only candlelight. The rest of the double, football pitch-sized area was total darkness and silence.

What hid in the darkness was actually the purified grape water. Thousands of litres bottled up, stored in cages and wine racks, along with the occasional cage of wine that does get harvested for the group. Why not? They were living in a vineyard after all.

Their footsteps echoed off the tiled floor as they paced to the stairwell, which corkscrewed through three more floors and eventually opened into the rooftop restaurant. It was one flight of stairs to the ground floor's cafeteria, which was half the size of the storage basement and had a fitted, dome roof of glass overhead.

The remaining dinner tables had been arranged into eight rows. Mikey pulled a chair out at the end nearest the stairwell. Notepads and pens were sprawled out, along with the familiar empty water bottles you'd see from anyone who was on a night shift.

"How's it looking out there?" Mikey asked without looking up, scribbling on a tattered piece of paper.

"Dark and quiet," Ryan replied, taking his black hoodie off and wrapping it around his waist. "What's up?"

"Doc thinks he can get the road lights working." Mikey didn't hesitate in getting straight to the point, referring to the third joint-leader of their community.

"Really?" Ryan knew Doc could easily find a grain of rice in a sandpit—the guy loved problem-solving and fixing things—but even this news was a shock.

"Yeah, the whole carriageway outside our eastern wall." Mikey leaned forward and picked up one of the notepads. "He's written down what he'll need here."

"Surely their circuits would've been fried?"

"Doc says the lights were shut off during the day of the bombs. Repairs were being done. So, it's likely they'd have been safe from the..." Mikey clicked his fingers trying to remember the phrase.

"E.M.P," Ryan interjected.

"Yeah, that," Mikey frowned. "Other than a few vehicles and all electrical equipment that was switched off at the time, the lights might have been one of the few things unaffected."

"Power source?"

"He's going for solar, there are enough panels still untouched in... let's see here." Mikey eyed over his notes. "Six warehouses in Surrey, assuming they haven't deteriorated. He says using the generator would be too loud, and we don't want to start eating into more of our oil supply."

Used vegetable and corn oil was the main source for running electricity generators since The Fast War finished. Not many other people seemed aware of that, which left a lifetime supply for the group to salvage, along with the methanol and sodium hydroxide required to make the fuel useable. It took Doc and Cooper five months of research to figure out the correct ratio; luckily, just in time before the syphoned petrol ran out.

Mikey handed the notepad over.

"Why do I feel like there's a 'but'?" Ryan groaned, pulling out the chair opposite his best friend.

"Because there is something else we need to talk about." Mikey put his hands together and leant on the table, his eyes showing a glimpse of anxiousness. The candles created dancing shadows across his stern look. "You know Doc and Cooper went on an excursion after you went to bed?"

"Yeah, I was asleep when they returned, too."

"Well, on their way back, they found one of our refuge signs, in Reigate."

The town of Reigate was a thirty-minute drive away.

"Okay, what does that mean?" Ryan asked, not really getting the point.

"We've never put a sign there."

"We had a big storm not too long ago, any chance it could have been blown there?"

Mikey exhaled sharply, clearly irritated that Ryan wasn't getting the picture. "Even if it was possible for a sign to blow perfectly along the road for twenty miles, it doesn't explain how it was found, standing up, pointing in our direction."

That hit Ryan in the gut, and he started to share Mikey's anxiousness.

"Someone's moved our signs, I get you," Ryan said, tapping his finger on the table. "Could it be more survivors just stretching the message for their friends?"

"I doubt it," Mikey answered coldly.

"Why?"

"If you're looking for refuge and you find it, do you walk twenty miles back to leave a sign for some friends, then walk another twenty miles back to the refuge?" Mikey used his fingers to imitate the walking part. "No, you'd go to the refuge and tell them about your friends."

Mikey was right, no sane person would risk a forty-mile walk when they could have instant access to food and water.

"So, potentially there are people out there, fed enough to do that and not let us know their presence. Why?" Ryan questioned.

"I couldn't wait until the end of your shift. I have to say this now."

"Okay."

"We need to go out and find who this is."

A silence fell after his suggestion, the two men staring at each other until Ryan gave in, rubbing his eyes. "Okay, I'm with you," he stood. "Can I get a bit of your water, please?"

Mikey stood with him and handed over an unopened bottle.

"How seriously should we prepare for this?" Ryan twisted the cap off the bottle.

"Very. We've made it clear on all our signs that if anyone requires help to go to the church in the town centre, ring the bell, then wait for us to come and aid them." Mikey grabbed his blue hoodie off the seat. "If these people don't need help and can afford a forty-mile journey to move our signs, what's their motive? And who are they directing our way?"

2

I f it wasn't for the discolouration on the sycamore's leaves, the sunshine and heat could have fooled anyone into thinking it was summer. The trees ran aside the battered driveway, following it in between the vegetable patches and animal enclosures and all the way up to the ground's perimeter.

Ryan stood in the top floor restaurant, overlooking the front of the vineyard with a smile on his face at both the safety and sight that his former workplace provided. Before the war ravaged the continent, he was head chef for the very room he was standing in. Serving fifty covers a night on a refined, fine dining taster menu, he even achieved a small bit of a local celebrity status.

The vineyard attracted customers worldwide who wanted to see the hidden gem on the border of the Surrey Hills, bringing tourism to the town of Maidville, and turning profits well over seven digits every year.

Supermarkets requested to brand certain wines. The finest of London's stand out restaurants begged for the prosecco being produced so they could add it to their lists of exotic and globally celebrated wine.

That was all in the past. Another life ago.

Nowadays, the grapevines were reduced to two separate growing patches. To the right side of the building lay 39 x 160 metres of vines. Behind the winery, 49 x 120 metres of vines. The two patches annually produce nine hundred bottles of wine between them. The grape's juices added with the collected and purified rain made ninety-thousand litres of grape water. The early days of survival required learning how to contain and purify rain, and fortunately in the UK, rain was never far away. The rest of the vines had been torn out and the ground cultivated and prepared for the necessary agriculture.

It was a strict vegetarian community, and rice provided just enough protein for all of them. Enough killing had happened over the years, and all animals on their grounds were treated like family.

On the left side of the main driveway lay the twelve-acre vegetable patch. Aisles of corn, beetroot, spinach, and vegetables that grew best in the unique, high-alkaline soil.

They also grew various berries, herbs, tea, tobacco, and even attempted to grow sugar cane. Rye corn thrived here too—the perfect grain for making bread with bicarbonate of soda.

Ryan had made a specific request to Cooper to grow the smaller sprouting vegetation at the far edge of the patches. The top-floor lookout needed constant visual access to the perimeter wall. The Texas-born man pulled it off.

"Y'all know I like my corn!" he'd say, smiling while chewing on a blade of grass, trying to give himself a redneck charm. It didn't work though; his shaved ginger hair, freckles and overly tall, lanky frame made him look more like a basketball player.

Raised as a carpenter by his father, a self-employed, Vietnam war veteran who hid out in a small, Texas suburb, Cooper had learnt at a young age to give his dad space when needed and acquired a part-time job on a nearby ranch. He loved caring for the horses, never feeling a connection with any animal before that. His childhood was then spent on helping his dad bring in money.

Ryan never told him that he considered the American to be the most irreplaceable member in the group of survivors, with his knowledge of vegetation, animals and craftsmanship. Without Cooper, it wouldn't be anywhere near as possible to keep the number of survivors they housed alive.

From the window, Ryan looked across the carriageway on the outside of their walls and took in the scale of the hill on the opposite side. Maidhill—the first of many meadow and pine-covered hills across the county. Its enormous presence gave the impression that they were always being watched by someone. Anyone.

The news that there could be people watching them right now sent a chill down Ryan's spine, but he shook off the paranoia and turned his attention back to inside their grounds. He saw Cooper throwing dried corn trimmings into the chicken pen, the furthest animal enclosure on the driveway's right side. Noticing a couple of smaller figures, Ryan pulled his binoculars up and veered in on the farmer boy.

Maisie, his own adoptive daughter and her slightly older friend, Jess.

The only memories the two girls ever had were of post-war survival, and yet their smiles and laughter showed that it is possible to overcome what the world had been through. The future was being created now, so they were going to make it a good one. A better one.

He saw the girls grabbing hands of corn and tossing them in, Cooper leaning over and pointing inside, teaching the girls how to keep the chickens well-fed, clean and safe.

The future, Ryan smiled to himself. Sights like those held the little happiness that the world had left to offer.

"Cooper seems in his element when he's teaching."

The voice from behind was Doc's, Ryan's former sous chef and fellow joint-leader of their community. His skin was always covered in red patches like he was allergic to air, fading into his short, dark, curly hair. His inquisitive eyes were magnified by his thick glasses, which rested on his bulky nose and under his bushy eyebrows.

Ryan nodded and turned; he was greeted with a bowl of thyme rice.

"Eat it," Doc ordered, looking over the top of his glasses. "Cassy told me you haven't been down for food today."

Ryan took the bowl, gulping down the first two mouthfuls without hardly chewing. "Sorry, things on my mind." He shoved in another spoonful.

Doc smiled, a rarity.

It wasn't his real name. Ryan tagged him with the nickname because Doc could've gotten a PHD in anything if he wanted to. He always wore a face of observant concentration. Everything he saw was a puzzle that could be solved or improved. Ryan used to joke that with his thick, curly, black hair, thick glasses, and lack of visible emotion, he could be the next Frankenstein.

"Mikey wants to hear your final thoughts on tomorrow's plan," Doc said, getting straight to the point.

Ryan had momentarily forgotten about the conversation in the early hours of the morning. He was lost in the moment of an unusually hot and beautiful autumn day.

"Yeah." He paused, retrieving a stem of thyme from the back of his mouth and throwing it into the bin on the floor. "We'll go out before sunrise."

Doc didn't say anything, silent in agreement.

"I want Sam to stay back. If we're being goaded out of our safe area, we need the best shooters on standby for an ambush," Ryan continued and picked up his bottle of grape water. "We can't underestimate that they won't plan to jump us."

Sam was the only member in their community with a criminal past, having spent most of his adult life being a jewel thief. His shooting skills were second to none, especially with his hunting rifle, and he was deadly stealthy—a trait that was sometimes needed in this backwards world. To look at him in the face, you'd never know of what he'd done for a living. He had the innocent youthfulness that Mikey possessed, the same pale skin as Ryan, and puffy, dark hair like Doc. He could've blended in anywhere.

"Keep everyone else inside the building?" Doc asked rhetorically, knowing that everyone's safety while the team was out was more than paramount.

"Yeah, and whoever has weapons training should be armed."

That was their reality. Any unidentified threat was treated with extreme prejudice; no stranger could be trusted. With no laws, no debt, no overpaid boss on their case, and no medication for anyone with mental health problems, people were free to do whatever they wanted.

"What about the search mission?" Doc said, pushing the issue like an impatient child.

Ryan wanted to keep a straight face, but the corner of his mouth started to rise as he attempted to repress the smile. This was the bit Doc wanted to hear, the 'action' part. Any excursion outside fuelled his underused brain; it needed constant stimulation. Ryan loved that about Doc. It was the main factor for hiring him as his sous chef over a decade ago, before all this.

"It's going to be a five-person-excursion. We'll head out just before sunrise as I said, but I don't want to be completely low profile. I want them to know we're out and think we're unaware of their presence."

"Risky bluff, even for you." Doc raised an eyebrow.

"If they're hostile, they'll expose themselves thinking we're off guard."

"Could put ourselves in danger."

"We're always in danger," Ryan said with a sigh. "We both know that."

"And if they don't expose themselves?"

"Then we'll make it look like a standard trip into town." Ryan pointed his right arm out the window. "You can check the cars before heading into town."

He was referring to the few 4x4's they kept in working condition. Since they only used them for supply hunting, the car park on the other side of the dual carriageway was the best place to keep them. They were visible from the top-floor window during all hours of sunlight, and if tampered with during the night, the alarms would rip through the silent sky.

"After the cars..." Ryan took a mouthful of grape water, "...you can look at the streetlights and whatever else it is you need for your new project."

"Oh yeah." Doc rubbed his hands together with a look of thrill in his eyes.

As exciting as it was to think that Doc could get the streetlights working, they had to put all efforts into finding out the motives of whoever was out there. That was their main objective on the mission. Find those who'd moved their refuge signs.

Ryan prepared himself for the next part of his plan, knowing it could spark an argument. "I'm going to break away from you guys while it's still dark." He quickly threw his hand up, cutting off Doc. Splitting up while outside was strictly against their protocol. "I'm going to make my way to the school, cross the train tracks, and come up to the back end of the church."

The same church that lost survivors were instructed to go.

"What?" The confused look on Doc's face was swiftly replaced by an angry one.

Ryan took a deep breath. If he was going to sell this idea, he needed to say it right. "Our signs clearly say to ring the bell. At some point, whoever is out there must be planning to ring it."

"I know," Doc growled. "Why go on your own?"

"I'll go when it's dark. When the sun rises, hopefully all focus will be on you."

"Then what?"

"I'll sneak up to the church. Whoever is out there will be none the wiser."

"I don't like this."

"I'll approach with caution," Ryan reassured as he drank some more grape water, spilling it down his white vest. "If there are people there already, you'll hear either the bell or gunfire. One of the two."

"What if no one's there?" Doc took the bottle from Ryan and drank some.

"I'll lay low and wait."

"For what?"

"You guys," Ryan smirked, walking over to the table against the central column's staircase wall, motioning for Doc to follow him.

Rolled up maps and various stationary covered the table. Doc recognized the notepad as the one he'd handed to Mikey the day before, outlining the potential plans for bringing the streetlights back to life. Ryan unrolled one of the larger maps and spread it out across the table, pinning down the corners with water bottles.

It was an ordinance survey map of Maidville. They had found it in the sewage plant across the road, along with every other thinkable map of the surrounding area.

Maidville's layout was simple: a mile-long high street of shops and restaurants. Apartments and housing off behind the southern side. Schools, a church, a football pitch, car parks and the Maidville flower gardens behind the opposite side.

Ryan placed three bullet shells on the map, marking certain locations. "I've been reading through your notes about the lights, and I can see you will need more tools, specific tools."

"Okay," Doc replied patiently.

"These three stores..." Ryan pointed to bullet shells, "...should still have a lot to search through." He paused again. "After the sun starts to come up, I want you to make your way towards town and go up London Road, you'll come to the pool service shop."

The first bullet casing.

"After that, cross over the high street and head to the radio repair shop on Moore's Road, that little shabby place opposite the police station."

The second bullet casing.

"The final place is Lenny's hardware at the far end of the high street." Ryan's fingers moved past the church and to the other end of the high street.

The final bullet casing.

"Hopefully, you'll find what you need in these stores, and at the same time, have a look around town to see if there are any obvious signs that we've got company."

"Should we communicate with you when we pass the church?" Doc rubbed his hands on his buttoned shirt.

"No, I don't want it to be known that I'm there."

"Shoot on sight?"

"If they start fighting first." Ryan pulled the lighter out of his pocket, slipping a cigarette into his mouth and lighting it. "I can't believe that everyone left out there is too far gone, I just can't."

"I know," Doc agreed. He pointed at the third bullet. "So what do you want us to do after we get to Lenny's?"

"Stay there." Ryan puffed on the stale cigarette. "Set up a temporary defence. Lenny's is on the hill. It's raised enough that you can see the church tower's window."

"Ok, I get the plan so far. What will we be waiting for, lunch?"

"Pretty much." Ryan's eyes widened, trying to hide the amusement at his immature response.

"I don't follow," Doc frowned.

"When the sun is at its highest, and if no one has shown their face, we're going to force them out of hiding." Ryan exhaled a large cloud of smoke. "If they don't want to ring that bell, let's flush them out and ring it for them."

3

The sound of twigs cracking pulled him out of his gaze. He'd been admiring the view from the woodland's border at the top of the hill. The meadow rolled all the way down the southern slope. The different shades of rusty yellow blended into wild red like a watercolour painting of wildfire. That combined with the hypnotic smell of apple and cherry would be enough for any poet to start writing lyrically of the British autumn.

"Ben just got here. He says the package should be here in a day, minimum." The voice from behind was his second in charge; he knew it better than his own children's.

Raising his hand to acknowledge, he continued to look over the raw beauty in front of him. All the hell that raged over the planet's surface still wasn't powerful enough to eradicate a spectacle such as this.

He wiped the sweat off his brow, and he pulled the binoculars back up to eye level, peering right and spying over the luxurious-looking vineyard. All the things that he was told about this place were true. A fully functioning society in a rural location with structured agriculture and protocols.

He could see two men in the top-floor room, about half the width of the building's base structure. The taller one, with light, dreadlocked hair and a cigarette in his hand, seemed to be relaying orders to the other. The smaller of the two had glasses and shorter, darker hair.

"I wonder if you two are the top guys here?" he mumbled.

He turned his attention to the perimeter that circled their land. The winery's land was surrounded by a deep, thick, bush-style border.

Not very car proof.

The layout inside the grounds was what got his attention and what really made him happy. On one side of the central driveway, there was a row of fenced-off animal enclosures, barns, and huts with water and feeding systems. Chickens, a couple of cows, horses, deer, rabbit cages, and a handful of cats were roaming free.

"Keep those cats away from the chickens," he mumbled again, aiming the comment at the tall redhead outside the chicken pen, who was helping two young girls throw in some sort of food.

The other side of the driveway displayed an outstanding variety of crops and what looked like herb growing patches down the other side of the building. This was a community to be in awe of.

Except for you.

His eyes locked firmly on the dark-skinned couple emerging from the vegetable patch, the smile fading from his face as his teeth locked in anger. A rage reminding him of the atrocities he'd witnessed at the very hands of those kinds of scum; they didn't deserve the blissful settings they now called home.

Fucking dirty Asians.

"They'd sell you out to save themselves," he snarled.

The fact that the people at the vineyard called them friends made his blood boil. He accidentally dropped the binoculars and resisted the urge to scream, aware he'd be heard like pin dropping in an empty school hall.

Regaining composure, he acknowledged that going in guns blazing wasn't going to work against these people. If they were tolerant enough to let those dirty rats live with them, they'd be diplomatic enough to talk.

If he had to fight to get what he wanted, then he'd fight to his last breath.

He brushed the binoculars off with his massive hands, blew away the dirt, and peered through them again. The Asians were now talking to the lanky redhead, exchanging laughs and smiles. The sight disgusted him. Shifting his view back to the top-floor window, his heart stopped.

For the first time in years, he froze with fear.

The dreadlocked guy was pointing a scoped rifle directly at him.

———

"You want to ring the church bell to flush them out, on your own?" Doc took his glasses off and rubbed the bridge of his nose, irritated at the idea. "Seriously, on your own?"

"Yeah," Ryan paused, aware that putting himself in that situation would sound stupid to someone like Doc. "You'll be able to see any movement on the west to north sides of me. There's no entrance on the east side of the church, so I'll just have to cover south from the bell tower."

Ryan walked to the window where he stood earlier, picking up an L96 sniper rifle he had left leaning against the wall, one of three from their salvaged collection of weapons.

"That's why I want these... for cover should we need it." An immature smile crossed his stubbled face.

"I've not shot one of these yet," Doc stated.

"Mikey has."

"Has he shot one in combat yet?"

"Yes."

"Any variables or traits I should know about this gun?" Doc huffed then asked. "In case I have to use it to save your mental arse?"

"Powerful kickback," Ryan said, positioning the barrel of the gun on the window ledge. "Much more powerful than the one Sam walks around with." Leaning down on one knee, he pulled the butt of the gun into his right shoulder, moving his head towards the scope.

"How do you know that?"

"Experience my friend, experience," Ryan replied, focusing into the scope.

"How many bullets do we have for these rifles?"

"About seventy each. Not a great amount, but our friends down in Lewes might have some extras for an exchange." Ryan referred to the only other community they knew, near the south coast. There wasn't a great deal of interaction between the two groups, just the trading of bullets for medical supplies every few months.

"Let me guess, trade ether for ammo?" Doc assumed.

"Probably," Ryan propped the rifle tighter to him and twisting the dials on the scope. "And we have a bit of an issue right now."

There was a brief silence. He let a long breath escape his lungs, remaining still for over ten seconds as he zoomed in on Maidhill across the road. His left hand flicked the scope.

"The sight is loose." Ryan stood, laying the weapon on the table. "Can't see shit through that."

"I'll get Sam to fix that tonight then," Doc said. "That's his bread and butter,"

Ryan nodded and rubbed his eyes.

———

He let out a huge sigh of relief when the long-haired one pulled away from the window and placed the rifle on a table.

Did the long-haired guy choose not to fire? Did the gun jam? Or had he not seen him at all?

He wouldn't risk standing outside the treeline again.

As he hurried back into the woodland and through the nettle pathways, the first clearing came into view.

His men had been waiting there for the order to start renovating the derelict mansion—what would soon become their new base of operations. They looked at their leader as he strode out the nettle pathway. A man they worshipped, someone to follow and make the world as it should've been, a man with the tenacious ability to rid the world of its disease. A man no longer called by his birth name or military rank, but rather by how they saw him.

A man called 'Father'.

He looked over his men as they saluted, which he returned. The newest recruit, Ben, was sat on a log and covered in blood, panting hysterically. His short, blond fringe was matted to his face and a look of pride was in his wide, yet hollow, blue eyes.

Not a single scratch on him; he'd done well.

The rest of the men, dressed in grey T-shirts and black cargo pants, stood around Ben, impressed with what was the harshest of initiations they'd seen so far. He was proving himself to be quite the addition to their unit.

"There's more coming, Father," Ben's voice rasped as his body shook uncontrollably. "Much more."

"They're all following the signs here?"

"Yes, Father."

"Good work, Ben." His own was voice deep. Even when he spoke softly, it felt like it was booming. "Let's get you washed up, and then some food. The first time is always the hardest."

4

"Why'd you have to stay out tonight? This would've been our first night alone in weeks," Cassy whispered in Ryan's ear as they embraced.

"Great, turn me on before I have to leave," he complained. "Wait, where's Maisie tonight?"

"Staying with your sister."

Ryan now knew why Cassy was wearing his favourite black jeans and crop top combo with her hair plated into pigtails.

"Please say she's still babysitting tomorrow when I get back?" he begged.

"You'd have to ask her." She pointed behind him. His sister exited from the cafeteria's double doors, joining them in the dark, wooden, panelled reception area.

"Ask me what?" Steph tucked her blonde hair behind her ears. She stood a couple of inches taller than Cassy, same green eyes and thin nose as Ryan. Her pale skin stood out against the dark, leather jacket and black chinos.

"How long have you got Maisie for?" Ryan leaned against the reception desk.

Steph grinned, knowing she could burst her brother's bubble.

"Please don't be a div!" he whined.

"I'll keep her tomorrow night, too," she said with a smirk. "You'll probably need sleep after tomorrow anyway."

"I won't be that tired."

"So, you want Maisie back tomorrow?"

"Oh no! No, no, I'll need sleep, yeah, sleep." He rubbed the bridge of his nose with his finger and thumb.

"Why does tomorrow have to be so extreme, plan wise?" Steph asked sincerely, changing the subject.

Ryan hated having to answer questions like this in front of Cassy, but it had to be done. "As much as I like the idea of finding people in need, I can't trust who could be out there. There might not even be anybody out there, and this is just overkill. We always have to take the necessary precautions."

Both women nodded.

"Anyway sis, this isn't the worst outing I've been on." Ryan winked with a warm smile.

During the peak of The Fast War, he had run the western train line to his sister's home... two towns away. He succeeded in avoiding getting caught in the crossfire between the military and the incursion enemies, pulling both her and his nephew, Lyndon, out from under the debris of their kitchen and escorted them back to the wine estate. Or at least, he told Steph that he'd avoided the cross fire. She'd never known what he'd really done to get to her that night.

"I know it isn't." She hugged her brother. "Stay safe out there."

"You know I'll be safe. I've got Cooper, Doc, Mikey, and even Jen volunteered for tomorrow."

"That's not surprising is it?" Steph laughed.

"What isn't?" Ryan asked.

"Jen volunteering,"

"Why?"

"Her and Mikey..." her voice trailed off, waiting for him to finish the sentence. Cassy burst into laughter.

"You don't know, do you?" Steph joined Cassy in hysterics.

"Know what?" Ryan demanded.

Steph slumped over the reception, head buried in her arms.

It took a few seconds before it all clicked in Ryan's brain. "No way? When? how?" he asked, swivelling his head between the two women.

"Ah, never mind now." Steph managed to recompose herself, fanning her eyes with her hands. "I'll see you when you get back tomorrow, div!" she giggled, waving and turning back to the cafeteria.

"What the fuck?" Ryan turned back to Cassy. She surprised him with a long, deep kiss, grabbing his hair with her left hand and his crotch with her right.

"See you tomorrow, baby, I love you." She smiled before skipping after Steph.

Ryan stood bog-eyed and dumbfounded. He liked to be focused the day before a mission outside, and now he was left confused and horny. "Women!" he shouted, pulling his hair in frustration.

Mikey burst through the double doors into the reception with his own look of bewilderment. "Why did your missus and sister nearly shit themselves with laughter when they just walked past me?"

"You tell me, bruv," Ryan shrugged. "You tell me."

———

Of the seventy-one post-war survivors who lived in the vineyard's grounds, Ryan, Doc and Mikey had been nominated as joint leaders.

They ran the community like a democracy, making sure everyone had the opportunity to share their input, ideas and have a say in the group's future, though at the end of the day, the final decision down to the three of them.

As far as emergency meetings went, the previous night's was perfect. A few groans could be heard when a lockdown had been implemented until the team's safe return. It had been a while since a procedure like that was put into effect.

The last fight had ended before it barely had a chance to start. It's not every day that you're confronted by a doomsday fanatic claiming to be the next antichrist, stating that this new world was the prophesized apocalypse, and he was the new rightful ruler.

Most of his followers had fallen to rifle fire from Sam and Ryan. The distance from the restaurant windows to the carriageway was measured at over five hundred metres, not bad shooting for civilians with zero military training.

If you're going to threaten to burn down their perimeter, don't leave yourself exposed in clear view. That's how Ryan justified the barrage of bullets that tore through them.

The standard emergency escape plan was reassessed for the unlikely event they had to bail out, detailing both the route and supplies to be taken to the contingency location: a farm on the outskirts of Gatwick Airport.

Sam was nominated to be in charge while the team was out, not only to secure the ground and people's safety, but with the added responsibility of poisoning the water and crops should they need to evacuate.

The two cows were to be put down, as gut-wrenching as it was. It would be impossible to move them out quickly, and they sure as hell wouldn't leave them for whoever to butcher them. The rest of the animals could be moved or freed, whichever the situation called for.

The thought of losing the animals didn't just affect their survival plans, but it also hurt emotionally. They were family too.

It required mass efforts to find those animals and bring them back to the vineyard, especially the two cows. Ryan and Mikey had found them on an abandoned farm when they first returned to the village they once lived in. Among the debris and aftermath that coated the village, the two cows, already named Thelma and Louise, had been found on the road just outside the apartment the two men once rented. Now, they were part of the future they were trying to create, and hopefully they'd find a bull before it was too late.

———

Not a single cloud had formed during the night, and the warmth left from the daytime still hung in the air.

Ryan sat on the floor against the stable doors, the building dimly lit with a single candle glued onto a saucer. The horse's faces peered over their gates, wondering what one of their feeders was doing in their home in the early hours of the morning.

He'd been in the stables since sundown, managing to catch a small nap during the night after chowing down a bowl of herb rice and a small loaf of soda bread.

All early morning stealth expeditions required the team to stay outside the night before; it would prevent anyone spying from a distance from seeing anyone leave the building, and the guttering spotlights wouldn't reveal the team as they left the grounds.

The barns and stables were constructed well enough to keep the candlelight hidden, along with the presence of whoever was inside them.

Ryan donned the usual excursion attire of all-black sportswear. His hood pulled up, sidearm ammunition in a makeshift utility belt around his waist, and a claw hammer tucked into the back of his pants.

Running trainers and sportswear had become a preference in the world now as no one was going on a date or job interview anymore, so comfort over trying to look A-list was the norm.

He counted the bullets in his third and final clip, slipping it into the utility belt, and pulled himself into a kneeling position, quickly checking his laces.

Looking at the seven horses individually, the candlelight flickered as they stared back. He cleared his throat quietly and approached each horse, giving them a nose stroke and some affection. He loved the horses, but in all honesty had no idea how to handle them, no matter how many times Cooper had explained it.

Next to the doors stood a small wooden stool; his pistol sat on top with the rifle upright to the side. Both guns were already loaded, checked and double-checked for good measure.

It was now a waiting game.

———

The morning alarm rang loudly. Henry the rooster was never quiet about it on any given day, and that morning he didn't disappoint. Ryan slung the rifle over his shoulder and gripped the pistol, blowing the candle out and canvasing the stables into darkness.

He ran his hands along the locking beam and unlatched it, pulling the door into the open right position. A slight glimmer of moonlight crept from behind the Earth's shadow, just enough for him to see the latch which he could tie the door's rope to. Hardly a breeze moved in the air with the stars shining down, telling him that another clear day was ahead.

To Ryan's left at the far end of their grounds, Henry bellowed his alarm again. The chicken could probably be heard in London, if was anyone alive there.

"Morning Henry," he whispered, walking left around the stable.

While patting himself over, he headed towards the chicken pen via the outside path between the enclosures and perimeter wall.

The two cows approached as he reached the end of their enclosure, and Ryan scratched the fence post loudly with the head of his hammer before holding it tightly and silently counting to thirteen.

A single thud followed. Mikey had struck the top of another fence post with the backside of his hatchet. It was the signal that he, Doc, Cooper and Jen had all gathered and were ready to meet at the chicken pen. That location was next to the only clean exit route out of the perimeter. Also known as section D1, the beginning of the pathway out of the maze that circled the whole of their home.

The maze pushed out at one hundred metres thick. It was divided into twenty-six areas clockwise and labelled alphabetically, starting with section A in the northeast corner behind vegetable patches. Section Z completed the circumference. It was then divided up ten layers deep, 1 being the inside and 10 being the outer.

One-hundred and sixty-three traps laid between one hundred and thirty-seven false routes and dead ends, and unless you knew the only way in or just happen to have a leprechaun with you, you'd likely die trying to find the only way in. In the case of quick evacuation, the part of the maze constructed over the driveway could have its traps set off by a release cord. The walls would collapse outwards and the salt-acid traps would disarm.

One other trap could be manually set off from a release cord hidden in the walls of section D9, leaving C10 unarmed for quicker on-foot access only. Even if an outsider knew the location of the release cord, setting off the trap would be loud enough to alert anyone outside or on guard duty.

The combination of Doc's brain and Cooper's practical skills had manifested itself perfectly into the organic, deadly, self-defence system that orbited their home. Constructed during the first spring after The Fast War, fashioned out of one hundred and sixty-five acres worth of grapevine wires, it took six months to shape and weave the multiple routes through dead ends and would later turn into the salt-acid traps. The next step was to line the edges and rows with any fast-growing seeds they could find in the abandoned garden centres.

After sifting through weeks of research, they learned that Griselinia seeds and Root Ball were to be the most effective linings, all growing faster than the average, quickly thickening and surviving the year-round. Minus the odd maintenance to prevent the pathways from joining into one large mess, it did its job effectively. No one had ever successfully made it inside without guidance.

During its construction, Ryan and Doc travelled the safe route repeatedly, mentally mapping it out and making it second nature. Once they felt confident, they inserted the traps.

"Sleep well?" Mikey asked, walking behind Ryan in the single-file formation.

Doc led at the front with Jen and Cooper bringing up the rear.

"As well as I could have in a shit-smelling barn with one fucking candle," he whispered back.

"At least you didn't stay in cow hut," Mikey complained under his breath. "Jen and I barely got a wink in."

"Doubt it was the cow's fault." Ryan did his best not to laugh with his response.

"Shut up," Jen hissed.

Doc cleared his throat, signalling for them to behave, though he sported a suppressed smile.

Mikey and Jen had tried to keep their relationship a secret. It was unfortunate that the locks on the dry storage room didn't work, and Sam was on lockdown duty that night. Ryan was the last to find out.

"How long, Doc?" Jen whispered, changing the subject.

"About three minutes. We're just into the ninth section." There was enough light starting to break that he saw each turning well enough.

Everyone had their main weapons in hand as they reached the tenth layer. Doc and Ryan with their familiar Glocks, Mikey and Jen held G36C assault rifles, and Cooper rounded out the group with his Remington 870 shotgun.

A knot tightened in Ryan's stomach, and his mouth dried out. One row of the thick bush now separated them from the outside world, the exit a mere twenty metres ahead on their right.

They moved slowly, listening for any activity or movement on the outside. Each step tightened the knot in Ryan's stomach. He thought he might vomit at any given chance.

This was the bit everyone hated: the first step outside.

Once outside, everything was fine, like dipping your toes into a swimming pool. Except their swimming pool was potentially filled with violent racists, disease, rapists, and religious fanatics.

Doc held his left hand up, spreading all five digits, and pressed tightly against the hedge wall. Jen moved closer to him, Mikey and Ryan paired up, and Cooper drew his shotgun, overtaking them to the front of the line. Doc's fingers disappeared as he began the countdown, the slowest five count in the world.

Two... one...

Cooper rounded the corner, eyes focused directly in front of him. Jen and Doc moved out to the right and took kneeling positions, facing west. Mikey and Ryan repeating the procedure on the left side facing east.

The team took a full 180-degree view of the desolate space. The area had once been a part of the original vineyard grounds but now served as a derelict space of nothing, all for the purpose of being able to see anyone trying to get close to the maze's eastern wall.

"Good west," Doc whispered from his side.

"Good south," Cooper confirmed.

"Good east." The last confirmation came from Ryan.

They kept low and tight against the outside of the maze, using the remaining darkness to keep them hidden. None of the other entrances were disturbed, and everything looked exactly like it should.

Rounding the corner onto the eastern wall, they checked the remaining entrances, until reaching the driveway that ran through sections C and D and up to the front door of the winery. Maidhill towered over them from the other side of the carriageway.

"It's gotta be mid-October." Ryan turned to the group, a puzzled look crossing his face.

"What's wrong?" Doc spotted his expression.

"It's not even remotely cold."

It was standard for that time of year to have the first chill in the air and light frost on the ground.

"I'd hate to interrupt your global-warming conference," Mikey butted in, "but you've got about twenty minutes before you're visible to anyone looking at us from over three hundred metres away."

The first glare of sunshine crept behind the horizon of Maidhill.

"See you on the other side." Ryan pulled his hood down and began a gentle jog up the road. After a minute, he disappeared into the darkness that coated Maidville.

"Stay safe, brother," Mikey whispered.

5

E very sign they had posted around the county all read the same; the message was clear:

Salvation: A24, Penbrook wine estate, Maidville.
We can help you, feed you, treat you.
Do not try to approach us unaware or sneak into our grounds.
We will see you as a threat and defend ourselves accordingly.
Ring the church tower's bell in Maidville town centre.
We will come to you.
We do not intend harm on anyone looking for help, we will defend ourselves only when necessary.
Ring the bell, we will be no longer than an hour getting to you.
Stay outside the church or in the main hall in harsher weather conditions.
We can rebuild, we can help, we can prevail.

So far, the signs had helped guide a reasonable number of lonely drifters to the vineyard, including Jen, though the number of survivors seeking refuge had declined over the past few winters.

Their last encounter with new faces was the doomsday cult a couple of winters ago, a group who threatened to burn down the maze unless they handed over their animals. Some of the road was marred with the rusty bloodstains of that group, and no one felt one ounce of guilt about it.

A lack of medication, the newer stresses, and the hell that surrounded them could have led to them becoming this. With all reasoning aside, they were a threat, and God only knew how many other survivors out there they could have hurt or killed.

Expendable.

Doc sat next to a streetlight with the access panel open, sorting through various wires as Mikey performed security sweeps beside him. Neither of the church's bell of gunfire had rung out, so Ryan was safe. Jen and Cooper had spent all morning inspecting the vehicles, being as thorough as they could given they had all morning available to them.

Mikey swung the high-powered rifle over his right shoulder and swapped it for the G36C, patrolling the carriageway while the others worked. The road was a mess of overgrown weeds, creeping out the cracked tarmac all the way up to the roundabouts at either end.

To their best of luck, the variety of deserted delivery and shipping trucks had proved a Godsend. Toilet paper, tobacco, tinned food, bottled water, soaps, prescriptions and other medicines had helped them survive the first year after the war.

The assortment of discarded cars, trucks and vans had been moved to each of the roundabouts situated at the end of the carriageway and arranged into blockades, which remained to this day. It was more of a mental tactic; they didn't know if they could withstand a haul of larger trucks, but at the very least it would slow down any would-be convoy.

Mikey felt the heat coming from the sun, knowing a sticky day of walking around in full gear was ahead. "How're the streetlights look-ing?" he called out as he approached Doc.

"Jen and Cooper are nearly done with the cars. We've got around three hours before midday, plenty of time." Doc huffed and rubbed his eyes. "I'm finished here."

The sound of the access panel closing made Mikey lower his weapon. "Know what you need for your shopping trip?"

"Couple of copper-based extension wires and some soldering metal."

"Sweet."

"All is good with the motors, gentleman," Cooper reported as he approached from the car park, his ginger hair glowing in the morning sun. "Tyres are in good check, considering Doc was the last to drive her."

They all checked their weapons, nodding at each other that it was time.

"So, shopping and rescue the mental one called 'Ryan?'" Jen rubbed her oily hands with a cloth before pushing it into her hoodie pocket. She wore the same all-black attire as the men which nearly matched her dark skin, making her grey eyes stand out even more. She was much better at tying her back than Ryan could manage with his messy dreadlocks, and she'd never stopped ripping into him about. Time alone on the outside had hardened her, but she never refused to try and lighten the mood, and Mikey loved that.

"Yes," Doc said, pushing his glasses up. "The quicker we get to the shops, the quicker I can get back and fix the lights."

"I wonder if you can get a discount for multibuy?" Mikey joked as they started walking towards town.

———

Hamsa kept running.

Not looking down for hours, his bare feet thumped on the road. The burns across his back and chest had faded into a chilling numbness as he kept moving through the early morning. His family escaped the slaughter, and he prayed that others had gotten out too.

The sickening laughter and cries of enjoyment echoed through his brain, the images flashing of people begging for mercy, a deal, a negotiation, or just anything that would make it stop.

A traitor on the inside had opened the doors for the devil to come in. To no one's surprise, the evil would not be bargained with. They had to be stopped, and Ryan was the only person he knew who would fight them.

———————

Ben felt his body regaining control, his breathing had slowed to a normal rhythm, and his sight sharpened.

"First time is always the hardest, kid," Father said from across the dining table. "But you did one hell of a job. You can consider yourself a man now."

Ben took that as a compliment of the highest kind. His new family were people who listened to him, people he could look up to.

"Thank you, sir," he managed to blurt, still trying to adapt to his new breathing problem. The ferocious withdrawals had caught him off guard since his initiation the previous week, but it was a small price to pay to be a member of Father's team.

Ben sat opposite him in the mansion's cobwebbed and dust-covered dining room, not even noticing the state the room was in, but in awe of Father's build. His shoulders could carry a camel, arms like elephant legs that disappeared under a grey T-shirt, a neck that no man could strangle with his hands alone.

The union jack, roses, bulldogs, and a mixture of military tattoo's canvassed Father's skin all the way from his knuckles to his jawline. Even his facial muscles were toned and chiselled finer than most men, with dark, brown eyes fading into their sockets. Slicked, grey hair tied into a ponytail hung between his monstrous shoulders, and he was clean shaved across his steely jawline, thanks to a few supplies Ben salvaged for him.

The men Ben now served with looked well-built and focused. His own mental image was nowhere near matching that. He wanted to be as superior as them, instead of the skinny, slimy, twitching moron he felt he was portraying. *Why would they look at you like a man? You just sold out the people who once sheltered you.*

Winning his new family over was his personal priority.

"Make sure you're fully recovered, Ben," Father's deep voice bellowed across the dinner table. "I, and everyone else, need you on your top game tomorrow."

———

The walk to the church always had an emotional sting while passing through the school's grounds. Under the rugby pitch's soil lay all the dead bodies they had found in the homes and on streets of Maidville. Eight-thousand, eight-hundred and thirteen bodies, to be exact. A mass grave, remembering everyone who died in the onslaught of The Fast War.

From families in their homes to children at school, police, firemen, ambulance drivers, paramedics, people at work, and non-locals passing through town to get to their destination, every dead body in Maidville were buried here. No one liked going into town when they had to walk past the remains of a mother holding her twin babies or having to see an elderly man trampled under his shopping cart.

Doc and Cooper theorized the mass grave is what keeps wildlife away from the area, as if their animal instincts could sense the emptiness that surrounded most towns, littered with decaying corpses.

From the church tower, Ryan watched the sun on its journey to the highest point. The other team was running a fine line, leaving themselves roughly half an hour until midday. His rifle rested against the wall next to the single window, which stayed propped open with his hammer. He could see Lenny's hardware store, the team's final destination, without the aid of the scope.

If you ignored the gaping holes that riddled the rooftops along the high street and the rest of the structural decay, the church tower's perspective of the town was outstanding. No doubt however that inside the buildings, like the church's bell tower, had succumbed to invading flora, coated in thick layers of cobwebs and suffocating dust. The stale smell of death that lingered years after the occupants' bodies removed, combined with the lack of maintenance, made the air mentally unbearable to breathe. The sense of hopelessness was unescapable—you just had to pretend it wasn't there.

Ryan wiped his brow and squinted his eyes when a flicker of light from across town caught his eye. He pulled the rifle into firing position and aimed towards the store six hundred metres away. Mikey's waving hand greeted him along with two, preassigned hand signals.

The first, a thumbs up followed by four fingers. This was the code for: *'Everyone had arrived without contact or conflict'*.

The second signal was a middle finger: *'Shopping had been successful'*.

Ryan responded with two lots of thumbs up: *'No contact on the way to the church and none since setting up defence'*.

So far, so good. He figured there was enough time for a cigarette to calm himself, the anticipation unbearable. In the next five minutes, he would announce to anyone hiding out there that he was aware of them and was ready to find out what they wanted.

6

A pathetic whimper escaped Hamsa's mouth, the lactic acid searing as he collapsed knee first into the middle of the moss-covered road. The tarmac cut into the skin at the joints, the rest of his body slammed forward, and the air shot out his lungs. His right cheek, elbows, forearms, and hands screamed with a burning pain.

The sobbing was barely audible as he tried to catch his breath. Maidville town centre was only half a kilometre ahead. Hamsa pushed hard to raise himself, only to be told by his body that there was no chance.

The frustration was torturous. His brain raced with the laughs of their attackers and the desperation to get to Ryan. His body was shutting down, too tired to even care about the pain he was in. For all his effort, Hamsa's eyes closed, drifting off into the world of sleep.

———

The sledgehammer jerked uncontrollably as it bounced back off the bell's surface, falling out of Ryan's hands and crashing on the wooden floor. The sounds of something like a runaway train shot through his head, causing pain to flash from his eyes to his jaw.

"I've gone fucking deaf!"

His own voice sounded like it was coming from deep inside an empty chasm while choking on the stale dust that exploded around the room. As he opened his eyes, a blurry double vision greeted him. Grasping his Glock would have proved tricky and potentially dangerous in this state. He could only hope that the dizziness passed quicker than anyone who could be on the way to his location.

Nothing had moved since the bell rang, although Mikey caught a glance of Ryan falling over and holding his ears in the church tower. The street itself remained lifeless.

Jen covered the ground floor of the shop, hiding behind an upturned table near the base of the stairs, scanning the shop window and entrance. Cooper and Doc peered out the windows facing north, overlooking the same gardens and car parks that Ryan passed through in the early hours of the morning.

"Anything?" Mikey asked.

"Nothing yet," the American answered back.

All were focusing like their lives depended on it until Ryan either gave the 'all clear' or needed their help.

The high-pitched ringing turned down from thunderous to irritating, but it became obvious it wasn't going to leave Ryan's ears for some time, no matter how much he tried to make them pop. Standing on the opposite side of the room from where his rifle and hammer were, he leant against the wall and peered out the window, surveying the side roads that ran south off the high street; all in a close enough proximity that his handgun would suffice, providing his brain would allow him to aim successfully. If people needed their help, it was the right time to come out of hiding and ask for it.

———

"Sleep well?" Father asked Ben as he sat at the top of the hill, hidden from view of the vineyard.

"Yes, thank you, Father," he replied.

"We've had an early arrival."

Through the binoculars, he saw the weary traveller stumble along the road, not far from the roundabout that joined the town centre and carriageway. So far, Ben had kept every word and was proving himself to be an excellent recruit.

"Can you give me an estimate for how many will come today?" Father asked from behind the binoculars.

"Four or five, sir," Ben answered. "Just one on their own at first. The others would group together and search for help later, in case the first one didn't make it."

"And they're all coming to the vineyard?"

"It's the only other community they know. That's why I moved their signs, to direct them here."

The smile on Father's face grew wider, watching the lone traveller stumble again and then collapse a few hundred metres away from his men's current base of operations: the hotel on the outskirts of town.

"It's not going to be a good day for you. Not good at all." He fixated on the solo traveller, taunting him from the safety of his current position. With the blink of an eye, his pleasant view and satisfaction halted, wiping the callous smile from his face as the church bell rang loudly across the open sky.

"Who the fuck rang that bell?" Father growled. "It's going to alert the vineyard!"

———

"What was it like when you rang the bell?" Mikey queried.

"It was like someone made a hole in my head and dropped that fucking rooster in it!" Ryan replied, adjusting his eyes to the sun as they left the church.

Mikey filled him in on their early morning shopping trip. "All gifts were purchased and not a single bit of traffic."

"Don't talk in code," Ryan groaned. "I don't think my brain can deal with that."

"We got everything we needed. And no problems anywhere, like absolutely nothing has been disturbed since our last outing into town."

Doc, Jen and Cooper stood on the high street, their weapons slung and carrying bags of various equipment.

"Did you start up the cars?" Ryan asked.

"We said we'll do that on the way back," Jen answered, her dusky skin glowing in the sunshine.

"You could get a tan in this sun," he joked.

"Racist twat," she laughed, jabbing Ryan in the arm.

Doc and Cooper smirked, turning to head back down the high street.

"Let's get back and sort the cars out." Ryan rubbed his shoulder. "Mikey can give you a foot rub or something."

Mikey jabbed him in the other shoulder as Cooper burst into laughter. The five of them chuckled all the way from the church to the roundabout, passing through the car barricade and on to the carriageway.

———

Father watched intently over the next hour. The lone traveller eventually picked himself up and tried hobbling pathetically towards the town. He turned his attention to the vineyard. The lack of activity puzzled him, the signs clearly stated that it would be an hour before their 'search and rescue' team made it to the church.

What the hell was going on? Who rang the bell, and why was there no rescue team?

"Sir, I think they've pulled a fast one on us," Paul announced from behind. "They know we're here, and they tried to flush us out."

"How so?" Father turned, and his voice boomed through gritted teeth, clearly annoyed with the idea.

"There." His lieutenant pointed towards a cluster of vehicles at the end of the carriageway. Father zoomed in with the binoculars, then his jaw dropped.

Five armed figures, all dressed in black sportswear, walking out from the town centre. One short, dark-skinned female, and four white males, including the tall redhead who was feeding the chickens yesterday. Also, unmistakeably, the two who were having a chinwag on the winery's top floor, and a shorter man he didn't recognise.

"They're not in offensive mode, Paul," Father pointed. "Their weapons are slung—they're not even checking their flanks."

"Yes, sir,"

"Are you sure they didn't send anyone out after the bell rang?"

"Not a single soul has left their community, sir," Paul reported. "Unless they have underground access."

Father lowered the binoculars, clearing the cloudiness in his brain and forcing himself to think on his feet like he was once able to. He rapidly assessed between the surprise of the bell ringing and the expedition team. Starting a fight would not be the answer, but he would have to draw some blood to get someone inside their grounds.

"We need to get back down to the hotel and intercept any other lone travellers." He cracked his knuckles. "Ben, you know what we have to do. This could be our only chance to get inside without confrontation."

"Yes, sir." Ben's voice echoed dread.

"Are you sure the rest are coming today?"

"Yes, sir."

"If not," Father locked his eyes into Ben's, "it'll be your neck that I break instead."

7

As the group walked home, Ryan had a paranoid feeling that they were being followed. He dismissed it, assuming that his ears were playing tricks on him from the lack of sleep with the added bell-based trauma. Yet, he was certain that he heard feet dragging in the distance.

Once they reached the maze's exterior, Doc immediately stuck his head into one of the lampposts openings and fiddled around with wires and other equipment that Ryan was clueless about.

Jen poured corn oil into the open petrol cap of the Landrover, closed the lid, and dropped the bottle in her bag. Keeping the vehicles fully fuelled opposite their safety wall was dangerous, so they filled them up accordingly.

Mikey and Ryan sat on the bonnet.

"So, when the fuck were you going to tell me about Jen?"

"She wanted to keep it quiet."

"Why?"

"She still feels like an outsider."

"Why? She's been living with us for three years now."

"I know, but during those first couple of winters while we were establishing ourselves as a community to produce food and water..."

Mikey paused, "...she had to do some very fucked up things to survive."

Ryan understood. He had heard the stories from Jen herself after they had taken her in.

She was pulled from the wreckage of her mechanic's office and only offered medical assistance in exchange for sexual favours. The two men didn't last five minutes in her presence. Her inner fighter and self-defence courses kicked in. Even after two days with no food, she bludgeoned them to death with a wrench. She then spent the next two years playing bait to such men, luring them to death in promise of non-resistant sex, then killing them and taking their food.

That should've been enough for Ryan to turn her away but given what he'd seen men do since the war ended, he had no motive to believe that she did it to unassuming, innocent men.

"All that matters is that since she's been here—she's been solid for us." Ryan jabbed Mikey in the shoulder, "That's for the one earlier."

"Fucker!"

They both laughed.

"Watch this for a moment." Mikey handed Ryan the medical bag.

"For what?"

"Need a piss!"

Mikey pointed at a row of hedges behind the car park and quickly scuffled towards them. The Defender's engine roared into life as Jen revved the accelerator. Ryan jumped off the bonnet like she was going to take off with him on the front. He could see her laughing like a child through the windscreen.

"You white boys are scared of everything!"

"Racist bitch!" he chuckled back.

"Just going to do a few laps of the car park." Jen leaned out the window, slowly edging the vehicle forward. "No point taking her out on the road."

Ryan saluted as she sped up and drifted left round the empty car park. He shouldered the medical holdall and walked out of the shade and onto the road, joining Cooper by the steel bumper. He couldn't wait to get back and have a decent night's sleep, or however much Cassy would let him have.

"Want some corn?" Cooper reached his arm out, offering a cold corn-on-the-cob.

"Not now, thanks."

Cooper shrugged, turning back to Doc who was kneeling face first inside the access point of a lamp post. "He said he'll be five minutes or so and not to disturb him until he's done."

"Puzzleboy," Ryan scoffed, while internally praying Doc could give them this gift. The first source of man-made light outside their grounds in over five years.

"Dead as a bird," Cooper said out of the blue.

"What?"

"Town. Like absolutely nothing has gone through there since the last time we went there."

"I know, you guys said earlier."

"Guess I was kinda hoping there was someone there, you know?" Cooper looked down, chewing on his corn, "People to help, more survivors and all."

"I know," Ryan nodded, understanding the American's deflated sense of hope. "We'll keep doing what we can, the guns might have been excessive today, but we always look out for ourselves..."

His voice trailed off, catching something in the corner of his left eye, someone approaching from the southern end of the carriageway. Ryan swiftly reached behind his back, pulling the Glock out and swinging his right arm in between Cooper and himself, pointing the gun back up the road.

"Do not fucking move!" Ryan rarely yelled, even in his chef years, but when he did, the person on the other end knew he meant every word. "I will drop you where you stand and not give two shits about how long it takes you to decompose on the railway tracks!"

Knowing it could be a potential ambush, it was impossible to tell what the individuals' intentions were from the hundred metres that separated them.

The figure paused, their knees shaking violently before their whole body started to tremble, their arms slowly raising towards their face like they were crying. Then a blood-curdling scream tore across the landscape.

"What, what the fuck did he just say?" Ryan stuttered.

"I'm not going to lie," Doc answered as he joined the two, pistol raised. "But I'm pretty sure he just screamed your name."

Mikey ran out from the bushes, nearly tripping over his feet as he hurdled the central barrier. "Jen's covering the base of the hill. Sam is scoping out the top." He pulled out the binoculars from the medical bag.

"Doc, Cooper, cover the north end of the road," Ryan ordered.

They both swung and aimed up the opposite end of the carriageway.

"Ryan!" The scream rang out again, the sound of agony and desperation was heart-breaking.

"That's Hamsa," Mikey blurted, almost falling over with the binoculars still up to his face.

"What?"

"That's Hamsa, from the fucking jail in Lewes."

"Ryan!"

"You three, keep eyes in all other directions," Ryan instructed Doc, Jen and Cooper. "Mikey, medical kit. Let's go."

Hamsa dropped to the floor and curled into a ball. Clothed only in grey chinos, his scorched torso became visible as they got closer. Half of his scalp was burned off.

"Ryan!"

"We're here, buddy!" Mikey said as they skidded on the mossy tarmac. "Are you hurt anywhere else?"

The response was a jumble of hysterical screams and crying.

"We need to get you inside." Mikey's urgency suggested that his condition was bad, observing what was left of the skin on his back. "You have exposure. You could get an infection."

"My family are coming... they're coming," Hamsa mustered through the panicked yelps.

"Get ready to drop the emergency hinge for C10," Ryan shouted back to the other three. "We have to move inside quick."

"But my family are coming... they're coming," Hamsa kept repeating.

Mikey pulled him to his feet, wrapping his arm over his shoulder.

Ryan was in a whirlwind of thoughts, trying to make sense of what was being said. If others were on the way, should he stay out? How quickly could they repair the emergency exit?

The answer was out of his control. Above Hamsa's cries, a dying engine being ragged beyond capability was approaching the southern roundabout from the outside of town.

"Are they driving here Hamsa?"

No response. The high-pitched rev grew louder.

"Hamsa." Ryan turned to the wounded man as Mikey held him. "I need to know if they're driving here."

"Yes. They're coming from Gatwick, my wife and children."

"Were you being followed?"

"No!"

"Were you alone?"

"Yes!" Hamsa drooled in anguish. "My wife is driving!"

An ear-piercing screech sharply followed by metal meeting metal with God-felt force ripped across the valley. Whatever vehicle it was had just crashed into the southern barricade.

Hamsa cried hysterically and fell to his knees, pulling down Mikey who tried to balance himself but accidentally put his hand on the exposed wound. The pain knocked Hamsa unconscious. The skin on Hamsa's back stretched off Mikey's palm like bloody string. Ryan stared in horror, and his weak stomach gave in making him vomit over his trainers. Doc arrived up under the other side of Hamsa and helped Mikey lift him.

"Keep him quarantined from everyone else." Ryan spat out the remaining vomit. "Cooper, you're with me. Mikey, get your hand washed then meet us at the barricade with the Land Rover. Leave Hamsa with the backup medical team."

"Got it," Mikey answered, his voice shaking.

"Doc, start getting C10's replacement ready once you've helped get Hamsa inside."

"Understood."

"Let's go." Ryan patted Cooper on the back.

The two of them started for the barricade with weapons drawn, legs aching, and muscles feeling the fatigue burning inside. What had started as a potential search mission in the morning had just turned into a rescue and defend mission.

8

"Do we know who attacked them?"

The question came from the back of the cafeteria. Ryan raised his palm to signal for silence as a wave of murmurs covered the room. He could feel the tension radiating off the crowd.

"No," he sighed loudly. His chest still hurt from the way his heart had thumped all afternoon. "Hamsa was in a bad way. I can't describe to you what had happened to him, and to be honest, it's making me feel sick just thinking about." He took a mouthful of grape water, "He kept saying that his family were on their way and that they were attacked. He then passed out through the pain."

"What's his condition?" another voice called out. It was Steph, who was standing next to the stairwell's double doors.

"He's currently under sedation."

No one said anything. There was a nervousness in the air, and no one wanted Ryan's job of having to tell Hamsa that his family had died in the crash.

"There was one survivor, not of Hamsa's family though. I can't remember their name, but I recognise them from Lewes," Ryan huffed, his hands cramping up through the stress. "I'll need night shift volunteers for the next fortnight, anyone with weapons training. If you need to tell your kids, then, by all means, do so,"

It was standard procedure to leave children out of the emergency meetings. Parents finding out bad news while having to console their young ones just slowed everything down. There was a strong show of hands for extra security shifts, one of which being his nephew, Lyndon. Ryan's heart sunk, feeling his sister's eyes burning through him.

"Good, thank you." He caught a glimpse of Mikey walking out the medical corridor and into the cafeteria. He was freshly showered after the past two hours of working on Hamsa's burns. "Okay, Mikey is going to take over from here. He's going to do a refresh on the emergency evacuation scenario and talk shift patterns for the volunteers. Food still runs at normal times until otherwise stated."

Mikey walked down the left side of tables and joined Ryan on the make-shift podium.

"Hamsa is stable for now, it's just a waiting game to see if his wounds are infected," Mikey announced. Then he asked, "What's for dinner tonight?"

"Sweetcorn rice and rosemary bread," Sandra shouted from a row of tables on the right.

"Energy food!" Mikey replied with a smile on his face.

"We're going to need it," Ryan whispered through his teeth before jumping off the podium and heading outside. He not only wanted to see how the trap replacement was going but needed to soothe his anxiousness with a stale cigarette.

———

Father sat in the bay window of the hotel's wedding suite, overlooking the remains of the car crash a few hundred metres down the road. Two of his men walked in, looking extremely happy with what they had to report from their afternoon observations.

Paul was the taller of the two. A little over six-foot, bushy-blond hair, broad shoulders and perfect military posture. He looked like a poster boy for a gym, though he was a dedicated soldier, serving with Father's men since they had formed their own unit after The Fast War.

Jake was much smaller in height and extremely lean, never building his body up even after he'd beaten the heroin withdrawals. His face was as greasy and saggy as the dark, dangly hair that covered his pale face. It was only pure chance that he met Father at the right time, and as much as drug addicts were overlooked by the military, this new world had a place for someone who could weasel and fight for another hit. Jake had proven invaluable over the years and was treated like one of their own.

"Well?" Father looked over the top of his coffee mug then took a huge mouthful. He sat in a Victorian chair behind a large oak dresser, providing him with a full view of the car barricade.

Jake stepped forward, his rotted teeth showing behind the sinister grin. His dark eyes ready to tell an ice-cold story. "The entrance and exit point they used today is emergency-based." He tucked his long, scraggly, brown hair behind his ears. "It seems they have more than one entrance, yet all are protected in some way as they refuse to use any others."

"Like a lottery for intruders?" Father put the mug down on the table and looked out the window.

"Yes sir, maybe even a maze," Jake continued. "When they took the injured one back, the black bitch went through one of the entrances. A couple of seconds later in the next entrance, something seemed to burst."

Father's head snapped back towards Jake. "Burst?"

"Yes sir, a liquid exposure of some kind. I couldn't make out what, but they had to wait a few minutes before they could get past it."

Father placed his elbows on the table, resting his chin on giant, balled-up hands. "All ways in and out are protected, an emergency point put in place for quicker access..." he whispered, processing the information. "How quick was their response team getting out?"

"They took the wounded one through the front doors. I'd say roughly five minutes passed before one man ran back to the perimeter," Jake stated. "I heard the start of an engine, then saw the vehicle arrive at the barricade, joining the two that ran out to the crash. The black bitch stayed guard at the perimeter's entrance." He stood straight as he finished his report.

"And you didn't get spotted?" Father asked with a haze of concern.

"No sir."

"The bad news, however, Father..." Paul stepped forward, arms behind his back and chest stuck out. "Once they returned, they immediately started repairing or replacing whatever it was that burst in the perimeter wall." He looked at Father, waiting for an angry response.

"Go on."

"That perimeter has to be a maze, sir. Only they know the way in and way out."

"Were they still repairing when you left?" Father asked with a glint of hope in his eyes.

"Yes sir. The tall redhead and the dorky-looking guy with glasses started to replace whatever had burst. Whatever they use for these traps, it's extremely volatile and takes a lot of care and handling when refilling."

Father slapped the desk hard, the coffee mug jumping off the edge and crashing to the floor. Both of his men jumped back, eyes wide, not sure what the reaction was for or whether they were in trouble.

"Perfect!" He stood, leaning palms first on the desk. "That means they'll have to show us their correct way in soon."

Paul and Jake both relaxed, understanding what Father meant.

After all, the package had already been delivered, and eventually, it would have to be returned to the sender.

"Also, just for your benefit of knowing, sir..." Jake started to do that hideous giggle of his, "...the redhead is a yank."

———

"That's done," Doc announced, veering away from the salt-acid trap. Two gas canisters loaded with pressurised butane positioned to burst into the sulphuric acid and rock salt combination had been stuffed into two old guitar speakers. They were hidden so deep in the maze's walls that you'd never see them.

"Nice work guys," Ryan said, looking to the sky. Cooper started heading back inside, and Doc waited until he'd been a couple of minutes out of earshot. "So?" He took his glasses off and cleaned them on his T-shirt.

"Just one survivor," Ryan shook his head in remorse. "And it wasn't his wife or one of his kids."

"Fuck."

"Yeah. Survivor got a broken arm, badly busted face, but can see and talk."

"Who was the survivor?" Doc asked, pushing his glasses back on.

"Can't remember his name, but he's that little gobshite I knocked out last time I was down in Lewes." Ryan scratched his head in anger. "He had a couple of lighters and a handheld radio on him."

"Trying to stay in contact with any other survivors from Lewes?" Doc theorized.

"I'd assume so."

"I don't remember them having radios in Lewes."

"Me neither, unless they never told us."

"Or he stole it from whoever attacked them?"

"Also, possible." Ryan rubbed his eyes. "We'll question him more when he's ready."

"What about Hamsa?"

"He's under sedation, enough to keep him out cold for a while."

Doc could only muster a nod in response as he knelt, picking up his handgun and tucking it into his holster. He saw that Ryan was concerned.

"We've done what we can for now. Let's go in, get some food and a couple hours of sleep before tonight's shift." Doc turned while pushing Ryan back into the maze.

Ryan made light work of the sweetcorn rice, taking him less than a minute before he'd finished the bowl. Sandra smiled at him from the other side of the hot counter that ran along the back of the cafeteria. Her teeth were outstandingly white considering the state the world had gone into, though her skin looked tired and worn. Her curly, red hair hung over her broad shoulders, and her pale blue eyes were always welcoming.

"You need some sleep, darling. You overthink that brain of yours, and you'll be in trouble." Her voice held a layer of sarcasm and concern within it. Ryan never knew when to take her seriously. He figured it must have been her South London accent that made everything sound sarcastic.

"Your husband says the same about you," he smirked back.

"Well, if I didn't do the thinking in our marriage, no one would," she retorted.

"Leave me alone!" Dominic yelled from his table, overhearing them while chowing down his own dinner. "Boss!"

"Please tell him to stop calling me that," Ryan groaned.

"I'm the only black man here. Gotta make sure I know who's in charge!" Dominic laughed. He loved making Ryan feel uncomfortable with racist jibes, knowing the dreadlocked chef didn't know how to respond to it.

Dominic stood well over six-foot tall. An unrefined, bulky frame and clean-shaven head made him stand out from everyone else, his skin colour making no difference. Though his stature was more imposing than others, he wore the warmest smile, just like his wife. He'd use the old library next to the reception to run a daytime school for the little ones, and at weekends, he'd use it for prayers and sermons. Maisie attended all of those with Sandra and Dominic's daughter, Jess, her best friend.

Like his wife, he was in his late forties now. Mikey joked they looked like extras off the set of the TV show, EastEnders. Sandra and Dominic bought good skills to the refuge. Before the war, they'd worked in a school on the rough side of south London.

Dominic's experience as a security guard in an area renowned for its knife crime and Sandra the old dinner lady who could feed hundreds of people at once were vital to keeping the place going. Her food might not have been the 'fancy flick stuff' Ryan used to serve, as she called it, but it was good, nutritious and she never ran out or wasted anything.

"Going for some rest now anyway, Sandra." He took a bottle of grape water from the display fridge. "I'll see you in the morning, thanks for the rice."

"Good night, Ryan."

He walked into the cafeteria and tapped Dominic on the shoulder. "If I'm not awake by the time Sam finishes his shift, come throw some water over me, please?"

Dominic looked up from his Bible and chuckled.

"No worries." His teeth seemed lightning white in the cafeteria lighting in contrast to his dark skin. "Get some sleep, and as the missus says, don't overthink too much."

Ryan smiled in return. He felt his brain shutting down yet wanting to stay awake and question the day's events. He couldn't help but think —it's what kept him and everyone else alive.

Doc seemed happy when they finished replacing the trap. Security was doubled, and the maze was strong, but something was bugging Ryan. His brain was telling him something, and he couldn't figure out what it was.

———

A few hours of sleep had done more damage than good as Ryan tried to wake himself up, cupping handfuls of cold water from the sink and drenching his face. He would have had a lot more sleep if Cassy hadn't been waiting in his night shift room, but he wasn't going to admit that to anyone. She left just after letting Ryan get to sleep.

"Anything unusual?" he asked, wiping his face with a towel which was overdue its weekly wash.

"Standard night shift." Dominic shook his head and looked down at the floor, noting the bloodstains on the carpet. "Have you covered those blisters, boss?"

Ryan waved an empty plaster packet in the air before flinging it into the nearby bin and tying his dreadlocks back.

"Can't have you walking round making yourself and everyone else ill with a blood infection."

Fighting infections and illnesses was half the battle since the end of The Fast War.

Ryan nodded and reached to the mattress, picking up his beloved

Glock and a black hoodie. Dominic opened the door, letting in a freezing cold draft.

"Fuck me! When did that happen?" Ryan gasped, pulling the hoodie on. Dominic looked back at him, his smile exposing his bright white teeth again.

Ryan followed him into the narrow corridor, which had once been the first-floor private dining room. It had once sat up to three hundred guests for conferences or weddings but was now converted into the bedroom corridor. Originally, beds were randomly sprawled about in the room as it served as just a giant dorm. The need to start growing crops, making the maze, burying the dead, and having clean water outweighed living arrangements.

As more families had been found or rescued, the need for personal space was eventually addressed. There was enough carpentry and plumbing experience among the survivors, mainly Cooper, to convert the entire first floor into private spaces. The old function room, meeting rooms, the staff offices, and furniture storage rooms were renovated to give each family and couples their own space.

All rooms had their own showers or baths fitted in, some had multiple rooms for children to sleep separately from their parents.

"How much bleach do we have? I need to clean that shower out at some point, Cassy's getting annoyed about it," Ryan asked, closing the door behind him and following down the corridor lit by the candle he was carrying,

"Plenty left, boss," Dominic whispered as they strolled past the various closed doors, rooms with families sleeping or trying to sleep after the day's madness. "Doc has the ingredients to make more when the time comes."

They descended the staircase all the way to the basement. Their footsteps echoed as they marched across the tiled floor and opened the door to the second reception.

An exhausted-looking Mikey greeted them; he remained sat behind the small desk as he briefed them on Hamsa and the car crash survivor's condition. He expected Hamsa to make a full recovery, albeit a slow and painful one, which could also bring with it a lifetime of survival guilt, most probably leading to mental health issues.

"Go to bed." Ryan looked over his fatigued friend. "Dominic will take over on reception duty."

"Okay, thanks," Mikey yawned. "I'll see you guys in the morning."

Ryan unlatched the door and stepped outside.

The wooden-panelled trench was dug eight feet beneath ground level. The inner wall was straight and lined with timber, whereas the outer wall had a five-foot ledge, allowing people to climb up and then step out the remaining three feet. No one wanted to jump down eight feet in the event of an emergency, and most couldn't climb that high if they had to get out quickly.

Two figures approached from the left, Rich and Fergie—two former bartenders in Maidville's cocktail bar, and two lost prodigies of the acting world who'd just got their first auditions as the war started.

Both were smaller than Ryan with slim shoulders, grey eyes and narrow faces atop their thespian postures. The only difference between them was their hair. Rich was clean shaved, whereas Fergie had thin blond hair parted to the right, always combed like he was about to start serving up a Margherita.

Like everyone else, they had never handled a gun before the war, never mind killed anyone.

"Where do you guys need me?" Ryan whispered.

"Point A." Rich nodded behind him, the guttering light shining off his perfectly shaved head.

"Doc thinks there's a storm coming. Say's we should break out the winter wear in the morning. Just so we don't get off guard," Fergie stated. Rich and himself looked up at the sky which was still crystal clear.

The winter fear was a real thing. Flu was a killer now, and no one wanted to lose a loved one to what was once cured with an over-the-counter prescription.

"Are you guys okay to do that after sunrise?" Ryan asked. His heart broke for them. They had lost their mother to illness a couple of winters ago.

They both nodded. "Are we under attack?" Rich asked as Fergie carried on past to point B.

"I think we're always under attack," Ryan said. "That's how I keep myself alive."

"But the people down in Lewes?"

"I honestly don't know, Rich. All I know and all any of us know is what was said at the meeting earlier, my friend. That's why we're doing these extra shifts."

Rich's eyes stayed peeled to the ground.

"Get back to Fergie. He needs you, especially this time of the year." Ryan didn't want to make it sound like an order. "And I need the cocktail twins to be ready to kick the shit out of something if the situation called for it,"

Rich forced a smile and followed Fergie, leaving Ryan under the footbridge.

Pulling a cigarette out from his righthand pocket, he lit it while thinking about how he once tried to quit. "You can't win every fight," he mumbled to himself before turning his thoughts to the day's events. "I really need some answers, Hamsa. I'm sorry you lost your family, but I need to know what I'm protecting mine from now."

9

A few families remained in the cafeteria, finishing up the last of their breakfasts of raisin porridge, soda bread and thyme butter.

"Morning report is a bit more lively than normal, as you'd imagine." Mikey managed to make the sentence audible through a mouthful of soda bread.

"Go on." Ryan sat across the table, finishing off his mug of tea. Doc sat to his left with a bowl of porridge in hand.

"So, Rich and Fergie pulled out all the winter gear. It's all there and in good condition," Mikey announced, looking up from his notepad. "Of course, we have extra's now because of the people we lost last year."

There was a silent moment between the three of them, remembering those who had succumbed to the flu.

"The burial ritual for Hamsa's family has already started," Mikey continued. "The bodies have been washed and wrapped in linen. Cooper dug three graves in our northwest corner, all facing Jerusalem of course."

"Facing Mecca," Ryan said correcting him.

"Sorry, Mecca." Mikey reached for the water again, hands shaking.

"It's okay." Ryan reached across the table, holding his arm. "Don't beat yourself up. It's been hard twenty-four hours."

"Sorry." Mikey inhaled hard, calming himself. "We're going to wheel the bodies into Hamsa so he can say goodbye."

Ryan and Doc nodded; they felt for him. Mikey shook harder as he drank from the bottle again.

"What time did Hamsa wake up?" Doc asked.

"Just as you guys finished your shift." Mikey glanced back at his notepad before slamming it loudly onto the table. Everyone left in the cafeteria turned to the three sitting at the end of the room.

"He woke up and was shouting about his family, saying they were driving here and would be here soon." Mikey rubbed the tears away. "He didn't believe there was a crash because his wife was a very careful driver."

"They could have been chased?" Ryan shared a glance with Doc.

"I had to tell him his family are dead. I had to tell this man who looks like he's been put on an open fire that his family is dead." Mikey's eyes started to water again.

"I'm sorry," Ryan tried to comfort him. "That should have been me that told him. I didn't know he was going to wake up so soon, and if I had known, I would have put you on night-watch and me in the med room."

"It's not just that," Mikey said, composing himself. "Hamsa ran from Gatwick airport to here, to find us and to get help for his family. Barefoot and tortured, just to wake up here and be told his family were dead."

Ryan stood and walked around the table, picking up the notepad Mikey was reading from. "You've kept him alive and helped arrange the correct procedures to respect this man's family. I'd say you've done everything in your power."

"It's true," Doc joined in. "A lot worse could have happened."

"Did you get any more information from him?" Ryan asked, running down the bullet points on the notepad.

"No. I left him to grieve alone, that's what he asked for." Mikey slumped his head in between his arms over the edge of the table.

Ryan knelt beside him. "The other guy is stable?"

"As much as can be, his left arm has been put in a cast, of which we don't have many bandages left for that kind of procedure." Mikey lifted his head and pointed to the bottom of the notepad—he'd made a list of food and equipment they were running low on. Ryan looked down the list before handing it to Doc.

"We're doing overly well on flour." Mikey wiped away the final tears.

"That's more than enough for winter." Doc adjusted his glasses. "Now, both of you go to bed. I had a long sleep last night, and Cooper did too. We can oversee everything today."

"Okay." Ryan extended his arm and pointed Mikey in the direction of the staircase. He obliged before disappearing upstairs. "Doc, will Lyndon be okay on his own in the medical corridor while Mikey's asleep?"

"I'm on standby if he needs anything. Plus, he may look like you, but he's a better learner."

"Very funny."

Both uncle and nephew looked almost identical in appearance, structure, and height. Lyndon had blond dreadlocks like Ryan, though he was still a way off growing facial hair.

"Your nephew will be fine. Go to bed."

"Can you wake me and Mikey before the burial, please?"

"Sure."

"Thank you." Ryan headed towards the staircase.

"I'll be in the medical corridor with Lyndon," Doc shouted. "I'll see if I can get some information from the passenger."

Ryan raised his arm with the standard thumbs-up before hesitating. Something bothered him about that sentence. Feeling the irritation on his brain again as it was telling him something was wrong. *Passenger?* He carried on, telling himself to get some rest, then it punched him in the face.

"He wasn't the passenger!" he shot a look back Doc, wide-eyed and alarmed. "He was the fucking driver!"

"Okay, so?" Doc queried with bewilderment.

Ryan pulled at his hair with both hands, screwing his face up in anger and frustration that he hadn't spotted it sooner.

"Hamsa said his wife was driving!" He burst across the cafeteria and kicked the doors open to the medical corridor. Doc's face dropped. He jumped from his seat and hurried after Ryan.

They rounded the corner into the unattractive, yellow corridor with blue floor tiles; the ugliest part of the building.

"Hamsa hasn't mentioned this guy once!"

Each of the downstairs storage rooms had been converted into individual treatment rooms for the sick or injured. The quarantine rooms sat at the far end. Their feet slid on the synthetic flooring as they arrived at Hamsa's room. Ryan slammed the door open.

"Hamsa, we need to talk," Ryan blurted, stumbling inside.

Hamsa lay face down on the bed, the white sheet that covered his back stained with blotches of dark red and yellow. His arms spread out on tables either side, and his feet were wrapped in bandages bearing the same discolouration as the cover on his back.

As he lifted his head, it was abundantly clear that he'd been crying since Mikey had left him alone. "My family..." was all Hamsa could muster.

"I know, I'm so sorry." Ryan tried to recover his breath. "Hamsa, I need to know who travelled with your family, and I need to know now."

"No one."

"We pulled four people out of the car, three were your wife and children." Ryan paused as Hamsa burst into tears again. Tears and saliva hung from his beard. "Your wife was not the driver."

"I left my family at the airport, I told them to drive here if help hadn't arrived by midday," Hamsa shouted in despair. "We were alone, there was no one else!"

"Could this guy have escaped from Lewes like you did?" Ryan kept pushing. "Maybe he caught up with your family at Gatwick?"

"Who?" Hamsa babbled through his tears.

"The fourth person we pulled from the car crash."

"I don't know who you're talking about!"

"That little prick who started getting mouthy last time I saw you. When I bought the prayer mats down, remember?"

"Ben?" Hamsa suddenly stopped crying.

"Yeah, Ben. That's who's next door and who travelled with your family." Ryan turned, pointing to the medical room opposite.

Hamsa's face blanked. It then formed an amalgamation of confusion and desperation as if he didn't believe what was being said.

"Ben went missing last winter." He dribbled down his chin. "We haven't seen him since."

Ryan's own face turned blank as the realisation washed over him. Why no one came when they rang the church bell and why Hamsa didn't know about the fourth person in the car. It was a set-up to get someone inside, and in all likelihood, Ben had led his new friends to his old home in Lewes and now to Ryan's home. The hidden threat was already here, close to his family.

"Hamsa, I'm so sorry for your loss. I'm going to leave you to grieve." Ryan stood from the chair as Hamsa's head sank back down, crying louder. The raw emotion reverberated as he walked past Doc into the corridor.

"Lyndon?" Ryan called.

His nephew jumped out of Ben's room. "What's going on?"

"Has that guy in there moved?"

"No. He's been asleep since Mikey patched his arm up." Lyndon looked back at the injured man.

"Get up to the restaurant." Ryan kept his voice quiet. "Tell them we have a breach situation. Get Sam to set up guards at the end of this corridor and rifles aiming all directions from the restaurant. Go, now." He emphasized the last part to get Lyndon alert.

He had never been given an order like that from his uncle before that day. Lyndon made a beeline towards the cafeteria. Ryan switched off the safety on his Glock, shuffled into the room, strode over to the bed, and pressed it against Ben's forehead.

The young mans' face was a mixture of dark purple and black bruising, running from temple to temple and down to his top lip. The left ear was torn at the lobe, his blond buzzcut matted down with his own blood.

"Wake up, Ben." Ryan pressed the gun harder. "You've got some fucking talking to do."

On command, Ben's eyes opened. The corner of his mouth started to rise. He had been awake the whole time, waiting for this moment. "Handy that," Ben rasped back. "I'm here as a messenger."

10

"A messenger for who?" Ryan's body begged to pull the trigger.

"Our leader."

"You're going to tell me who you're with, and you're going to do it with the next fucking sentence you say."

Ben glanced to the radio that sat atop the bedside table. "He's expecting your call."

"What happened down in Lewes?"

"They refused to join us."

Ryan felt someone grab his shoulder as the gun shook violently in his hand. Fortunately, it was Doc.

"We're going to need him if we're going to be talking to someone out there." Doc started to pull him away.

"Are you the reason your leader is aware of our home?" Ryan asked Ben, ignoring Doc's suggestion. The words failed to pierce the disgust and anger that he felt.

Ben nodded.

"Ryan, don't do it." Doc reached over to the bedside table, picking up the radio. "Make the call Ben."

He threw the radio on the bed as Ryan reluctantly lowered the pistol to his side.

Ben fiddled with the dials and pulled it up to his mouth. "Father, they know," he announced. There was a click of static and a moment's pause.

"Are you with any of them now?" a deep voice responded.

Ben locked eyes with Ryan. "Yes sir. The long-haired one and the one with glasses."

"The two that were having the conversation on the top floor two days ago?" the voice sounded pleased. Ryan and Doc stood in shock, knowing they had been watched closer than they realised.

"Yes sir."

"I can guess by the silence they are unaware we've been watching them?"

"Yes sir."

Ryan snatched the radio from Ben's hand. "Care to watch us in the same place?" he snarled.

"Who is this?" The voice was taken aback.

"The long-haired one. If you want negotiations, your first one begins with Ben's life. We'll be up at the top floor." Ryan turned the radio off.

"You're going to consider letting him go?" Doc asked.

"I wanna kill him, I can't lie about that."

"Then why haven't you?"

"Because you're right," Ryan frowned. "We can find out more about this group if we keep him alive."

"Glad you see it that way."

"Just keep me away if he tries to provoke me. I'll happily shoot that weasel piece of shit if given the chance."

"I'm a soldier for a better future," Ben hissed at the two men standing over him. "You have no idea what's going on in the world."

"Then your new boss can enlighten us." Ryan yanked him up from the bed.

Doc made a point of standing between them and holding his own gun to the back of Ben's head. Ryan would kill him out of rage and vengeance, whereas Doc would kill him if it were the logical thing to do. Ben's life depended on his own actions.

"I suggest you and 'sir' be honest about everything," Doc whispered. "You still have a lot of blood to spill."

"I already got the paki's blood," Ben laughed, feeling proud with that torturing remark. His self-indulging moment got cut short with Doc spinning him around and driving the butt of his pistol into his already-bruised jaw. A mouthful of blood and two teeth shot across the wall.

———

"We'll be back before sundown," Paul shouted as he burst out the revolving doors of the hotel entrance.

They followed the same protocol every time they initiated contact with a new group. In the event of things going sour, they were to abandon their current post at the hotel and head for the next prearranged destination for attack preparations.

In this case, the prearranged destination was the mansion in the centre of the woodlands at the top of the Maidhill. Directly opposite the vineyard.

———

Ben was led at gunpoint to the top floor, not daring to say another word.

"Where was he watching us from?" Doc asked, pushing the pistol into the back of Ben's head.

Ben's good arm raised, finger outstretched to the top of Maidhill.

"You better pray he's there now." Ryan glared hard into Ben's eyes before talking into the radio. "Are you ready to negotiate for Ben's life?"

"Very much so. Can I ask your name so this conversation becomes somewhat more formal?" The deep voice sounded overly cocky, yet respectful. Ryan's skin crawled at the arrogant naivety.

"Ryan, and you are?"

"Father," the voice replied bluntly.

"Yeah, I'm not going to call you that. Tell me your name, or I won't be having any discussion with you at all." Ryan turned his attention out the window and focused on the massive expanse of Maidhill.

There was another long pause of radio silence before the voice replied. "This is Captain Morgan Jeffries, SAS task division 205."

"With a title like that, why would you insist on being called Father?"

"Our children will make the future what it should be, and I'm the one who's going to teach them how to make the future."

"Whatever you say, Captain. You sound just as deluded as some of the other people we've met since the war." Ryan continued searching across the hill's peak. "Seeing as you've been watching but haven't fired a shot, I'm guessing you aren't in a good situation of ammunition, or you're being forced to listen to me out of desperation?"

Ryan was hoping he could get under his skin. He already hated the man, but he was going to have to play this smarter than his anger issues begged to.

"The war is still happening Ryan, or are you so dumb to the outside world that you have no idea how screwed everything really is?"

The war is still happening? It finished only months after it started!

By the window, Sam used his hunting rifle to scope out Maidhill. He clicked his fingers and pointed to the top of the meadow. "He's standing out of the treeline. He's not even hiding himself, and he's got binoculars."

"Why are you not hiding yourself when you know we're armed?" Ryan asked into the radio.

"Why would I? You've played everything safe so far, including your trip into town yesterday. You're not going to gun down someone who has the answers you need."

Ryan could practically hear the captain smiling as he made that remark. He raised his pistol to Ben's head.

"Okay then. Answers, now." His eyes remained locked on the tree-line, hoping the captain was staring back. "Why Lewes? Why'd you attack them?"

"They refused to give up the non-British part of their community." The radio crackled. "We can't have any Asians or Africans living free."

"Why not?"

Doc was now crouched on the left side of the room with a rifle of his own, aim fixed on the hill. Though the temperature had dropped slightly, the sky was still clear.

"The invasion across Europe consisted of Middle-Eastern and African Muslim immigrants. Therefore, they can't be trusted."

"We have trust and faith in ours," Ryan replied. "No matter who it was that invaded and began to slaughter the population."

A bead of sweat dripped off Ben's nose. Ryan gripped the pistol tighter while ignoring his impulse to fire.

"They can't be trusted," Father growled.

"So, you attacked a community because they have Asian and African members?" Ryan shouted, starting to lose his cool. "You just sound like a racist cunt!"

"It's more than that."

"How so? Enlighten me, Nazi-boy!"

"When my unit were captured, the Muslim brothers we fought with were given a deal," the captain said calmly. "Defect and fight for them. Even British-born Asians are scum. Your Asians will betray you when the war reaches here."

Ryan didn't know what to say. Anyone could make up a story to get people on their side. He decided to change subject, trying to force the Captain to slip up, "You said the war is still happening?"

"Last we heard was that French, Belgian, Swiss, German, and Baltic forces are holding off the outland invasion across the French-Spanish border up to the German-Polish border," Father answered. "My unit held off an attack coming from over Scandinavia."

Doc and Sam both looked back. It was the first confirmation in years that a war was still happening.

"Will the war reach here?" Ryan pushed.

"Not if we have anything to do with it," Father paused. "We're not here to fight you. Your life is in as much danger as ours if the war manages to reach down here. We'll need each other."

"What do you want then?"

"The immigrants you have with you and the safe return of our boy Ben, that's all."

"Is that all?" Ryan laughed in disbelief.

"That's all."

Even if Ryan believed everything he'd heard, the man called Father and Ben were family killers, topped off with extreme racism.

"After what you've done down in Lewes, give me one good reason why I shouldn't remove Ben's head now and let our shooter put a hole in you?" Ryan retorted.

There was a chuckle before the reply.

"Should you be idiotic enough to kill me and Ben, you'll have my people to deal with. We may be outgunned, but I assure you we outnumber you, and my people are highly resourceful. Even if you are lucky enough to win against my people, you're not going to be left in good shape for when the war reaches here, and your immigrants will betray you in exchange for their lives." Captain Jefferies made sure he delivered that part as clearly as he could. That was his pitch.

Doc stared at Ryan, shaking his head. Though it could be a bluff, they didn't have the manpower to call it.

"What do you suggest?" Ryan asked Doc.

"I can blow his head off now, Cuz." Sam suggested.

"No, Sam." Doc rubbed the bridge of his nose. "Give them Ben back and tell them to leave."

"Are you fucking crazy?" Sam shouted. "Look what they did to Hamsa."

"Sam's right," Ryan said nodding. "How do I justify to Hamsa that I let them go?"

Doc took his glasses off and stared back at Ryan. "Tell him that you were protecting your family," he said coldly. "Hamsa would've done the same."

The words hit hard, and as much as Ryan hated it, he was right. To prevent a battle they weren't prepared for, he was going to have to take the high ground. But he was going to make sure he had the last laugh.

"You can have Ben back, then you have two days to get out of here," Ryan rasped. "Our Asians will remain as our family and help us to grow and flourish, even when dealing with simple, narrow-minded pricks like you."

"They'll betray you and will happily kill you just to save their own lives." The captain's response was shouted this time.

"He looks pissed," Sam said from behind his scope.

"If you're angry now, it's best that you know that our two Asians are preparing the burial of Hamsa's family. The bodies have been washed and wrapped according to Islamic tradition and will be buried." Ryan turned and smiled at Ben. "Facing Mecca of course."

The other end of the radio remained silent.

"Do you want Ben back?"

"Yes." The captain's blunt answer made it evident that he was repressing rage.

"Meet me in the middle of the road tomorrow at sunrise then. I'll have enough rifles on you should you try anything." Ryan switched the radio off.

"He's just thrown his radio on the ground. He's fucking fuming," Sam laughed.

Doc pulled away from his window and stood the rifle up against the wall. "I'll take this prick back downstairs." He grabbed Ben's good arm. "I'll put him in the cellar cage. He won't be going anywhere."

The cellar cage was a small room in the basement, once filled with ridiculously expensive wines, guarded with a jail-like, iron bar door.

"Okay." Ryan kept his gaze on Ben as Doc led him away. "Sam, switch windows with Dominic for now," he ordered. "And keep changing position every hour."

————

Up on the hill, Captain Morgan Jeffries bent down and yanked his binoculars from a patch of dandelions before storming back into the treeline. He adjusted the dial on top of the handset and clicked the receiver.

"Did they buy it?" he asked.

"Yes sir," Paul replied. "One of the riflemen was laughing while still looking at you. He's moved to the back now, and another one has taken his point. Some big, black guy. The guy with glasses has taken Ben out of sight, and the guy called Ryan has just followed them."

"Perfect. You haven't been spotted?"

"No sir. They were all focused on where you are."

"Okay Paul. Do you have everything you need for tomorrow?"

"Yes sir, well in range. They didn't notice Jake the last time he was in this position."

"Good. You know where to rendezvous after the meeting tomorrow?" Father smiled as he asked.

"Of course, sir. That's why you trust me. Out." The radio clicked silent.

Father couldn't contain his excitement as he looked at Jake, who was lying behind a fallen log with binoculars up to his eyes, gazing back at the top floor of the winery.

"Didn't see you either?"

"No, Father. It should be a walk in the park for us tomorrow, if we have to resort to it," Jake answered.

"These people have a final chance to side with us. They won't be even remotely ready for what we at throw at them."

———

"Give me one reason why I shouldn't kill you and your Father tomorrow?" Ryan screamed, ripping Ben away from Doc as he snuck up behind catching them both off guard. Ben crashed to the floor, his skull thudding off the tiles.

"We don't know what we're up against," Doc warned as Ryan picked Ben up by the collar.

"We're up against this little, rat-faced cunt's new friends. We're up against a group who kill anyone who doesn't give them what they want."

"You have no idea what's coming," Ben managed to say while spitting out a mouthful of blood.

Doc forced himself between them, trying to push Ryan away without provoking a physical response. "This isn't a group of crazy people who are standing out in the middle of the road in full view of our guns," he rationalized while Ryan backed away. "Don't give them the chance to attack us."

Ryan tried to take in what Doc was saying as images of Hamsa flashed through his mind, glazing over his eyes like a mist of hatred. "I should've killed you when you tried to stop us giving prayer mats to Muslims in Lewes."

"The prayers they sing on those mats are the ones they'll sing on after raping your children here!" Ben yelped while holding eye contact.

Ryan sprang forward, grabbing Ben's injured arm and a handful of hair, kicked the cell door open and threw him inside.

"You have no idea what they'll do to you. Father will stop that happening to the world."

"I might not be killing you," Ryan forced through gritted teeth as he slammed the cell door, locking it once in place, "but I have no issue cutting your tongue out."

"I'd listen, Ben. I'm not stopping him." Doc pulled on Ryan's arm, leading him away from the cage before whispering, "Just take your eyes off him and follow me."

Ryan reluctantly followed. "We'll need someone down here to watch him."

"I'll start organising that now."

"Why can't I just kill him now?"

"The same reason you can't kill this Father guy tomorrow."

"Why?"

"Because this enemy seems more of a threat and better managed than some random, desperate murderers," Doc said, keeping his tone cool. "Go through with the plan tomorrow, I think we'll find out more about them when Father talks."

"Do you think they'll accept our terms?" Ryan already doubted it. "Just get up and leave because we say so?"

Doc ran his fingers through his thick hair and removed his glasses, cleaning them on his white shirt. "I think he will if he wants Ben back," he answered, putting his square rimmed spectacles back on.

"No mention of food or water," Ryan pointed out as he untied his hair. The dreadlocks dropped down his back; he felt the adrenaline starting to burn off.

"Exactly. Whoever he has with him must be well-fed, disciplined and focused." Doc led Ryan into the staircase. "Give them the option to leave and start getting ready for a fight if they don't. This is the biggest threat we've faced in years."

11

As much as Ryan wanted to sleep, the sweet bliss of a good night evaded him. The thought of standing close to someone who'd openly confessed to killing the only other community they knew ate away at him. Ryan wasn't a saint by any means, he'd taken enough lives since all of this started, but it had always been in self-defence. Never once did he contemplate wiping out a society because they housed someone he didn't care for.

Doc was right, however. Avoid the bloodbath and tell them to move on. If the war was truly coming, then Father and his people would be busy with their own problems.

It still didn't put Ryan at ease though. He got out of bed and showered, put his all-black sportswear on, and checked his Glock. Cassy joined him as he headed downstairs, though she skipped the shower, and helped Sandra to cook the day's breakfast of spinach on toast and scrambled egg. Ryan didn't feel like eating, instead, he said good morning to everyone else as they made their way downstairs, doing his best to stay positive.

Doc and Mikey pulled Ben from the cellar-cage and led him up to the main reception. Cooper took over watching Ben, the barrel of his shotgun constantly aimed at the young man's forehead.

The sun was starting to rise; Ryan breathed in hard and cleared his
mind. It was time to go.

Cassy met Ryan by the table nearest the hot counter where he
stood and watched Maisie eat her breakfast.

"Come straight back, baby." She kissed him.

"I will," he said with a hesitant smile. He wanted to keep her reassured, even if he was about to meet a horrible piece of shit. "I love
you."

"I love you, too."

"I like the tomatoes, Daddy," Maisie said as she dropped a slice on
her white, pullover dress.

"Well, at least you're pronouncing it correctly." He rubbed the top
of her head and scuffed up her hair. "There's going to be a lot of other
new things growing outside after winter. I can teach you to be a chef."

"Cool!" Maisie exclaimed.

"Is that the same stuff you wore two days ago?" Cassy pointed at his
outfit.

"Maybe." Ryan tried to look innocent. "It doesn't smell too bad,
considering."

"You never smell. Not even of fear. You always make the right decisions, even if you don't agree with them." She sat next to Maisie.
"You're making the right decision today."

Ryan needed to hear that—more than he realised. *I'm gonna propose
to her when I get back.*

He headed for the main reception where Ben was held at gunpoint
by Cooper.

Doc tied a blindfold around Ben's eyes. "We set?" he asked, pushing
the main entrance doors open.

"I'm good," Mikey nodded as he slung his G36C over his shoulder
and picked up a bucket of rock salt.

"Ready." Cooper pushed Ben in the direction of the doors.

"Yeah," Ryan said as he tied his hair.

In full view of Maidhill, the four men proudly exited the building
with Ben in front. Ryan hoped that someone was watching this display.
If anyone tried anything, Sam and Dominic would take them down
from the restaurant windows.

. . .

That morning finally provided a chill that you could associate with autumn. Moody clouds hung overhead bringing the promise of much-welcomed rain after the heatwave of the week before. The sun was rising, hiding in the grey sky as a faint morning dew covered the ground and bushes.

Ryan had his pistol pressed between Ben's shoulder blades, guiding him through an alternative route to C10. There was no way they were taking the correct route out to J10. Cooper led the party with Doc just behind. Mikey filled in behind Ryan.

They set off C10's trap via the pull wire in D9, releasing the mixture with a sudden roar as it forced its way out of the canister and exploded through the speakers. Once the corrosive mixture dissipated, they rounded into C10. The ground beneath them had turned to mush after exposure to two lots of acidic salts in two days.

From behind, Ryan saw Cooper step outside the exit and raise his shotgun. Mikey and Doc placed the buckets of trap-replacement chemicals on the ground and brandished their pistols.

"Stop," Ryan ordered Ben as he stepped around his left-hand side, pressing the gun against his temple. He caught a glimpse of a gargantuan figure casually leaning against the carriageway's central barricade. He was dressed in a simple grey T-shirt, black cargo pants and black boots.

"I suppose these aren't the only guns you have aimed at me?" Father smiled, his voice even deeper than it was through the radio. It had a slight Geordie accent hidden in the depths of it all.

He was a mountain of a man, well over six foot six, and a muscular frame which screamed he could crush a man's head with his bare hands. His eyes were a dull brown, though appearing black and icy, buried in the sockets where the bone appeared prominent through the wear and tear of malnutrition. At some point since the end of the war, this man had experienced the hunger that followed.

How the hell did he keep his muscular frame after that?

Cooper kept his gun firmly aimed at him. Mikey and Doc swept their weapons between Father and the background.

Ryan pulled Ben's blindfold off with his free hand. Ben squinted for a minute, adjusting his eyes to the breaking daylight. The bruising around his face prevented him from smiling.

"How did you kill the family in the car?" Ryan directed the question at Father. "How did you get Ben in the car?"

There was a moment's pause, like the giant was figuring out whether to be honest.

"Quick and painless," Father answered, fearless of consequence. "We intercepted them at the shitty, little hotel up the road."

Ryan knew the hotel well. He had poached Doc from there in his cooking days.

"They recognised Ben, and they stopped. They got out, I broke their necks, we put the bodies back in the car, and Ben drove it into the barricade." Father listed off the process like nothing had happened. Ryan's body refilled with yesterday's rage, courtesy of a man who had just admitted to killing a woman and her children.

"Take Ben, take your group, and get the fuck out of here," Ryan said, controlling his rising anger. "You have two days."

Father rubbed his hands before clapping them together. "I was hoping to talk."

"I thought you would, but talking to a child killer isn't my idea of a good time," Ryan lashed back.

"I've got two people with me in that building next to the car park," Father pointed behind him to the sewage plantation. "They're not armed, but you need to see one of them."

"What the fuck are you talking about?"

Father waved his left arm in the air, and the fire exit opened.

Cooper swung his aim over to the building, while Doc and Mikey kept their guns on Father.

"Take it easy." Father raised his hands into a surrender position. "I'm being honest when I say my people genuinely mean you no harm."

"Let him say what he needs to say," Doc whispered to Ryan.

"You try anything," Ryan snarled, pressing the gun harder to Ben's temple. "You all die now."

"I know," Father nodded. "I'm not stupid, I just want to talk."

Two male figures emerged from the water treatment building, the first draped in grey scraggy overalls, with dark skin and tattered, brown hair. The second dressed in the same grey T-shirt and black combat pants that Father was sporting, although this man was much skinnier with dark, greasy hair tucked behind his ears. They joined Father in the middle of the road.

"Do you recognise this man?" Father asked, pointing at the man in rags. Ryan looked the man over, who was clearly of Middle Eastern heritage, before shaking his head.

"Now, when I asked you to hand over your own immigrants, I get the feeling you thought I meant to kill them." Father pushed himself off the steel barrier. "What good are these people to us if they're dead? They make a fine workforce, isn't that right Aslan?" Father slapped the ragged individual on the back.

"Yes, Father," the man replied. Ryan frowned at the response. The man called Aslan seemed to be submissive, his eyes never looking up from the ground. "I have over five hundred of them. They renovate buildings for us to stay in. We clothe them, feed them, and even provide a roof for you, don't we?"

"Yes, Father."

"If the new world ever gets fixed," Father continued, "these people can't be trusted to run around and make decisions, so they might as well graft and do all the shitty jobs that we shouldn't have to do. Just like the useless, little, sand-dwelling scum you are, isn't that right Aslan?"

"Yes, Father."

Father now grinned at Ryan, showing off his almost perfect set of teeth.

"Sounds like you have slaves," Ryan answered coldly.

"Call them what you want," Father shrugged. "We call them 'Termites,'"

The greasy, long-haired guy started sniggering. Aslan twitched at the mention of the word.

"Termites?" Ryan scoffed at the absurdity of racist slavery and comparing them to bugs.

"They work, they build, every day." Father grinned. "Until death."

"Why wouldn't they betray you for freedom?" Ryan blurted. "Like you claim our immigrants would?"

Father crossed his arms and hesitated, calculating what to say without giving too much away.

Doc noticed the delay. "Answer him."

"We have something they all need," Father responded vaguely. "Just hand yours over. They'll be looked after, and there is no issue."

"Like I said, no deal." Ryan put his left hand on Ben's stronger shoulder, pushing him into the road. "Take Ben and go."

Father's smile faded, and the sky seemed to get darker with his mood.

"Do you actually know what these terrorist cunts did to people during the war?"

No one answered.

The war in the southeast of England was over before the first winter. It lasted less than half a year. And until yesterday, they didn't know the war was still ongoing.

"They use male rape as a form of torture to try and break a prisoner's spirit and make them the dominant race." Father's face turned serious, his eyes trying to drill into Ryan's head. "If you even try to resist, they'll start removing your fingers, teeth and ears. They'll make you watch as they rape your friends, your women..." he paused, his teeth locked together, "...your children."

Ryan swallowed hard. "How'd you get out?"

"The non-obedient are burned alive." Father ignored the question. "They fuck you every day, make you eat their shit, drink their piss, and then eat your vomit when you can't keep it down." He turned to Aslan, "You're fucking lucky we don't do the same to you."

"Yes, Father. We're bad people," Aslan mumbled.

There was a long pause; what Father had just told him was muddling its way through Ryan's brain. He tried to process what he actually believed. Father's words hit all the right notes, in a possibly clever manipulation to get people on his side. Henry the rooster interrupted, snapping Ryan out of the haze.

"Leave."

"Fine." Father raised his hands again. "I bought Aslan out here to show you that we actually treat them well and that I'm capable of catching fucking big fish."

"What the fuck does that mean?" Ryan replied.

"Aslan here, is the reason the world went to war, minus the useless fucking Americans of course," Father laughed, like that comment was directly aimed at someone.

Ryan saw Cooper tense up in the corner of his eye, then looked back at the submissive Aslan. It hit him, like a slap in the face. He did recognise him. That was the man who announced the start of the war, condemning Europe to its fate.

I don't fucking believe it.

"Keep the radio in case you want to chat." Father placed his hand on Ben's shoulder and directed him towards town. Aslan and the long-haired, scruffy one followed.

Ryan lowered his gun and exhaled loudly. He was torn inside, resisting the urge to open fire on the four of them. Father was running his own slave trade, using a common enemy as his own workforce, and the common enemy was what sent the world to shit.

Cooper and Doc side-stepped over, keeping their weapons raised.

"I recognise Aslan," Ryan said to them. "I know who he is, and I was doing my best not to shoot him."

"Who is he?" Doc asked.

Ryan lowered his head and closed his eyes. "You guys remember the day the war started?"

"Why?

"I do." Ryan struggled to process the shock while his memory kicked in. "I remember everything about that fucking day."

APRIL 24TH 2024; THE DAY THE FAST WAR STARTED

It was the hottest start to spring that Ryan could remember as he stood in the garden, feeling the sunburn against his pale skin.

Try and burn me you big, yellow bastard. I work next to stoves on a regular basis.

Two bees buzzed frantically around the flower bed opposite the wooden decking. Ryan silently swore as he flicked cigarette ash off his white T-shirt, creating a grey smear across the stomach.

"For fuck sake!"

He made his way back through the patio doors into the kitchen, grabbing a dishtowel off the counter and wiped his top. At the end of the narrow, white kitchen, the 12" inch flat tv displayed Prime Minister Coogan with the rest of Europe's elected leaders. They were holding a press conference outside of Buckingham Palace as a symbol of hope and pride that the people of Europe should still feel. Even in the wake of what was happening in America, they were doing their best to deliver comforts. Comforts that were falling on deaf ears.

Ryan increased the volume so that he could hear it from outside.

"There has been no threat so far on European Border Battalions. I ask everybody of Great Britain, including our Muslim citizens, to carry on with your lives as normal whilst the leaders of Europe try to find peace and justice for

the wrongdoings committed to the people of the Middle East," Coogan reported.

Ryan scoffed behind his bottle of beer listening to the Prime Minister's wishful thinking.

"How can we carry on as normal when two nuclear bombs have already been set off over a holy land, creating a death toll that's into the millions?" one reporter shouted out from the crowd.

"Exactly." Ryan took a sip of beer.

"The nuclear destruction of Mecca is nothing to do with us. We are not involved, nor wish to have any involvement in such atrocities."

There was an eruption of questions before another reporter was allowed to ask. *"What will become of America? Are we allowed to intervene?"*

There was a pause. The question hung in the air like an evil spirit.

"America is responsible for its own current situation. They lied to the world to justify a war in the east for oil. On September 11th, 2001, they sacrificed over three thousand of their own citizens. The false flag event of the world trade centre has landed them where they are. China and Russia are trying to bring order to America during their occupation."

The Russian and Chinese invasion of America had the whole world on the edge of fear. All the United States had to do was admit its involvement in what was now known as *White Flag Trade Centre* and admit they had falsely attacked their own country to justify a war in the Middle East. A war for oil that lasted nearly two decades causing untold amounts of casualties. A war of greed.

When the first public light was shone on the inside job, America screamed lies of faked footage, and Russia's attempt to finally dethrone them as the world's dominant super-nation. An hour-long video had been plastered over the internet and was finally analysed by the cyber and tech departments of the UN and NATO, who proved the video was genuine. After the *Trade Centre Bombings*, February 26th, 1993, as structural engineers worked frantically and insurance companies surveyed the damage, another team had been sent in. One lead by a former CIA operative.

Terry McPherson and his team, dressed as insurance inspectors, took four days to dig, bury and plant the military-grade thermite throughout the steel columns of the twin towers. They documented each step: where they got the supplies, CIA credentials, and videoed themselves planting the devices.

"We know the world will come after us for this, the rise of Islam must be stopped," McPherson explained. *"For our president, our country and our allies."* The video finished with all five men saluting.

It didn't take long for the American population to crack right down the core. Millions rioted, attacking any form of policing, silencing any government attempts of an explanation.

Martial law couldn't be implemented, and the whole country was retaliating. Americans had been lied to for long enough by those in the highest places. With military and police control fading fast, militant ethnic groups started to unleash their hatred on each other. Nation-wide looting and lynch-mob style executions were broadcast on the internet for the world to see. It was like the Gates of Hell had opened across America. Russia saw that as the perfect time to attack, sending in wave after wave of aerial assaults, the ground patrols swiftly following from over the Canadian border. China attacked from the southwestern states, bursting up through the Baja peninsula and Mexican border.

No other nation was friends with Uncle Sam anymore, and the president was looking at no other option than surrendering and confessing to the biggest and most costly hoax of all time.

The backlash in the Middle East had reached levels that threatened to take the world into an all-out war. The Islamic revolt saw a complete overhaul of Israel. All forms of Muslim tribes or factions that had spent centuries fighting each other now joined in the fight against the common enemy to their homeland: the West.

The Hebrew state couldn't last while their biggest ally was under occupation. All trading seized, and Israel crumbled from the inside.

Syria attacked first, attracting all the military attention to the northern parts of the country with Egypt following from the south. What started as tactical strikes against Israel's defence soon turned into a massacre of the Jewish people. No one was spared.

Israel would not fall without taking a part of the Arab world with it. A huge part.

Two nuclear missiles achieved this dying wish of Mossad and Tel Aviv, aimed at either side of Mecca. The Islam world cried in anguish, vowing to finish off the western poison that was destroying the world. Europe was next.

The onslaught was coming from the borders of Bulgaria and Macedonia, all the way along the North African coasts of Egypt, Libya and Tunisia.

Unlike America, they had enough time to prepare themselves, and a full-scale lockdown of borders was in effect, unable to spare any military personnel for America. It was a lost cause. They had to defend themselves.

"As far as we know with Russia, their actions on U.S soil are to gain control and re-establish order. America will remain a Russian/Chinese occupied country until such times that America can become the country it once wanted and claimed to be," Prime minister Coogan answered the second question.

"Is America officially a communist state now?" another reporter shouted.

"No," Coogan continued. *"Russia and China are going to get what the world needs and deserves out of America. And when they do, we can pay our debt to the people of the Middle East also."*

Ryan shut the patio door so he didn't have to listen anymore. It made him feel sick knowing that the world was on the brink of war, yet everyone had been asked to go to work and pay their taxes. He finished the last of his beer and set it on the floor next to the ashtray.

The silence of Surrey Hills offered a surreal calmness, knowing exactly what was going on in the world. Ryan had heard of a few small riots in London, Birmingham, Manchester and Leicester, but nothing on the scale to the other side of the Atlantic. He hoped that the country wouldn't fall into the downward spiral of racial segregation and prejudice. If ever there was going to be a time for the far-right idiots to start stirring the pot, it would be now.

The patio door reopened. The overly exhausted look on his flatmate's face was quite welcoming. Mikey always looked tired after a night shift at the hospital, and as a creature of habit, he started the beginning of his day's off with a strong Southern Comfort and lemonade.

"Getting busier?" Ryan already knew the answer.

Mikey nodded as he took his first sip. "Few protesters, suicide attempts are rising," Mikey sighed. "Even had a survivor of 'The Bully-Killer'."

"They haven't caught that guy yet?"

"Nope."

"Jesus."

"And the prick in charge of this country is saying we should carry on like nothing is happening."

"I heard. Will you be awake for movie night?" Ryan tried to distract him from the day's work. "I'm getting pizza."

"Damn straight I will. You're paying?"

"As always, Mikey. As always."

Ryan finished placing the pizza order and slipped the phone back into his jean pocket, smoking the last bit of his cigarette and flicking it in the ashtray. He guessed Mikey was out of the shower as the singing had finally stopped.

The TV came back into earshot as he reached inside the back door, pulling another bottle of beer out of his shopping bag.

"We, the United Kingdom, are not obliged to pay compensation or investigate ourselves until the true perpetrators, America, have been brought to justice first," Coogan announced.

The sound of moans and angry reporters was suddenly followed by screams and panic. Ryan's face turned perplexed as he leaned inside and looked at the screen. The microphone podium was empty, apart from the lifeless figure drenched in blood on the floor behind it. Prime Minister Coogan was dead.

There was an eerie dread that associated itself with the image on the screen. It wasn't just the execution of Great Britain's leader on the doorstep of the Queen's house, it was a message. Whatever calm and normality that people were being told to carry on with was now impossible.

Ryan stood in silence, eyes wide and blank of awareness. An over-whelming fear and numbness blanketed him, not even noticing that he'd stopped breathing.

"Mikey? Mikey?" his voice barely left his mouth, followed by a wave of vomit. He made it to the sink just in time.

Mikey appeared out of the living room and into the kitchen doorway dressed in blue loungewear, towel in hand. "You puking already? When did you become such a lightweight?" he teased as he dried his face.

"TV," Ryan mustered his response, pointing towards the screen.

Mikey tossed the towel in the living room and looked at where Ryan's finger was pointing. "What am I looking at? Empty seats and dropped paper? Who the fuck is that lying down?"

Given the fact he was a gifted emergency service worker, he still had the capacity to be amazingly slow.

"That's Coogan." Ryan's words were followed by another batch of stomach content.

"Is he... Is he fucking dead?"

"Can't you see the fucking blood?"

It took about half a minute before the cogs started working in Mikey's head. "What happened?"

"I don't know, I was outside." Ryan gargled a mouthful of water and spat it into the sink. "Just screams and stuff. I looked in, and he was like that."

"Who though? What the fuck is going to happen now?" Mikey's hands griped on top of his damp hair.

"I don't... don't know," Ryan stuttered.

The shock didn't have enough time to settle before the TV screen went blank, sharply replaced with a video that was digitally streamed into the BBC network. A plain, white room with a square, blue table, a single desk chair, a notepad, and a series of photos neatly placed in the centre. A closing door was the first sound followed by echoing footsteps, suggesting that the rest of the room was bare apart from the camera.

The individual came into shot: a tall man. Dark skin, shabby, brown hair, and bearded, sporting a black, combat sweater with sunglasses tucked into the collar.

"Who I am is not important. How I'm being broadcast over Britain is also not important," he said, calmly pulling the chair out. They sat and crossed their arms on the table. *"What is important is the reason why this video is being shown to all of you."*

Ryan and Mikey stared silently at their screen, listening to the words of a focused and very sincere looking individual. He had a Persian appearance and the voice of an Eastern European.

"At the turn of the year, a video had been broadcast across the motherland of Russia. This video was from the narrative of this man, Terry McPherson." He held up the first photo from the stack on the table.

"This man was a decorated CIA operative involved in missions across the 1960s and 1970s." The bearded man let out a long breath, building up the suspense for what he had to say. *"Terry McPherson dedicated his life to the stars and stripes. A 'true' American. He served his country, never disobeying orders."*

He placed the photo facedown next to the stack and picked up the next one—an image recognised globally. Two skyscrapers, one with a hole punched into the side of it, black smoke billowing upwards, and a plane a few hundred feet away from the second building.

"His patriotic devotion resulted in this," he said, pointing at the photo. *"The day thousands innocent of American civilians were slaughtered in order to justify a two-decade massacre of hundreds of thousands of Muslims."*

His voice grew angrier yet remained in control.

"America is well on the path to where it needs to be. Russia and China will crush what remains of their arrogance and transform the land of the free, into the land of the behaved."

The left corner of his mouth twitched upwards like he was trying to repress a smile.

"Israel, well, it was only a matter of time. A country where the wealth of the world is controlled. A global bank that stole from once peaceful countries free from the US dollar," He held up the next photo, a collage depicting

Saddam Hussain, Colonel Gaddafi and a few oil fields. The next photo
he picked up was of Prime Minister Coogan, posing outside 10
Downing Street with his family.

*"This man, instead of looking to make peace with Islam, chose to hide
behind Satan."* He leaned forward, looking deeper into the camera. *"This
man had a chance. A chance for all of you to be forgiven and blessed by Allah. If
you're watching this video, he didn't take that chance."*

He picked up a final photo, the most horrific saved for last. The
photo represented a global nightmare for months, the identity of the
victim unknown. Somewhere in America, silhouetted outside a
burning mall, hanging by the neck from a street sign.

"People in America are burning in hell now." He paused. *"This is what
will become of Europe. May your God be with you."*

The last words hung in the air with a demonic sentiment. The man
stared coarsely down the camera. The image froze before a burst of
static bought the picture back to life, returning to the blood-drenched
podium outside Buckingham Palace.

Emergency news broadcasting resumed, and two news presenters
tried to explain the events of the past ten minutes, being re-fed pieces
of information from off-screen. The wrath coming from the borders of
Europe had found its way inside, promising on delivering everyone to
hell. The war was already there.

The next hour was a blur. It started in Islington, a frenzy of live news
reports and phone footage. Mosques and family-run stores were
attacked, streets filled with ugliness, anyone who appeared to have any
sign of Asian heritage was a target. Some of the men fought back as
women and children looked for safety. Screams came from inside a
supermarket; hundreds of desperate people who locked themselves
inside were facing the fury of makeshift petrol bombs and Molotov's.

Bodies scattered on roads and pavements. Flames, smoke, gunfire,
explosions and screaming. A camera concentrated on a single Muslim
man, held up by two thugs and hit repeatedly with what looked like a
hammer. His white robe turned redder with every blow.

The frenzy spread rapidly across the country. News came in from
Birmingham, Leicester, Portsmouth, Sheffield, Nottingham. The mobs

of Britain who took it upon themselves to retaliate against Islam and the relentless nature of all Muslims to defend their religion was an explosive cocktail of death.

"Is everything locked?" Ryan yelled.

"Doors and windows are, should we cover up the glass?" Mikey shouted back from the hallway.

"Maybe. We don't know how fast this will spread."

People were dangerous at the best of times, but when filled with the mixture of ignorance, panic, and rage, they were capable of anything. Mikey had seen it enough working at the hospital. An addict having morphine withdrawals wouldn't hesitate to slice the throat of a toddler for their next hit.

"Fucking hell." Ryan pointed at the TV. A pack of topless skinheads were beating their way through the carnage in Leicester. It was officially a free-for-all.

"Jesus," Mikey's voice shook.

Ryan looked through the kitchen drawers, trying to pick out the sturdiest chef knives he kept at home. Every anxiety that the nation previously shared was now a reality.

About half an hour had passed when the West Midlands news went off the air.

"We can confirm we have lost contact with our West Midlands Studio. No initial reports of the building being attacked or targeted, but we have lost all communication and broadcasts in that area."

"I've taken the coffee table apart, I'm gonna board up the front door." Mikey popped his head through the kitchen doorway. "The front windows should be covered enough, too."

Ryan pointed at the patio doors that led to the back garden, "We'll leave them as is, quick way out if needed, and if someone decides to come through the back then they are sitting ducks in the kitchen."

Mikey liked his way of thinking. They had different lines of work, but both fields required being able to think on your feet and act quickly.

"Whilst you're doing the door, I'm gonna check on everyone."

Ryan walked towards the back of the kitchen with a wooden-handled blade in his hand.

"Everyone?" Mikey asked.

Ryan pointed to the house next to them, referring to their landlords.

"I don't think the Spencer's are home, but Claudia might be next door with Maisie. She's probably scared to death." Mikey ran back through the living room and into the hallway. The hammering against the door frame started shortly afterwards.

Ryan's first step outside made him sick. There was a wall of warm air mixed with the amplified fear. People were being killed on live television, and yet here he stood under a cloudless, silent sky and summer-like heat, with the sound of a pheasant somewhere the other side of the garden fence.

The next batch of vomit followed. If he was aiming for the ashtray, it was a good shot. His throat felt like he'd eaten a sandpaper sandwich, and the small ash stain on his T-shirt was now covered in whatever he'd eaten for lunch. Taking a mouthful of the beer he opened earlier, he gurgled it and spat it onto the patio. Forcing what little composure he had left, he walked across the decking to the wooden fence.

Ryan peered his head over and looked down the driveway. No car. He hoped the Spencer's were somewhere safe.

He opened the side gate and walked onto the back end of the driveway. There he stood between their converted barn and the Spencer's picturesque farmhouse. The mud track driveway was dry under his feet. He'd forgotten to put shoes on.

Turning his attention back the barn, the sound of hammering wasn't too loud. Someone would only be able to hear if they knew it was happening. He walked along the porch to the door at the furthest end, leaning right hand first against the wall and knocking heavily. It seemed ages before the door opened.

Claudia answered the door, looking relaxed in a grey hoodie and red tracksuit bottoms, her daughter in a cradle position. Her ice-white hair and blue eyes shone vibrantly compared to the dread that Ryan felt he was living in.

"I've just got Maisie to sleep so we'll have to be quiet," she whispered from behind her smile. "What's that hammering noise?"

Ryan stared back in disbelief before clocking that she must have had the television turned off. "You might want to bring Maisie round ours, and bring anything important with you," he managed to huff out his lungs.

"What are you talking about?" She tucked a lock of her blonde hair behind her right ear. "You don't look too good."

"Can't explain, turn your TV on."

A concerned look spread across her face—the guys next door usually only knocked for either milk or the plunger. This was the first time she'd seen one of them in such a deranged state, unable to hold eye contact and reeking of vomit. Especially Ryan. She thought he could walk through the Sahara and still maintain his boyishly good looks.

"Just trust me, Claudia, you need to stay with us."

She frowned, leaving the door open for him to follow through the child-gate and into the living room, which was always immaculate, especially for a single mum working from home. Claudia reached for the remote, but Ryan insisted, making sure she wouldn't accidentally wake Maisie.

"Ladies and Gentlemen, we can confirm that Prime Minister Coogan has been fatally wounded during the European leaders' speeches earlier. All efforts to revive him have proved futile."

Claudia shared the same gobsmacked expression that her neighbours had shared an hour earlier.

"The identity of the individual in the videotape remains unknown—it seems the war we have been fearing for months now, is already on our shores. Mass riots, chaos and hysteria have broken out across the capital. Nottingham, Birmingham, Leicester, Sheffield, Bradford, Manchester, Blackpool, Portsmouth, Norwich and we are now hearing in Newcastle and Liverpool. There seems to be absolutely no effort from the police or armed services to try and gain order or control, we can only advise you to stay in your homes and avoid any areas of high-level danger."

"What... what happened?" she stammered.

"Think Coogan got shot. Then some video played, some guy saying

about Coogan had the chance to rectify America's lies and failed."
Ryan paused for breath. "He said we're going to suffer the same fate as
America."

*"We're getting images in now from Torquay. A large number of what looks
to be like Middle Eastern men, heavily armed and dressed in military uniform,
are opening fire at anyone in sight. This is the most awful thing I've ever
witnessed."*

A video taken from a mobile phone displayed the horror and panic
in a sports shop as two men in military uniforms opened up on the
people inside, spraying gunfire into anyone they could see.

"Whoever is behind all of this is clearly steps ahead of everyone else."

"We're boarding up our flat, the Spencer's aren't in, and we don't
know how long this will last or how far it'll spread," Ryan said to
Claudia.

*"More reports of these groups of armed men coming in from Tonbridge,
Wakefield, Preston."*

"We'll keep you safe, Claudia. Just come with us."

"We've now lost contact with our North East and Cumbria studio."

"Let's go, now."

She grabbed her travel bag of baby care products, mobile phone
and purse.

"It's okay, go around the back," Ryan reassured. "The gate and
doors are open, and Mikey knows you're coming."

Claudia peered into her bedroom as if to suggest she would need
more supplies. "There's some wipes in the bathroom and a multi-bag
of nappies in the airing cupboard," she sobbed. "The baby bed has
wheels. I need to get my insulin from the fridge."

"It's ok, Claudia, I'll grab it. I'll meet you round ours in a minute."

She nodded, repressed the urge to cry, and inhaled one large breath
before stepping outside.

Ryan grabbed the bag of nappies and baby wipes, dropped them
into the baby bed, kicked the locks on the wheels, and pushed the bed
into the living room.

*"What we have feared since the beginning of the Cold War has now become
a reality. This image came in from Nuneaton shortly after we lost contact with
our West Midlands studio."*

Although the footage was shaky with low resolution, the mushroom cloud dominated the screen.

"Oh my God." Ryan's pulse thumped; he didn't want to believe it was real.

"It seems we are on our own now, may God have mercy on us."

As he ran towards the front door and pushed the bed through, a blinding light screeched across the sky. He covered his eyes and saw his own hands x-rayed through his eyelids.

Moments later, a hurricane-force wind slammed him into the wall, shattering the glass on the front side of the barn. Trees screamed under the strain, and the wind roared as it tore into the buildings, destroying anything breakable inside. Dust and debris consumed Ryan in a suffocating blanket of heat and dirt as the air felt like it was being ripped out of his body.

Then, almost as quickly as it started, it stopped.

A haunting silence followed with a continuous rumbling of something like thunder. Ryan couldn't tell how close or far away it was.

A few branches fell, fences toppled over, car alarms wailed, and dogs barked uncontrollably in the distance. A relief came over Ryan as he heard Maisie cry from inside their flat and Claudia trying to comfort her.

Finally opening his eyes, still horrified after seeing the bones in his hands, he felt the dirt choking him with every breath. What was a scenic, clear day was now painted in a dark brown, red dust.

Still lying on the ground, Ryan turned in the direction from where the flash had come from.

London.

There it was. Everyone's fears since the bombing of Mecca. A nightmare in real life. Although the capital was thirty miles away, the mushroom cloud loomed over the whole area, looking back down like it was a sadistic trophy.

12

"R yan's right, that's the guy off TV when the war started," Doc grunted as he pulled the gas canister out the hedge wall.

"I didn't see the broadcast gentleman," Cooper said, standing guard at the exit of C10.

Ryan stood in the carriageway, gazing south where Father had headed. "That's the guy, isn't it?" he asked into the radio.

"I was wondering how long it would be before you asked," the now familiar voice at the other end responded. "And yes, it is."

"How have you got him now?"

"What do mean?"

"The guy who announced a new world war is following you around like a whipped fucking dog." Ryan thought he caught a glimpse of movement from behind the car park.

"We'd intercepted one of his home-grown army groups on the day of the bombings. A fast and efficient interrogation lead us to where he planned to rendezvous with his own personal squad."

"You found him straight away?"

"Two days after."

"You didn't kill him? Why?"

"We kept him alive, tried to bleed information out of him. He's a tough little bastard, I'll give him that," Father continued. "Tougher than the previous squad we interrogated, but eventually we found out how he got the bombs to the desired locations."

"He was responsible for the bombs, too?" Ryan asked.

"The bombs, the ground assault, the invasion of America, the training given to the enemy, including the male rape and finger removal I told you about," Father answered.

"He's responsible for all of it?"

"Yes. The SAS kept him alive even after I was captured."

The wind had started picking up as the sky turned darker,

"So, how have you got him obeying you now?" Ryan walked past C10 where Doc and Cooper were fitting the lid on the speaker.

"As I said, I have something they need," Father retorted. Ryan could feel the satisfaction coming from his comment. "When I escaped and made it back to base, I made a choice."

"Which was?"

"Death would be too easy for him and his followers—a lifetime of servitude is more humiliating, to embarrass Allah's name."

"And the SAS went for that?" Ryan laughed while questioning, scratching his head. Mikey joined him in the road.

"Of course not," Father answered. "Well, not everyone was on board."

"What did you do?"

"We infected Aslan and his people with something. We have the antidote. They work for us to have access to the antidote."

"Infected them with what?"

There was a long pause. The wind rippled through the trees on the opposite side of the road. Mikey pulled his assault rifle into a firing position.

"Classified."

"You got your hands on a disease? How?"

"That's also classified."

"How did you get hold of an antidote?" Ryan pushed.

"It wasn't hard getting the antidote," Father laughed, "It's everywhere."

"If you're talking in riddles, I can only assume that I'm calling your bluff?"

"I'm telling you the truth."

"How did you infect so many?" Ryan stayed on track.

"Some of the other officers in the SAS agreed with what I was doing, and they provided their own prisoners to be infected."

"Slaves," Ryan interrupted.

"Call it whatever you want. You sound like the officers who didn't approve. Said I should be court-marshalled when all I've done is turn our enemy into a non-threat," Father continued adamantly. "There was a mutiny as you can imagine which resulted in my team, new followers, and the now infected ragheads breaking free of the bullshit politics."

"And now you go round killing survivors?"

"Let's just say... people who oppose us." Father waited, then added, "You all serve a big purpose for us, whether you want to or not."

"Go fuck yourself."

"I'm going to give you one last chance to hand over your dirty ones and join us," Father's statement was blunt. A direct call-out.

"I already told you, no deal."

A branch cracked to the left of the car park. Mikey swung his gun in the direction of the noise.

"Then your lifestyle and systems, which I might add are still way too diplomatic for this world, have cost you," Father responded under a heavy breath.

"Make sense if you're going threaten us, you cunt!"

Another branch cracked; Mikey gripped his gun tighter.

"I told you, I have no sympathy for Americans." Fathers voice changed to cold and flat. "Your systems and lifestyle have just cost you yours."

A crushing feeling burrowed its way down Ryan's spine as the threat sunk in. He immediately turned to Cooper who had his back to him. Doc recognised the fear on Ryan's face.

Mikey caught a glimpse of two people running out from the tree-line with spears. He fired two shots, followed by backup fire from the restaurant.

Ryan saw the next spear as it flew over his head towards the opening of C10. Doc instinctively reached over, grabbed Cooper's shoulders, and pulled him away from the trajectory. Ryan dropped the radio, pulled out his Glock, and turned to the direction the spear had come from.

The figure ran from behind the Landrover towards the fire exit of the sewage plant. Ryan calmed himself, channelling all focus into his hands, and aimed slightly in front of the runner. The body flung violently to its side, both feet lifting off the ground and hurtling through the air. The explosion of red mist was clear from the fifty metres that separated them. He'd witnessed the force from a bullet of a hunting rifle enough times to know what had happened. Sam put that guy down.

Ryan scanned the windows of the sewage plant. Mikey pointed to the trees where the first attackers had sprung from, signalling Sam and Dominic to cover that area from the top floor.

Mikey ran over, his barrel aimed over the back of the carpark. "Two down that side didn't get a chance to throw their weapons," he reported.

"One down this side got a chance to throw. Doc pulled Cooper out the way in time," Ryan replied.

Slowly stepping backwards, not looking away from across the road, they gradually made it to the maze wall, a few metres right of the opening. The man that Sam shot began to move, his arms failing to pull forward like they were trying to crawl away.

"Doc, let's finish this and get inside," Ryan shouted around the wall. No response. The pair side-stepped towards the opening. "Doc?"

Mikey shuffled back inside. "Oh my God," he gagged.

A wave of dread engulfed Ryan, shuffling quicker until he made his way back into C10. The sight that awaited broke his soul.

Cooper's lifeless body lay face down, the spear puncturing through the back of his neck and into Doc's thigh. Blood mixed with the chemical mixture from the morning, forming into a brown mess. Doc's eyes were open. He was wheezing hard, and his skin was turning whiter by the second.

"Sam!" Ryan screamed. The rifleman would be able to hear from the restaurant. "Help!"

Mikey had crouched beside Doc examining the entry wound. "Judging by the bleeding, you've not had an artery hit, you're going to make it, trust me," he reassured, holding back his own emotions. He looked at Cooper, his head twisted upwards and held in place by the spear that entered through the back of his neck and exiting just below his chin.

Ryan fell uncontrollably to his knees beside Cooper, all energy sucked from his body. Doc managed a faint groan as Mikey pulled him up into a sitting position, kneeling behind for support.

"Sorry, I need to keep you upright for now," Mikey choked. The sound of frantic running could be heard on the inside. "Help's coming."

Ryan checked Cooper's pulse, holding onto little hope that he was still alive and that Mikey could miraculously save him. The charming American's skin was already cold as he held his finger to Cooper's wrist. He was gone.

Sam burst around the corner at such speed that his feet lost traction, and he slipped onto his back. Lyndon followed with the fold-up stretcher and Mikey's medical bag. The boy froze. His bright-green eyes widened behind his dreadlocks. It was the first time he'd seen a victim of foul-play having spent the past five years inside the maze walls.

"Lyndon, I need that ether now," Mikey ordered calmly.

Sam pulled himself up, staring in horror at the scene.

"We're going to pull that out of his leg and make a quick run back, quarantine room one," Mikey instructed. His eyes hadn't left the entry wound. "If he's had an artery hit, I'll need to close it here."

"I should've been quicker to the trigger," Sam blurted.

"This isn't your fault Sam."

"It is."

"Sam!" Mikey shouted, clicking his fingers, "I need you. Doc needs you. Focus!"

"Who's up on top floor?" Ryan brought himself upright, his arms covered in bloody mud. Anger swelled from inside.

"Dominic and Fergie," Sam sobbed, moving beside Mikey.

If anyone else was coming to attack, gunfire would be their alarm.

Mikey held the cloth of ether over Doc's mouth as Lyndon pulled the stretcher off his back.

"Ryan, I'll need you to remove that." Mikey pointed to the spear.

Rain began to gently patter down along with a fall in temperature. It felt like the brightness of the past week had dropped into a chilling hell before their eyes.

"Lyndon, hold his leg as firmly as you can." Mikey reached to the stretcher, unfolding it next to Doc. Ryan gripped the thick, wooden spear with both hands.

"The ether has set in, hold him tight," Mikey instructed, ready to put pressure on the hole in Doc's leg. "Ryan, three, two, one,"

The spear exited the leg. Mikey put his hands on the wound with force. Ryan fell back, pulling the spear all the way out of Cooper's neck, and blood poured all over the ground.

"Lyndon, put pressure here." Mikey grabbed the boy's hands. "Sam, gently lay him down but keep your hands under his shoulders."

"Okay," Sam's voice quivered.

Mikey laid the stretcher parallel with Doc, stepped behind Lyndon, and held Doc's ankles with both hands. "Ready?"

Sam nodded and they heaved Doc onto the stretcher. Lyndon nearly tripped backwards as Mikey started wrapped bandage around the wound, making sure Lyndon kept sufficient pressure.

Ryan stood with his hands behind his head, blood and mud painted across his face. A mixture of relief filled him that Doc had a possibility of survival, combined with hatred and anguish for Cooper's murder. A vision of Father flashed through his mind. *I'm going to kill you.*

"Okay, I'll take point by his feet. Lyndon, stay on the same side as you are now," Mikey sniffed, moving his hands to the handles at the foot of the stretcher. Sam and Lyndon tried to compose themselves, preparing for the lift. A faint sound of a radio crackled somewhere outside the maze.

Ryan glanced at the three of them beside Doc. Tears rolled down their faces, lips shaking and bodies trembling with sorrow and desperation. For the first time in years, he felt the rage again. All logic and emotion evaporated out of his soul,

"Go, I'll set the trap," he wheezed, trying to wipe the blood from his face.

Mikey looked up to acknowledge him, but Ryan had already exited the maze with his gun hand.

"Ryan, what the fuck?" Mikey shouted. "Fuck!"

They were left with no alternative other than to get Doc back, leaving Ryan on his own with only backup support from the top floor.

Ryan ran across the road, jumped the steel barrier, and went into the car park where the second radio was audible. Cooper's warm smile flashed through his mind.

The radio was a few feet in front of the crawling man. Ryan kept the gun aimed at the individual as he rushed past and picked up the device.

"Paul?" The voice coming from the other end was Father's.

Ryan marched to the injured man and kicked him over onto his back; there was a gaping hole in his hip from where the bullet had hit him.

"Paul?"

Ryan clicked the receiver, holding it to the offenders' mouth.

"Father," Paul gurgled in his own blood as a callous smile spread across his blood-soaked face. "The yank is down."

"Good. Where are you?" Father replied.

"I'm..."

Ryan fired a single shot into Paul's left knee. The scream shredded its way across the landscape.

"You'll find him in where we had our conversation earlier," Ryan snarled, clenching the radio. He drove his fist into Paul' jaw, feeling the bone crack against his knuckles and knocking him out.

Clipping the radio to the neck of his hoodie and grabbing Paul's ankles with both hands, he started pulling him out of the car park, waving towards the restaurant window.

"Keep an eye on the treeline!" he shouted.

As he forced Paul's body over the steel barricade, he picked up the other radio he'd been using earlier and attached it to his hoodie next to Paul's device.

The weight of the man he was dragging bought involuntary groans.

He shuffled urgently back into the maze before shooting a bullet into both of Paul's shoulders and throwing him against the speaker hidden in the wall. Yanked out of unconsciousness, Paul tried to cry in pain but was thwarted by his now-shattered jaw.

Two shots bellowed out from the restaurant window. There was incoming danger.

Ryan picked up Cooper's shotgun and threw it around the corner, then placed his hands under Cooper's armpits and pulled his body out of sight of the exit. He caught a glimpse of Cooper's dead eyes. Suppressing the urge to cry, he jumped back into C10, ready to set the trap.

This man killed Cooper.

"The people down in Lewes was one thing." Ryan bent down, holding eye contact with the man who'd killed the community's most beloved member. "It was only out of regard for my people here that we didn't wage an unnecessary fight with winter approaching."

Paul tried to respond, but Ryan cut him off with a punch to the bullet wound in the left shoulder.

"You're either going to rot in this spot, or you're going to help kill a few of your people if they come for you."

I'm going to kill them all, in every way possible.

Ryan stood, reached into the hedge wall, and pulled out the retracting cable until he had a few metres leeway.

I will taste their blood and make them watch if it's the last thing I do.

"Ryan?" Sam's voice caught him off guard.

"Here."

Ryan led the tripwire through the hooks embedded into the ground, remembering the correct pattern around C10 before bringing the slack back towards Paul.

"Ryan, we have to fucking go now!"

"Don't come in here, Sam! Ryan yelled back cautiously. "I've set the wire!"

"There's a shit load of them coming down the hill."

Ryan looked up. Sam poked his head around the corner, his eyes burning red, snot hanging from his nose. He had a stretcher folded up in his left hand and Doc's handgun aiming out the exit.

"Get Cooper on that stretcher," Ryan ordered. "I'll be thirty seconds."

Three more shots rang out from the restaurant.

Ryan tied Paul's hands up with the cable, leaving enough excess to run through the remaining hooks next to the open-faced speaker. He then carefully reached into the wall and ran the cable through the last hook—the one connected to the valve on the gas canister.

If he slipped or tied it loosely, the cable would spring out of his hand and release the valve, exploding the contents in his face. He'd be dead within a minute. An awfully slow and torturous minute.

As he stepped over the wires, he moved back inside, catching a quick glance of a few figures darting between the trees across the road. He realised he wouldn't have time to set the emergency release cord in D9. Sam had already rolled Cooper onto the stretcher, shotgun placed on his chest.

The gunfire then exploded from the top floor, and the screams of the victims were heard from where Ryan and Sam stood. Their adrenaline was so amped that they hadn't noticed the rain had started coming down heavier.

"Let's go," Ryan said, heaving as they lifted Cooper.

Sam started to lead the way before being cut short in his tracks. A spear crashed through the hedge to their right, exposing a foot of sharpened wood inches away from his face.

"Holy shit!"

The sound of spears impacting the thick hedge walls and thudding into the ground was all around them. They were playing their own game of battleships with the enemy outside.

Ryan's subconscious showed him an image of a spear potentially hitting one of the traps.

"Go, fucking go!"

They ran faster than they could've imagined, taking each corner so sharply that they nearly slipped or accidentally dropped the stretcher. Their feet became soaked as the puddles got wider and boggier, the ground giving way beneath the sheer force they exerted on themselves.

An acid trap exploded somewhere to the left, erupting even more violently as a spear penetrated it. Another pierced the wall behind them and shot straight through the bushes in front.

"Keep going!" Ryan roared, lungs burning behind the strain.

"Fucking hell!" Sam screamed.

It wasn't until they reached the sixth section before the gunfire stopped, and the thuds and tears of the bushes had thankfully subsided.

Both Sam and Ryan's muscles ached like never before. Their clothes were soaked with mud, blood and rain.

"Is there anyone waiting for us?" Ryan tried to shout, though exertion caused his breath to grow thin.

"Rich," Sam huffed backed. "He's on the quad."

A crack of thunder deafened from overhead. Ryan felt the vibrations through the floor, the rain shifting to torrential as they nearly collapsed out of D1.

Rich was waiting, his face turning pale as his eyes scanned Cooper. They lifted the stretcher onto the back of the quad, wrapping the straps through the handles and across it. Ryan burst into tears, reaching for the American's dangling arm and bringing it up to his chest, securing it in place with the last strap.

"Rich, drive carefully with him please."

Rich could only nod, horrified.

The quad slowly took off down the driveway, Ryan and Sam watching as Cooper left their sight.

"I should've been quicker." Sam held his face in his hands, sinking to his knees.

Bellowing thunder met with flashes of lightning ripped across the darkened clouds.

"This wasn't your fault Sam." Ryan's legs gave away, falling to his backside. "It wasn't any of our faults."

They sat in silence for minutes, numb to the rain and cold. The cocktail of hate and anguish bubbled inside as the adrenaline began to wear off. Ryan faced the stone reality that one of his good friends was taken from him. He'd never have a conversation with him, never see him smile, learn from him or say thank you to him ever again.

Ryan looked over to the chicken pen, Cooper's favourite of the animals, hoping they hadn't seen his body. He had to blink twice, making sure he was seeing correctly before realising Sam and himself were still in potential danger.

"We need to get inside, Sam. We're still in range," Ryan sniffled through his tears.

"Huh?" Sam wiped the snot from his nose.

"There." Ryan pointed left.

Embedded between the maze wall and chicken pen, over a hundred metres from the road outside, a spear stuck out from the ground.

A few candles offered minimal light against the darkening storm outside. The wedding suite's Tudor beams vanished behind the flickering flames.

Father held Paul's George Cross in his left palm while taking another swig from the hip flask.

"This one's for you, Paul." He'd never mourned for a soldier who was still breathing. "One hell of a fucking soldier, my friend, one hell of a soldier."

Resting the flask on the windowsill, he analysed the updates he'd received from Jake, who had hidden out of sight as the gunfire had torn across the road.

The lanky American had been eliminated. Paul's final act of valour before he had succumbed to a gunshot and then dragged into the walls of their perimeter and tied up as bait.

"Is he still breathing?" Father asked through the radio.

"Yes father, I don't think it'll be long," Jake answered. "I'll let you know when he's gone."

"Get back to the mansion once you've confirmed," he ordered, fighting every instinct to give the order to bring Paul's body back. He'd lose more of his workforce if they tried to return his body. The years after the war had turned this particular civilian group into much more of a threat than originally anticipated.

Sitting back in the Victorian armchair, he grabbed the hipflask and finished off the scotch inside. The alcohol warmed through his body as he looked out the window to the lightning display above, remembering the day Paul had been awarded the George Cross.

"One hell of a fucking soldier."

————

Perched on a wooden stool, Ryan sat inside the kitchen's delivery entrance with a boning knife in hand. He was in no fit state to be seen by anyone.

The opened doors crashed against the outside wall as the wind and rain reached tropical levels. Cooper's smiling face looped through his head like a tape on repeat. The mixture of anger, guilt and fear increased with every roar of thunder.

"Everyone's terrified." Steph approached Ryan who hadn't heard her come through the cafeteria doors.

Looking at the corkboard to his right, the carved-in names of those who'd passed throughout the years had a fresh one to accompany them.

"I should've killed them." Turning to his sister, face bright red, he said, "Then Cooper would still be here."

Steph could only watch as Ryan began to well up.

"It wasn't your fault," she said, trying to reassure him. Her eyes teared; she hated seeing her brother like that.

In their new world, there was no access to medication, and Ryan could not calm himself down. Any good he had ever achieved would eject from his memory, leaving him with his rage to punish him relentlessly, and his natural way to fight it would be to destroy anyone who got in his way.

The schools where he wound up in trouble for protecting his sister from the childish taunts of teenagers who mocked them for being the 'new kids with no parents', were an early indicator of Ryan's anger issues. And now, every second passed like a stab in the heart because he failed to protect his friend, and his body ached as it fought between mourning and revenge.

"Cooper was one of the best people I've ever met. Look at what he's helped us achieve," Ryan cried. "He was killed for being American."

"You couldn't have known that he was a target."

"I'm gonna kill that cunt!" He launched a soup pan across the kitchen into a stack of plates, smashing them across the pot wash area.

"Last time you let it get to you, Maisie couldn't be near you for a week," Steph pressed, trying to switch his focus. "When was the last time you spent time with her? Before Claudia died, you promised you'd do everything in your power, not only to keep her safe but also happy," she reminded him.

"I'm not a superhero!"

"To Maisie you are." Tears streamed down his sister's face. "To me you are. You haven't just kept me safe throughout our lives. You were brave enough to come and find me and Lyndon when the war was at its worst. You risked your life to help get us here, where you'd knew it would be safe,"

Ryan fell to his knees, his cries turning into a hysterical, child-like bawling. "I love you, that's why I did it," he blurted through his tears.

Steph rushed over, kneeling down and embracing him. The kitchen seemed to enclose around them. "We know." She pulled out of the hug, hands on her brother's cheeks and making eye contact. "Right now, everyone needs you. Maisie needs you. Cassy needs you. Mikey needs you—he can't hold it together on his own out there. You know this is what Cooper would say."

Ryan stared back, wanting to laugh at her audacity of using Cooper to try and calm him, even if she was right.

"He'd want you to keep everyone safe. That's what you need to do now. Make everyone feel safe." Steph handed him an oven cloth to wipe his face.

"Fuck sake." His voice muffled as he rubbed the cloth across his mouth and stood.

Steph closed the delivery doors and locked them in place.

"Okay, okay," Ryan whispered.

He could hear Mikey explaining Doc's condition the closer he got to the cafeteria doors. He breathed in deep and slowly pushed them open. All heads turned towards him, a crowd of faces painted with fear and hurt.

His anger briefly rose as he thought about the man who put his community in that situation. He reminded himself of what Steph had said and strode around the outside of the tables towards the podium, avoiding eye contact with anyone until reaching his best friend. Sandra was crying from the right side of the hall where she normally sat with Dominic, who was currently upstairs on scout duty.

Mikey's words expressed urgency; he needed to get back to Doc. They shared a quick hug before he took off towards the medical corridor.

Ryan looked over everyone, placing his hands on his hips and holding back the urge to scream.

"Today..." He paused to clear his throat. "Today, we've been attacked by people who don't agree with how we've been living our lives." Staring across the room to his sister, she nodded to continue. "They've taken away someone who we'll never replace. Cooper was the heart of what we have here." Tears streamed down his cheeks. "They killed him because we didn't give in to their demands."

"What do they want?" Fergie asked from the back.

Ryan looked down, wanting to clench his fists. "They want us to give up some people to join their workforce. Anyone who isn't English." He resisted punching the podium stand. "We must prepare ourselves for a conflict because I won't give them what they want, and I will not let Cooper's death go in vain."

The room was cast with a sobering silence. That was the first fight that Ryan intended to take to the enemy.

"I won't ask anyone to go outside our walls who feels they can't. I'd rather you were here looking after our food, animals, children, and elderly." He felt their apprehension. "If I have to go out and kill this man myself, you know I will, but he has an army, so we need to be prepared."

Ryan used his sleeve to wipe the tears. "Until then, hug your loved ones, remember how lucky we are to have each other and stay inside.

We'll cremate our friend the first day after this storm passes. I love you all." Ryan had to turn and hide his face.

The cafeteria started to empty as everyone headed upstairs to grieve for the rest of the day. A figure emerged on the right side of Ryan's peripheral.

"You're not going to sleep anytime soon, are you?" Sam asked, holding Cooper's shotgun.

"I don't think I could if I tried," Ryan sniffed.

"I've left my rifle upstairs. I'm going to stay on patrol down here. Fergie and Rich have started a trench watch," Sam explained. "They'll be covered from the storm on points A and C, assuming the drainage is still working."

"Did Steph ask you to organise this?" Ryan huffed.

"You know I'd never step on your toes," Sam said, nodding. "While Mikey was talking, she asked me to arrange shifts that didn't involve you."

Ryan looked over Sam who barely made eye contact in return. His thick, black hair was still dripping, and his beige, zip-up tracksuit and black pants had been coated in mud.

"Is there a night shift plan?" Ryan growled, unbeknown to himself.

"Yeah. Jen and yourself in the trench, and Lyndon in the second reception," Sam answered, still not looking up. "Dominic and I will sleep upstairs in case we're breached during the night."

Ryan felt anger towards his sister, getting Sam to hand out shifts without his knowledge and without him in the picture. *Am I really that bad?* Steph would never want to anger him; she'd only ever looked out for his best intentions. *She's only trying to help you.* It dawned on him that Sam truly feared him at that moment. Ryan came to his senses,

"Fuck, Sam. I'm sorry." He walked forward and hugged him, feeling disgusted with himself. "You've done the right thing,"

"I knew you'd be mad with me."

"I'm not. You know I have emotional difficulties, why would you think I'm mad at you?"

"One, I didn't spot the killer," Sam cried.

"That wasn't your fault."

"I should've spotted him."

"Sam, Cooper's death isn't your fault." Ryan pulled out the hug. "And Steph was right to get you to organise security."

"I didn't want to offend you," Sam exhaled. "She was adamant."

"Yeah, she can be." Ryan rubbed his eyes with a minute chuckle. "Have any of those cunt's tried to rescue the guy I tied up?"

"No." Sam shook his head and brushed the shotgun. "We're going to kill them, right?"

"You know we are."

"I'll be ready next time," Sam began to sob again.

"Don't you dare punish yourself."

They shared another quick embrace before Ryan left to head upstairs.

Thunder shook the walls and lights flickered sporadically as Ryan walked down the bedroom corridor. Opening the door to his night shift room, he picked up a pillow and screamed into it, smothering himself so tightly that it nearly choked him as he inhaled. The smear of bloody hand marks on the white fabric told Ryan to look at the mirror. His eyes and teeth shone behind the reddish-brown coating across his face. Maisie shouldn't have to see him like this.

Locking the door and switching the shower on, he started to strip down, placing his gun and both the handheld radios inside the ceiling tile before tossing his clothes into the empty laundry bin.

The heat awoke his skin from the cold numbness as he stuck his head under the water, feeling it run down his back and body. Another thunder quake caused the lights to flicker.

The crimson and mud blended into a marble watercolour, covering an inch of the shower floor.

I'm going to kill them for you Cooper, every fucking one of them.

He scrubbed his face, arms and chest furiously with the homemade soap, wanting to get out of the shower as quickly as possible. Finishing off his legs and feet, he rinsed the suds off, grabbed the towel and closed the shower door again, drying himself inside the steamy glass cubicle.

"Daddy!" The door handle twisted.

"Fuck." He jumped out, drying rapidly while looking for a pair of jogging bottoms.

"What's for dinner, Daddy?"

"Fucking hang on Maisie, I'm getting fucking changed!"

The handle stopped rattling.

Ryan wrapped the towel around his waist, unlocked the door and pulled it open. Maisie sat in a ball, sobbing to herself.

"I just wanted to see you, Daddy."

"Why are you crying?"

"You shouted at me." Her cheeks blushed red, and her eyes were pouring.

Did I? He concluded that he must've shouted. Maisie never cried apart from when he was angry. Even Sam had been scared to talk to him earlier. *Fucking get it together, Ryan.*

"I love you, baby, I'm sorry." He picked her up.

"Why did you shout?"

"The thunder is very loud, I didn't think you'd hear me," he lied. "And I'm still stressed about the gun practice earlier."

None of the children were aware of the gunfight or Cooper's death. They were told it was a weapons training day.

"That was very loud too," she mumbled into his shoulder.

"I know, I know." He placed her back on the floor. "Can you do me a favour? All my washing is back in our family room. Can you bring me a clean pair of pants and a hoodie please?"

"Okay." She rubbed her eyes.

"Thank you. Then when I'm dressed, you can help me in the downstairs kitchen."

"Is Sandra okay?" Maisie showed genuine concern.

"She's okay, I think she just needs a shift off. So, we'll cook together and have story night after, yeah?"

"Yeah," Maisie smiled, her sadness vanishing at the thought of spending the night with him. She then skipped off towards the far end of the corridor.

The lights flickered again. Ryan watched her turn left and disappear, guilty that he'd made her cry. Now wasn't the time to plan for blood. Everyone needed to see the stronger side of Ryan.

"Steph was right," he whispered. "Don't let it get to you now."

Cassy waited for Ryan to wipe down the stainless-steel workbench before she dried the twenty-litre stockpot and placed it on the surface.

"Is this the one?" she asked.

"Yeah, Sandra says can do a two-day batch of rice in that." Ryan leant elbow first on the counter, burying his face in his palms.

"Will she be okay to work tomorrow?" Cassy hugged from behind.

"I doubt anyone will be."

"We're all going to miss him." She kissed his shoulder. "I can't believe he's gone."

The delivery doors were reopened. Ryan glanced at the rain that had persisted through the entire afternoon. It felt like the end of the world. He wasn't surprised that many didn't eat or even came down for dinner at all.

"Will you sleep before shift?" She kissed his shoulder again.

"I'll try."

The cafeteria doors opened, and small footsteps hurried across the floor.

"Beetroot and eggs is funny!" Maisie exclaimed from the other side of the stoves. Her happy voice bought a vague smile to his face.

"What do you mean 'funny'?"

"Pink eggs," she giggled, appearing with her dirty plate.

"You should've seen the food Daddy used to cook. I've heard it was even funnier," Cassy smiled, taking the plate and heading towards the pot wash area.

"What's funny about what you heard?" Ryan asked, picking Maisie up and following.

"Red snapper and honeycomb?" she shouted.

"That was a customer favourite!" he protested, veering right to the delivery entrance.

"Your customers were pretentious arseholes then!"

"What're arseholes, Daddy?" Maisie asked, loud enough for Cassy to hear.

"Oh no," she gasped, scrapping the plate into the bin.

Ryan laughed as he leaned out to close the delivery doors. His smile dropped as he saw the corkboard. Cooper's name stared back.

"What wrong, Daddy?"

Ryan blinked and looked away, forcing a smile at Maisie and remembering his priorities.

"Sorry, just had a sleepy moment." Feeling a tear build up under his left eye, he pulled the doors shut and locked them.

"Bedtime?" Cassy dried the plate, placing it on the rack where Ryan had demolished a stack earlier.

"Yeah." Ryan kissed Maisie on the cheek.

"Already?" Maisie queried. She had seen it wasn't completely dark outside.

"You can stay up with mummy, but I need to try and sleep." Ryan held Cassy's hand, and the family of three headed out of the kitchen and up to their family room.

———

"He's gone," Jake announced solemnly.

Father closed his eyes, pressing the radio to his forehead and remembering when Paul threw himself into the wreckage of an IED blasted vehicle, saving his commanding officer from the flames.

"Jake, time to leave." He put the radio back to his mouth and stood from the chair. "Connor will be meeting us with the rest of the food in a couple of days."

"Understood, Father," Jake replied, "The other supplies are delayed slightly. They encountered a small group of survivors as they circled around London."

"Okay." Father exited the honeymoon suite. "Make sure a few beds are made up for Connor's team."

"Yes, Father."

The radio clicked silent. Father descended the curved stairs into the hotel's reception. The red wallpaper and carpet appeared brown as Ben stoked a fire in the middle of the open room. A pan of water boiled, suspended above the open flame. The beige pillars disappeared out of the flame's reach and into the high ceiling.

"I have a question, Father," Ben asked, pouring a cup of coffee from the pan.

"Go ahead." Father took the cup.

"In Lewes, why did we let everyone loose?"

Considering Ben's involvement with breaking into the jail and his unquestionable loyalty, along with how new to the team he was, Father pondered how much he let Ben know about their process.

"One key reason," he said, drinking the piping hot coffee like it was a milkshake. "We had to tire them out, let them build up lactic acid before we recaptured them."

"Lactic acid?"

"When Connor arrives, you'll see why that's important." Father finished the coffee and placed the cup in his duffle bag.

"Understood, Father."

"Good." He picked up the bag. "Finish your drink and pack up, we need to get to the mansion while we have the cover of this storm."

———

Ryan kissed Cassy on the cheek, pulling the blanket up to cover her shoulders as she slept silently. He picked Maisie up and cradled her out of their bedroom and into her own, gently lowering her onto the single bed and pulling the duvet over her. Lighting a candle that he found on the bedside table, he then tiptoed out of their apartment. Sam was waiting in the corridor.

"Thanks for knocking gently."

"No problem, Cuz."

The rain hammered the roof above as they walked quietly down the corridor, reaching Ryan's night shift bedroom.

"One sec, need to grab my stuff." He opened the door just as the overhead lights turned off; the basement generator was powered down.

"Was that Dominic in the basement?"

"Yeah." Sam pulled out his pocket watch, it was midnight.

"How long did I sleep?" Ryan tucked the Glock into his waistband and pulled a red hoodie over his head.

"Think you went upstairs around 17:30. Well, that's when I turned the kitchen lights off."

"I wanna see how you and Dominic have set up upstairs, just for peace of mind."

"No worries." Sam led them up the stairwell, turning right when they reached the top floor, ignoring the door to the left that led into Ryan's old galley-style kitchen and into the L shaped seating area.

One in every two windows had been boarded up. There was a sleeping bag by the east window and another around the back.

"How's the ammo looking for you both?" Ryan opened the window nearest the stairwell and stuck his hand out, feeling the rain pound against his skin.

"Dominic used twenty-five L96 bullets. My rifle is four shots less. Fergie used fifty bullets from the G36C's," Sam reported.

"We killed fifteen of them in total, using five times the number of bullets." Ryan pulled his arm back in. "If there is over half a thousand of them, do we have enough bullets?"

Sam didn't reply, his eyes widened towards southern windows.

"Sam?"

"What the fuck is that?" He pointed across the room where two white lights shone through trees in the distance. "Where is that? The barricade?"

Ryan ran across the room, picking up a rifle, and opened the window in the southeast corner. He zoomed in with the scope, trying to get his bearings in the pitch black before the lights moved outwards from the town and vanished into the night.

"No mate, that's the hotel."

"Isn't that where they're staying?"

"It could be." Frustration flooded over Ryan. "Unless they're leaving."

He might not get the blood he silently craved, but there was only one way to find out. They would have to go and check the hotel themselves.

14

Cassy had given herself the gruelling task of collecting beetroot as the rain continued its violent downpour for the next two days. Rani and Sanjay provided extra hands during the picking. Sam watched from in the restaurant, his eyes searching for anyone on the outside of the maze.

Ryan wasn't keen on the idea, but Cassy insisted time alone with Maisie would do him good. While she was in school lessons, he'd spend time in the rice room, learning how to maintain the makeshift rice paddy and also how to convert the spare corn into generator fuel. Doc could easily learn all those tasks, but Ryan didn't want to dump all the responsibility on him after he recovered.

"When's Cooper coming back?" Maisie asked as she ran behind him.

He held the double doors open into the water purifying room, and she trotted underneath his outstretched arm before he gently let the doors reposition, following and avoiding the question.

"No running Maisie. This floor gets slippery."

The wine distillation room bared the same blue mat flooring as the cafeteria kitchen, designed for the least amount of slippage with the correct footwear, which only Sandra chose to wear.

In the ceiling to their left, a forty-foot-wide hole loomed over the two-storey wine pressing tanks, their tops removed to collect the rainwater. Their rusty, beige colour matched the walls and remaining ceiling. Two gridded drains sat at the back, leading the excess rainfall into the drainage system and out into the river.

"Is that the grape water in there?" Maisie pointed.

She stood in bright blue dungarees over a white, long-sleeved T-shirt, her ice-blonde hair tied in Ryan's best attempt at pigtails. Ryan chuckled to himself realising it was going to be another day of answering questions. Most of which he would have to make up answers for, but it was better than facing the pain of losing Cooper.

"That's the beginning of the grape water." He folded his notepad in half and pushed it into the back pocket of his blue jogging bottoms. "They used to make lots of wine in here."

"Is that the adult drink?" She carried on walking down the length of the room.

"Yes, or dizzy juice as Mummy calls it." Ryan sped up to her until he could hold her hand. "We used to have more of those big machines, but we had to get rid of them to make room for all that." Pointing ahead to the left to a sealed, glass room that once served as the wine bottling station before being converted into Doc's laboratory.

"What's in there?" Maisie jumped, trying to look through the windows.

"That's all of Doc's magic equipment." Ryan couldn't name any of the equipment if he tried. "He makes soap and toothpaste in there."

"What's through those doors?" She pointed at the end of the open expanse.

"Those doors take us into the end of the medical corridor. That's where Doc is recovering."

"And what's the other side of this wall?" She pointed right.

"The cafeteria, laundry rooms and library." Ryan stopped. "This long area of our home uses the most amount of electricity from the generators, that's why we need so much corn oil."

"How do you make corn oil?" she asked.

"I'm not explaining that today."

"How come you've never bought me here before?"

"Because I'm never normally here, Maisie. This is Doc's area of work."

"And where do you work?"

"Everywhere but here."

They reached the doors to the medical corridor where Ryan knocked twice.

"Why do we have to knock on these doors?" She looked up at him.

"We have to make sure that no sick people can accidentally get in the medical rooms. That might spread infections and sickness to those who are already sick," he said, faking a heave of vomit at her.

"Yuck!"

The left door creaked forward with Lyndon poking his head out. His bum fluff had been shaved off, and his blond dreadlocks were perfectly tied back. He looked like a younger version of Ryan.

"You look fresh!" Ryan said.

"Mikey made me have the day off yesterday," Lyndon smiled. "I just want to make sure I'm good when you need me on duty."

"Good man."

Ryan and Maisie both stepped into the corridor. Hamsa's room was directly to the left while Doc was in the room opposite. The same room they had treated Ben in. Lyndon took Maisie's other hand, leading her away.

"Maisie, I wanna show you something cool. It's in the cafeteria though, and Daddy isn't allowed to see it."

"What the fuck?" Ryan whispered as Maisie let go of his hand.

"Go in Doc's room," Lyndon said with a wink.

Ryan felt a lump in his throat. He pushed the door open and found Doc asleep under a thin white blanket, his right leg slightly raised on some extra pillows. Mikey sat in the armchair, his white clothes also pristine, though he was visibly sporting bags under his eyes.

"He's just nodded off—missed him by a couple of minutes," Mikey said looking up.

"He was awake?" Ryan's face lit up.

"Briefly. His wound was easy enough to stitch. He just needs to rest before he puts any weight on his leg. He should be good to uses crutches within a week."

"Any signs of an infection?"

"None as of yet, but I'll keep monitoring it."

Mikey stood while Ryan looked over the leg where the wound hid behind the bandaging. A sudden wave of sadness hit him.

"Does he know about Cooper?"

"Yeah, I think he knew before he woke," Mikey nodded. "We should leave him for now. The more rest he gets, the better."

"Okay." Ryan stepped back into the corridor. "Have you been getting rest, too?"

"Yeah, I've been sleeping in the spare bed next door." Mikey closed the door. "Your sister covered my rest time, and I gave Lyndon a full day off. Didn't see any good in overworking him while he's still learning."

"Was a good idea." There was a pause between them before Ryan continued, "I haven't told Maisie about Cooper. I don't know how to. Steph said she'd do it for me."

"Your sister's a fucking legend," Mikey said. "She wants to keep any added stress off you."

"She was with Fergie this morning, helping to dig a hole for Cooper."

"Is the wood not burning?"

"No, the storm ruined it all. They're digging a hole next to Hamsa's family." Ryan looked up. "How is Hamsa?"

"His wounds are scabbing." Mikey rubbed his chin. "Haven't seen any signs of an infection, considering."

"Considering?"

"The wounds came from necklacing."

"Necklacing?" Ryan hadn't heard the term before.

"It's a torture method. I'd only ever heard about it in books."

"Do I want to know?"

"If you still want to keep your emotions in check, no." Mikey stared him down, knowing keeping it to himself was the best option.

"Okay."

Mikey was one of the few people who could hold a leash on him. Though Ryan could beat him in a physical fight, disappointing his best friend proved to be the kryptonite between them.

"Hamsa wants to stay here. He's got nowhere else to go."

"Of course," Ryan acknowledged. "And he'll be near his family."

"Exactly." Mikey pushed the door to Hamsa's room open slightly. He was in the same position, face down with his arms spread out onto tables, the room lit with candles in the opposite corners. "He walked for the first time yesterday. His feet are still painful and his legs sore from the run here."

"Let's not rush him," Ryan whispered, remembering Hamsa's tortured screams. "He's got a lot to get through."

"Already seeing signs of survival guilt." Mikey closed the door. "He blames himself for leaving his family."

"Know anything about how to deal with that?"

"I can look at therapy books," Mikey suggested. "But that's never really been my department. I know how to calm people during emergencies, but actual treatments, you probably know more than me."

"I had medication," Ryan replied. "Saw a therapist occasionally. I think Sam could also benefit from that now."

"Why's that?"

"He keeps saying that he should've spotted Cooper's killer."

"I remember him saying that at the time," Mikey nodded.

"He's not eating properly, barely leaves the lookout window."

"Does he seem a danger?"

"Danger?" Ryan pondered before shaking his head. "No, not as such. He's focused on spotting someone, but he's not erratic and can hold a stable conversation."

"Could just be his way of mourning." Mikey walked away from the door. "Give it time, then we'll assess if we need to take it further."

"Did he tell you about the car lights we saw?" Ryan asked.

"Yes, and they were leaving?"

"Looked like it, headed away towards Reigate. I wanna check the hotel, maybe burn it down if I have to."

"You'll have my blessing when Doc is mobile and we've said goodbye to Cooper," Mikey said firmly. "You're staying here till then."

"Thank you."

"One small thing though," Mikey added. "Hopefully it'll add a silver lining to this whole situation."

"Go on."

"We know their main source of weaponry, it's very basic."

"I wouldn't underestimate it." Ryan looked back at Doc's room.

"What do you mean?"

"They can throw those spears over a hundred metres." He shuddered, remembering handling the spear. "The one we picked up next to the chicken pen weighed over ten kilograms."

"That's well over Olympic distances," Mikey tried to mention without sounding impressed.

Both stood in silence, absorbing the reality of unheard human capability.

"Maybe it's best if they've gone," Ryan huffed.

"True."

"Half a thousand people that can throw like that?"

"We'd have a big problem," Mikey agreed. "Anyway, put that at the back of your mind, concentrate on Maisie."

Ryan put his hands on his hips, wondering where Lyndon had actually taken her. "Is Lyndon taking over your shift?" He looked back up the corridor.

"Yeah, I've got the night off. Jen and I are having a sweetcorn-broth and wine night," Mikey yawned.

"Good to hear. Enjoy your night, I better go see whatever Lyndon is showing my daughter."

They shared a fist bump before Ryan headed to the cafeteria. He found his nephew by the serving counter. "Where's Maisie?" He looked out over tables.

Lyndon pointed into the kitchen. Maisie was with Sandra, rolling bread on the backbench by the stoves.

"She looks entertained." Ryan looked through the hot counter.

The past couple of days had been torturous on everyone, but they grouped together and cracked on with what had to be done. That's what Cooper would've wanted.

Ryan remembered his smile. It could lighten up anyone's day.

"Just want to say thank you for what you've done. Mikey couldn't have done it without you."

"That's what I trained for." Lyndon approached the display fridge, taking two bottles of grape water. "Just glad he's got a night off."

"Same. The guy would work every hour if he could." Ryan opened the bottle that Lyndon handed to him.

"We used to say the same about you." Steph's voice from behind made Lyndon jump. "When Uncle Ryan was a chef, he'd never leave the kitchen."

"Same working hours like Mikey?" he asked.

"Yeah, I never saw much of Mikey when we lived together," Ryan reminisced. "We made sure we had Thursday night's off for movie night, but other than that, we both worked."

"Sounds stressful."

"Stressing yourself in a kitchen isn't the same as saving lives. That's what Mikey does, that's why I want you to learn from him."

"He's a good teacher," Steph interjected. "He showed Lyndon how to stitch Doc's wound."

Ryan raised his eyebrows. "Really?"

Lyndon nodded. "Tonight, I have to change Hamsa's dressings, on my own. Mikey's shown me before."

"Good lad," Ryan leaned forward, scuffing Lyndon's dreadlocks.

"I'm going to tell Maisie about Cooper now." Steph tied her hair up. "Cassy has just finished beetroot picking if you want to wait with her."

"Okay, thank you." Ryan was grateful Steph took the responsibility.

"No worries."

"Don't tell her near Sandra—she's just got her smile back."

"Sure."

"Okay, I've gotta go see the missus." Ryan patted Lyndon on the back. "Have a safe shift, yeah? Fucking proud of you mate."

"Will do." Lyndon beamed from ear to ear,

Knowing Cassy was likely soaked, Ryan picked up a tea towel on his way to the main reception. It was better than nothing.

Cassy finished locking the doors as he approached. Five large bread trays of beetroot lay spread across the tiled floor.

"Is there much left to pick?" he asked, handing her the towel.

"Not a huge amount," she said as she bolted the locks. "Maybe two more trays worth. Rani and Sanjay said they'd take care of that tomorrow. They've gotta check the spinach anyway." She dried her face with the tea towel. "I can't go out in that weather again."

"I don't blame you. There's only so much security we can provide from the windows." He took a swig of the grape water and handed it to Cassy. She tossed the cloth on the beetroot and took a mouthful.

"It's not just that." She handed the bottle back, her wide eyes glazed with sadness. Tears began to form in the corners.

"What's wrong?" He held her cheeks and kissed her.

"I think I'm pregnant." She bit her lip looking back at him, not knowing what reaction to expect.

Ryan heard the words, knowing they were both speaking English, yet his brain was struggling to translate the sentence. Falling into the back of his own mind, time stood still. Shock started blending with guilt, knowing he should still be mourning for Cooper, but he had just had his heart set on fire.

"That's fucking great news," he puffed out with a nervous laugh. She responded with the same and kissed him. "Of course you're not going back out in that weather, or outside again. I'm going to lock you up in our room. Who have you told?"

"No one." She wiped the tears with her soaked sleeves. "I wanted to tell Steph, but she's telling Maisie about Cooper."

"Oh, yeah." Ryan felt himself land back on earth. "I'll take Maisie after. You can tell Steph then."

"Okay," Cassy whispered as she caught her breath. "I love you."

He hugged her again. "I love you too, Cassy."

They held each other for what felt like an eternity, each passing second added another ounce of calmness. He had never felt so safe in her arms. She'd been an amazing mother to Maisie, while keeping Ryan calm when needed.

The undeniably recognisable sound of kitchen clogs interrupted the moment.

"What's up Sandra?" Ryan didn't even need to turn.

"Just finished showing your daughter how to roll soda bread. She said I'm a better chef than you."

He could sense the banter in her voice; she was starting to sound like herself again. "This is the same girl that thinks beetroot omelettes are funny," he remarked, feeling Cassy laughing on his chest.

"She's an amazing learner." The wooden bench creaked as she sat.

Ryan broke from the hug and faced Sandra. Her black apron and chef trousers were covered in rye flour, yet her hands were immaculate as always. Her dark, curly, red hair rested on the shoulders of her chef whites.

"She's only as good as her teachers," Ryan smiled, which Sandra returned.

"We just put some rolls in the oven." She rubbed her hands. "Steph asked if she could have a few moments with her. Didn't say why."

Ryan stiffened, desperately trying to think of something to say other than that Maisie was about to get the bad news.

"I think you'd better go see our daughter." Cassy pushed him in the back, sensing his apprehension. "In the meantime, I've got some good news for you, Sandra."

"Oh yeah? What's that?"

Ryan turned and hugged her. "I'll tell her to keep it quiet," Cassy whispered in his ear.

"I love you." He kissed her one more time and before jogging back to the hot counter, wondering how he'd juggle the varying emotions the next hour was about to throw his way.

———

The rain had finally eased to a misty drizzle. Large drops burst loudly as they hit the marble stairs next to Father's feet, falling from the archway overhead. Nights were now coated in total darkness. Any moon or starlight that tried to penetrate would be foiled by the clouds above.

Leaning against the pillar, he followed the headlights as they danced through the trees of the mansion's front entrance. The truck's engine ran silently, weaving up the asphalt driveway, circling the fountain and pulling up in front of the grand entrance.

"Nice new gaff we have here, Father." Connor leaned out the driver's window. "Can't wait to see it during the day,"

He wore the same grey T-shirt and black combat pants combo as the rest of the men, standing a little over five foot and probably just as wide at the shoulders. A fully-shaved head and piercing blue eyes, Connor was the most ruthless soldier Father had ever seen in combat.

"Wait till you see inside," he grinned, drinking a freshly-poured cup of coffee.

"Our new neighbours know we've moved in?" Connor asked, jumping out the driver's side and slamming the door shut behind him.

Father shook his head.

Though they were at the top of the hill opposite the vineyard, they were a mile away from the western slope, surrounded by dense woodland.

"They can't know for certain we're here, although their lead guy probably has a hunch." Father watched another drop land at his feet.

"What's the security between us and them?" Connor stubbed his cigar out.

"Parker's on that—he's got Termites running perimeter watches while we begin to build their barns. There's enough wood here." Father leant off the pillar, finished his drink, and pointed to the back of the truck. "Cargo okay?"

"Yes sir. Martyn and Pikey are five minutes away with their half." Connor looked at the truck. "We picked the rest of them up near Gatwick. They followed the signs like Ben said they would."

That inflated Father's satisfaction. The vineyard signs were originally made to direct survivors to safety, but he had used them to guide the survivors of Lewes into the hands of his men, full of fear and lactic acid.

"I'll get Parker. He can help unload them," Father said. "Ben has made rooms up for you and your men. The beds are comfy as fuck here. Go to bed once you're done unloading, and I'll see you in the morning, son."

Father opened the large oak door. Connor saw the mansion's stunning grand hall reception under the chandelier light. A water-like reflection danced on the marble flooring, rippling down the central fountain, which the Termites had cleaned and refurbished before Connor's arrival.

"Parker!" Father called out. "Delivery's here."

15

Father had sat with Connor in the dining room since sunrise, taking on the responsibility of telling his sergeant that Paul was dead, murdered by the new enemy. Even Father didn't look forward to this, especially while the most recent butchery was happening a couple of rooms away. The sounds of saws hacking through flesh and rubber mallets thudding on bone rippled through the grand hall to the dining room. Even with the lounge in between where they sat and where the activity was, the sheer amount of work was deafening.

The dull, grey morning's sun broke through the large windows. Connor rubbed his temples angrily and sat next to Father at the circular table.

"When do I get to kill these people?" he asked. "He was like a brother to me, sir."

They held back on breaking the news about Paul when Connor first arrived. Father wanted him to have a decent night's sleep first.

"This is for you." Father placed Paul's George Cross next to Connor's bowl. "I'm so sorry. He was an exceptional warrior, loyal friend, and we wouldn't be as strong as we are now without him."

Connor held the medal in his palm and stared. "I'll kill these paki-loving cunts for you brother, I swear." He closed his hand and pressed both fists against the top of his head.

"He'd have loved this place." Father looked around the dining room.

"Yeah, he loved his historical buildings, didn't he?" Connor laughed behind the tears. "Fucking dork!"

Father raised to toast, and Connor obliged. Both teacups filled with scotch. "To Paul." They swallowed the alcohol.

"I'll never get used to that shit." Connor gagged and quickly gurgled the coffee next to his bowl.

"Goes well with the broth," Father joked.

Connor nodded, beginning to eat his breakfast.

He'd rested the best he had for a long time, waking up fully refreshed before sunrise. Jake had given him a quick tour of the mansion before showing him around the grounds. The front entrance to the east stretched for over half a mile, the driveway weaving in and out of an array of weeping willows. Tennis courts, a swimming pool and a summer house dominated the northern side of the grounds. The back garden was the biggest he'd ever seen, a spectacular football-pitch-sized lawn with a stable that backed onto a display of fir and oak trees. The southern side had a terrace, almost looking ideal for a barbeque or afternoon tea, over-looking more and more weeping willows.

Connor realised why Father had chosen this spot. Not only was it walking distance from their next target, but outside the garden's border lay a lush, thick woodland, over-grown with nettles, weeds and grass. It was hidden from the enemy, and no one could sneak up on them.

A sick irony as the vineyard people applied the same tactic to defend themselves, though, they had an unidentified, corrosive material hidden throughout their perimeter.

"When did the first supplies arrive?" Connor drank some more coffee, trying to vanquish the scotch after taste.

"The day before you. The preserved meat, generator, veg oil, filtered water and coffee all came in the morning." Father stretched. "The candles, alcohol, tools and rest of the Termites came sometime in the late afternoon."

"Yesterday was Ben's first slaughter?" Connor swallowed down a mouthful of the broth.

"Yes." Father stood.

"I didn't hear any of it. I think I passed out when I got into bed."

"I told you the beds are good. I do have another piece of bad news though."

"What's wrong, sir?"

"Two Termites ran away last night."

Connor immediately sat up, alert.

"Jake knows this area, he scouted it for weeks." Father cracked his knuckles. "When you're ready, I want you to go with him and track them down."

"Why are they stupid enough to run away now?" Connor started hurrying through the broth.

"Maybe they got scared after seeing the slaughter. It's the first time we've done one this open." Father turned back to Connor. "I need you to find them before the vineyard people do."

————

"How does it feel?" Mikey stood at the end of the medical corridor. Doc manoeuvred the wheelchair up the yellow passageway, gliding along the floor.

"Pretty good, left wheel's a bit stiff." He pulled up beside Mikey.

"It's only for today, tomorrow you can go onto crutches and even stay in your room." Mikey opened the doors to the cafeteria.

Doc was greeted by a round of applause, and a rare smile appeared on his face as he looked around.

"Thank you, everyone." Doc blushed behind his glasses. "I really want to thank both Mikey and Lyndon. They've been amazing. I've heard you've all been chipping in with the extra workload. Cooper would be smiling at you all."

There was a soft applause from everybody before they began to greet him one at a time.

"Uncle Doc, Uncle Mikey!" Maisie ran over and hugged Mikey's right leg.

"It's so good to see you." Mikey rubbed the top of her head.

"It's good to see you, too." She looked up. "Did you help Uncle Doc when he was sleeping?"

"Yes, I did. He snores really loudly!" Mikey imitated the noise.

"Like Daddy!" she chuckled, letting go of his leg and standing next to Doc's left side. "Did you really sleep that long?"

"I think so, Mikey kept waking me up with his farts!" Doc in turn imitated the bodily noise.

"I got scared you wouldn't wake up, like Cooper." She held his hand, looking down at the floor.

Doc leaned forward and held her other hand. "You don't have to be scared. Mikey will always keep me awake, especially with his magic farts!" He bought her smile back. "Did you say good night to Cooper?"

"Yeah, he has a comfortable bed in the ground outside. Mummy says he'll always be with us."

"He will be. I've also heard you want to learn how to grow more tomatoes and other new food?" Doc raised his eyebrows, impressed.

She nodded.

"Well, when we start bringing in the fruit at harvest, do you want to help the team?" Mikey suggested as he held the wheelchair's handles. "If your mum and dad are okay with it?"

She nodded again.

"Talking of which Maisie, where are your mum and dad?" Doc looked around the cafeteria.

"Daddy's up in the shooting room." Maisie meant the top floor. "His eyes got sick after saying goodbye to Cooper. Aunty Steph is looking after me in the kitchen with Sandra. We're making bread again!" She jumped excitedly.

Doc looked back at Mikey. There was every chance Ryan could be losing his shit again. "Is Mummy looking after him?" he asked.

"Yeah."

It was a relief that Ryan was not on his own.

"I'm sure your dad will be fine. Can Doc and I try some of your bread?" Mikey turned Doc's wheelchair and pointed it towards the serving counter.

"Yeah, it's the best bread ever!" she exclaimed.

Maisie skipped beside them as Mikey wheeled Doc to the counter. Sandra and Steph greeted them from the other side.

"Well then," Mikey smiled. "Three orders of the best bread ever, please."

"Have you told anyone about the baby?" Ryan held Cassy from behind as they looked over the back of the vineyard. Behind the herb patches in the northwest corner, Cooper's freshly dug grave was visible to them.

"Just Sandra and your sister," she whispered.

They kept the conversation quiet, not wanting to put Sam off from his duty on the front side of the restaurant.

"How can we raise another child with this threat still alive?" he asked.

She pulled his hand up and kissed it. The last of Ryan's tears rolled down his cheek. Steph had suggested they spent some alone time together until he felt comfortable being around people.

"How many trees would you cut down next year?" Cassy tried to put his brain into productive mode by pointing over the part of the maze behind the winery.

The area in question had a small woodland and country house, formally occupied by the wine estate owner. Half of the trees were chopped down both for timber and for security reasons. There was no visual blockage for fifty metres between the treeline and the maze. It would be impossible to sneak up from the backside without the restaurant lookouts spotting you.

"I'll let Doc do the maths on that, which should keep him occupied while he's recovering." He pulled his hand away and wiped the tear from his cheek. Ryan couldn't take his eyes off Cooper's grave.

A motor started and broke the silence. Cassy leaned out the window and saw the tractor driving out to the western vines.

"Sanjay's starting the grape harvest," she said.

"Good man." Ryan sniffed. "Rani is probably cleaning the grape tanks now."

"I'll be helping with the bottling of this harvest. It keeps me indoors. That okay with you?"

"Of course." They held hands and walked away from the window. "I'm not comfortable with anyone working out the front, with either the veg or animals, but we have to."

Dominic entered from the stairwell door. "Doc's in the cafeteria if you wanna see him," he interrupted. "Maisie is making the 'best bread ever' with the missus. I'll cover the backside if you want, boss."

"Thank you." Ryan nodded.

The big man approached with a smile and hugged Cassy. "Sandra tells me everything," he whispered. "Congratulations."

Cassy held her mouth, overwhelmed with happiness. It was all starting to sink in.

"Thank you," Ryan whispered back, shaking Dominic's hand before calling out, "Hey, Sam?"

"What's up, Cuz?" he answered, still not looking away from the window.

"Dominic's covering the back, Cassy and I are heading downstairs if you need anything."

"Understood."

"Doc's down there if you wanna see him?" He patted Sam on the shoulder as they passed. "I can cover you later if you want."

"I'll see Doc when the sun's gone down. I don't wanna take my eyes away from the hill," he replied stubbornly.

"Okay. Let me know if you change your mind." Ryan noticed the dried blood on Sam's hands—blisters and sores from gripping the binoculars for hours on end. "Or if you need a rest."

"Will do, Cuz."

Ryan and Cassy disappeared into the stairwell and out of earshot.

"Poke your head out from those trees, and I'll blow it clean off, cunt," Sam whispered to himself.

. . .

Doc had his back turned, eating a bread roll next to the hot counter as Ryan and Cassy strolled over.

"Is the bread as good as I hear?" Ryan asked.

"She's a better chef than you," Doc joked bluntly, turning his chair around.

"It's fucking good to see you." Ryan laughed as they shook hands.

"You too. Cassy, how are you?" Doc turned his attention as she leaned over and kissed his cheek.

"All the better for seeing you." She eyed him over. His white track-suit bottoms and baggy T-shirt hung over his body. "White really isn't your colour though."

"Mikey's orders." Doc pushed his glasses up. "Should be good to start using crutches soon."

"I feel less guilty about ransacking the hospital now." Ryan reached for a bread roll, breaking it in half and sharing with Cassy.

"Thanks for the notepads." Doc looked up, but Ryan stayed silent and bit into the bread. "Had a quick look through them. I'll be able to carry on with Cooper's plans. Fergie and Rich have both offered to help set up new developments by next spring."

"The fruit patches?" Ryan asked, using the bread's fresh-baked smell to block out the pain of hearing Cooper's name.

"The fruit patches and the maze interior," Doc stated. "I'll start calculating the timber project tonight."

Ryan nodded and swallowed the first mouthful, and he looked over to Cassy. "Looks like our eldest is going to be a baker." He smiled as she wiped the crumbs from her mouth and kissed him.

"Eldest?" Doc asked with bewilderment.

Ryan's faced dropped. *I'm a fucking idiot.* "Yeah." There was no point lying to Doc. "It's looking that way."

"Looks like you're ready to tell everyone," Cassy said out the side of her mouth.

Doc stared with his mouth open. Letting out a sigh, Ryan turned for the podium, saying hello to a few families, and strode down the middle aisle, stepping onto the platform.

"Everybody?" All eyes stayed with Ryan as he began. "This isn't an official meeting, so your children can stay." His heart began to race.

"Firstly, I want to say thank you for everyone holding it together during the burial of our good friend. He'd be immensely proud of how you've all come together." He paused, then added, "He'd want us to look at the good, and we have a great blessing with our local genius on a full recovery." Everyone applauded as he pointed to Doc, who still stared, mouth open at Cassy.

"A massive thank you to Mikey, Lyndon and everyone who volunteered to help with extra hours in the medical corridor." He paused again, looking down at the podium stand.

"And finally, thank you to everyone who's been picking up extra shifts for security, too. Dominic, Fergus, Rich, Jen and lastly Sam. From what I hear, he's been exceptional when in charge."

Another round of applause followed Ryan's words.

"Other news for those who aren't aware, Rani and Sanjay have started harvesting the vines now that the weather's calmed down. If anyone has some free time to help with loading, transporting, and processing the grapes, please see Steph, and she'll let you know what's needed." A few hands raised from rows in front of him. "Thank you. And one final bit of news." Ryan smiled, looking at his girlfriend, then over the crowd. "I need my daughter for this."

Cassy disappeared into the kitchen, reappearing while holding Maisie's hand. She'd been covered from trainers to eyebrows in flour, and everyone smiled as they walked through the cafeteria.

They stepped up onto the podium, Ryan picked her up with his left arm and hugged Cassy with his right. He noticed Mikey, Sandra and Steph standing at the back next to Doc and was glad they were there.

"The good news is, apart from Maisie being an amazing baker..." His comment was met with cheers and laughter, "...it's looking like she's going to be a big sister, too."

The room erupted. Everyone stood, clapping and cheering.

"Really?" Maisie asked, wide-eyed.

"We think so." Cassy leaned across and kissed Maisie on the cheek.

The family of three hugged closely. Ryan looked over the top of

Maisie's head and saw his sister and Sandra hugging. Mikey and Doc high fived with laughter.

The warmth and love of the room engulfed Ryan. For a moment, he was able to enjoy some inner peace. Cooper wasn't here to celebrate with them, and when the time was right, he'd make his inner peace with Cooper's death by taking Father's life.

16

The dreary clouds displayed the same depressing mood as the storm of the previous week. Wind speeds constantly changed bringing the occasional misty rain. The back garden of the mansion hadn't stopped bustling with activity.

"You need to have that last barn up by the end of the day," Jake ordered.

"Yes, Jake, sir," Aslan whimpered, heaving a large, wooden beam on his shoulders with the aid of two other Termites.

"You want Father angry at you again?" His rotted teeth gritted behind his greasy hair.

"No, Jake, sir."

The mansion's back garden now boasted four freshly erected barns. A fifth had yet to be completed, and each served as sleeping quarters for the Termites. The collection of fir and oak trees behind the lawn had been near enough depleted.

"Any news on the runaways?" Connor asked, presenting a coffee to Jake.

"Thank you." Jake took the mug, blew on it and took a sip. "And no. The Termites saw Aslan take five whips yesterday. If anyone knew anything, they would've said by now."

"I need you to help me find them."

"Understood."

"We'll check the whole grounds first." Connor pointed around the massive garden perimeter. "Then we'll head out."

"Think they could still be here?" Jake asked.

"Possibly. There's a lot of hiding spots in and just outside the grounds." Connor spat on the mud. "How well do you know the town and surrounding areas?"

"Good enough. I managed to map it all out a few weeks before Father got here."

"Didn't get spotted?"

"Not once," Jake boasted.

"Good. We'll head out tonight and check the hill's surrounding areas, then we'll get to the town tomorrow."

"Understood, Connor."

"Good. Make sure you're armed."

"Won't Father want them alive? To make an example of them?"

"Last resort," Connor stared him down. "You should know what the Termites are capable of when not kept on their leash."

"Yeah, sorry."

"Good. Don't question me again."

"Sorry." Jake knew of Connor's lack of respect for civilians. Unless you were military, you were an insect to him.

He and Ben were kept safe by Father from Connor's disdain, but he felt like he'd proved himself enough, being a loyal and efficient scout over the past few years to earn some credit. On the other hand, they had just lost Paul, and he already pitied the person that would feel Connor's wrath for it.

"Be on your top game tonight, Jake."

"Yes, Connor."

———

Behind the gloomy sky, the sun set with random bursts of red, purple, yellow and orange streaking through the clouds, adding a colourful dusting to the dismal weather. Mikey, Jen and Sam sat at the table in the centre of the top floor.

"Sunny day tomorrow," Jen said, looking out the window.

"I doubt it," Sam replied. "It's been the same for a few nights, all those colours at sunset and then each day after has been cloudy as fuck. Never seen anything like it."

Doc's crutches echoed, accompanied by the occasional mumble as he climbed the stairwell.

"Need any help?" Mikey called.

"No!" He wouldn't have admitted it anyway.

Sam lit two candles, sticking them to a saucer at each end of the table. Doc entered and placed his crutches on the floor, sitting in the chair nearest the exit.

"How are you coping?" Mikey asked.

"Fine, where's Ryan?"

"In your old kitchen," Jen answered.

Ryan's kitchen was converted into the weapon storage room. The thin galley was stripped down to multiple shelves and racks, all organised into different weapon classes with their own ammunition and an inventory log.

Ryan and Doc only had to serve fifty covers a night, whereas the cafeteria would serve hundreds per day with sandwiches, salads and various hot food items—not quite at the refined detail as the top floor's twelve-course tasting menu.

Ryan entered the restaurant with some rolled up notepads, sitting at the far end of the table. "It's good to have everyone here." He looked up and everyone nodded in agreement. "We have a lot to discuss."

———

Father sat on a bench, watching the sky overhead change multiple colours before eventually fading to black; a magical sight to an unaware individual.

The horrifying reality, if the rumour was true, was that this display had been created by men. Certain men who had just caused the most destructive explosion the planet had ever seen. A single act that rede-fined the occupation of America and altered the world as the human species ever had known it.

The weather had already changed drastically, now the fight would too.

Father wondered where the next fight would come from. *Was the rumour true? Did China really start a new war three weeks ago?*

"Father, the last build is up," Jake said as he stepped out the mansion's front doors with Connor. "Interior renovation begins tomor-row. Parker and Martyn know what needs doing."

"Good work. When do you both go out?"

"Half an hour, sir," Connor informed him. "We've swept the grounds. We're checking all the roads and derelicts outside of town tonight, then we'll move onto checking the town tomorrow night."

"What if you don't find them?" Father asked without looking back.

"Aslan has a scope set on the road in between the western slope and the vineyard," Connor continued. "He's ordered to shoot without hesi-tation if they're intercepted by the vineyard people."

"Who's with Aslan?"

"Pikey."

"Good. Do you have the pig blood if Aslan disobeys?"

"Bagged in the freezer, sir."

"Perfect," Father chuckled. "Bring the runaway's back if you can. Only kill them if it looks like they're getting captured."

"Yes Father," they both replied, then headed into the mansion for a final gear check.

———

"We all know why this chat is happening?" Ryan asked the table. It was a rhetorical question. "We have to find out if we still have a threat nearby."

"How do you want to do this?" Sam asked.

"Just Mikey and I will go out."

"Just the two of you?" Jen sat up.

"If anything happens to us, Sam will fill my position and Lyndon can pick up with his medical education," Ryan stated. "Jen, you'll be in charge of the ground defence if it's needed."

"Agreed," Doc approved, turning to Sam. "Yourself and Dominic would also slow down any attack on us, should one happen during this excursion."

"Okay," Sam said softly.

"I know you wanna be out there, Sam, but everyone would feel safer knowing that you're the first line of defence," Ryan assured him. "You're still the best spotter and shooter we've got."

That line was intentional, designed to puncture the obvious self-doubt Sam had after Cooper's murder.

"When do you want to go out?" Mikey asked Ryan.

"Tomorrow night."

"Tomorrow?"

"The quicker we know whether they've left or not, the better," Ryan explained. "It gives us time."

"Time?" Sam asked.

"Time to prepare for when they come back." Ryan cupped his hands together. "They could've left when we gave them the chance instead of starting a fight."

"It's likely our firepower put them off striking back straight away," Doc added. "They've regrouped, getting reinforcements and weapons."

"Live now, fight later," Mikey said under his breath.

"What's the search plan?" Doc pushed.

"Straightforward. We go out at night," Ryan answered. "We know the roads and terrain better than they do. Check the hotel and town centre. If it's clear, we come back and begin to prepare defences for when they return."

"And if not all clear?" Jen asked.

"We'll come straight back before being spotted," Ryan promised, knowing she was concerned. "Then we'll organise an attack plan."

Jen bit her lip.

"This isn't a trip for a fight." Mikey held her hand. "Have you started a plan if we do have to attack?"

"We'll cross that bridge if needed." Ryan cleared his throat then added, "Until then, everyone needs their heads screwed on while Mikey and I are out. We still don't know what we're up against."

Everyone nodded. Ryan placed the two radio's they'd obtained on the table.

"They've been calibrated to the same signal. We'll contact you asking for times. Do not contact us unless you're being attacked, understood?"

The table nodded again.

"We'll be moving slowly because we'll need as much silence as possible." Ryan tapped the table with his finger. "Doc, during this mission, stay downstairs with everyone. Keep their morale up."

"Sure."

"Jen, can you start organising the inner defence with Sam?" Ryan asked.

"On it," she nodded.

"Thank you," Ryan said, standing. "The quicker we deal with them, the quicker we can get back to living our lives."

"Nothing," Connor groaned, shouldering the M16 and rubbing his temples for a third time.

"Still getting migraines?" Jake asked as he switched the torch on.

"Occasionally. Stay focused."

They stopped halfway down the mansion's winding driveway. The road looked intact and devoid of any natural erosion. Black asphalt sparkled from the previous downpour, and dangling arms of weeping willows hung around the edges.

"Fucking Termites," Jake snarled, performing a 360-degree scan before flicking the torch off. "What if we bump into any of our neighbours?"

A silence hung in the air, and Jake nearly walked straight into Connor who had stopped still, aroused by the thought of a fight, especially with someone who killed his friend.

"We can only hope we do."

17

The damp off the ground soaked through Ryan and Mikey's joggers as they knelt inside J10. Autumn seemed to have held its mild weather and refused to enter the bone-chilling season of English winter. The clouds had vanished, and the nearly full moon shone as they both stared at the bush in front of them. The fine layer of shrubbery separating them from the outside.

"It's midnight," Sam voiced over the radio.

"Okay, stay silent from now until we call in," Ryan answered back.

"Understood, Cuz."

Ryan stood with the radio in his hand, clipping it to the side of his jogging pants.

"Ready when you are," Mikey whispered.

"Same."

They were travelling light with one sidearm, a G36C automatic rifle and an extra clip each. Mikey had the added extra of a small medical bag and his fold up stretcher across his back in case of an emergency.

The usual gut-wrenching nausea resurfaced as they prepared to step outside their safe zone. "Three, two, one," Mikey counted down.

They swung out and quickly scanned the south side's derelict field before pushing left towards the road, slowing as they reached the southeast corner of the maze and tiptoeing onto the asphalt.

Synchronising their steps, they moved south at a precise and silent pace, passing between the sewage building on the left and the derelict field on the right before the first rows of houses eventually appeared on both sides. The abandoned silhouettes were haunting. Screaming reminders of how many families died; each house represented a different voice lost in the Fast War.

The footbridge loomed above as the carriageway merged into single lanes, and the dividing steel barrier ended. The train station hid just out of sight to the left.

Remaining patient, timing each step with each other's and resisting the urge to rush, they eventually stopped under the bridge.

"Heard anything?" Ryan whispered to Mikey.

"No."

"Me neither."

"Ready again?"

"Yep."

They restarted their slow-paced march towards the barricade.

———

"Jake, get that fucking sand-loving-cunt!" Connor shouted as he ran down the stairs, his torch aimed at the hotel's revolving doors as Jake burst after the escapee. *Where's the other one?*

The Termites had lured them up to the first-floor landing, creating a chance to make a break from below. The second Termite was still inside.

Connor approached the reception desk, turned the torch off and closed his eyes, knowing what to listen for. After days without the antidote, the withdrawals would eventually reveal the hiding Termite, whether they wanted them to or not.

Jake reached his full speed, keeping his torch up and turning right as he exited the hotel car park and onto the main road, the adrenaline burning under his skin.

He didn't want to shoot, but if the Termite turned right again onto the road that led to the vineyard, he'd have no choice.

The stacks of cars ahead were now visible as the trees on either side became a blur in his peripherals. He almost forgot about the euphoric sensation that engulfed the body when the side effects kicked in. Better than any drug he had once killed for.

Connor remained silent. The more they tried to hide a withdrawal, the more violently another bubbled to the surface, especially when the biggest side-effect causes full loss of mental stability. The wheezing came from deeper inside the hotel's darkness, then the giggle, followed by the maniacal laugh. He flicked the torch on, shining into the restaurant through a glass partition. The laugh halted briefly, then exploded when the torch switched back off.

"You're in for a bad time," Connor shouted. "Can't wait to see what Father does to you."

The laughing continued.

"Yeah, you won't be laughing later." He added, "You fucking rat."

As he tried to pinpoint how deep into the restaurant the Termite was, something unexpected caused his skin to crawl.

"Ding dong!" the Termite shouted back hysterically.

Connor stood to attention. They never spoke back, especially when in trouble.

"What the fuck does that mean?" He placed his left hand under the M16's barrel and raised it.

"Ding dong!"

Connor gripped the gun tighter to his shoulder.

"We'll ring the bell at the church!" the Termite screeched in a blood-curdling rage. "The other people can kill the rest of you!"

Connor flicked the safety off with his thumb, clicked the torch on and gasped. Halfway up the restaurant in full view and ready to fight him, the Termite stared back. Arms dropped by its side; its lips chewed off completely. Their eyes wider than most people could physically replicate, and its shoulders heaved in time with the rapid breathing.

The Termites rags had turned a rusty brown, covered in dried bloodstains.

"Ding dong!" It laughed, glaring into Connor's eyes.

Jake felt a light relief mix into the God-like confidence that soared through his veins; the escapee Termite didn't turn right. He sped behind the car barricade towards the town centre and past the first rows of shops when the Termite clipped a displaced waste bin, sending it crashing into a phone box on the edge of the pavement.

"Got you!" Jake exhaled under his euphoric wheezing.

He rammed shoulder first into the Termite at full pace, but in the process lost his footing and skidded to the floor. The torch and M16 flew out his hands onto the cracked concrete. Jake's head cannoned off the road, knocking him unconscious.

––––––

Ryan and Mikey halted as a flicker of light came from the far end of the road.

"The petrol station, move," Ryan barked under his breath.

They shifted to the right, hiding behind the first petrol pump, keeping eyes on the light which zipped behind the barricade and towards the town centre.

"What the fuck?" Mikey gasped. "That's too quiet for a vehicle."

"Too fast to be human," Ryan thought out loud. "Pushbike?"

The sound of glass shattering echoed over the buildings around them. They listened for anything else. Footsteps, voices, vehicles, radio chatter.

Nothing.

"Go through the school grounds. We'll come up behind the church. We can cut them off without letting them know we're out." Ryan used his hand to turn Mikey's head, facing the road leading off the petrol station.

"Can you navigate that in the dark?"

"We're gonna find out," Ryan said, pulling the radio up. "Sam, we've had something with lights move into the town. Too fast to be a person, and too silent to be a car."

"You going to check it out?"

"We heard glass smashing. If it's one of them, we'll head back without a fight."

"Okay." Sam sounded nervous. "Let me know asap, please."

"Will do." Ryan tucked the handgun into his waistband and switched it to the G36C. "Ready?"

Mikey did the same with his weapons. "Ready."

They climbed through the school's twisted front gates and rounded the main building to the rugby pitch. They stepped onto the soil with a familiar guilt.

Since the burial of thousands of bodies, the air always seemed like it turned pungent, a cross between a rubbish dump and a morgue—though strictly speaking, the odour had long disappeared. For those who had been there during the weeks of burial, the stench always came back to haunt them.

Ryan always took the route around the sports field, avoiding walking directly over the bodies. It was a matter of respect for those souls.

"Here." Ryan pulled the fence open, and both slipped through, sliding down the small verge onto the train tracks and traversing up the other side. "You good?" he asked, pulling Mikey up as he held onto the metal fence.

"Yeah."

The moonlight shone over the flower gardens, revealing that the grass was a few inches shorter than Mikey. Ryan climbed the wire fencing, easing himself to the ground.

"We'll come out by the back end of the church, then take the side road onto the high street."

The grass cracked as they pushed through, forcing them to move slower than originally planned. Coming back alive, unharmed and undetected was the priority.

Jake opened his eyes and turned his head both ways, searching for the M16. His torch shone on the unconscious Termite ahead.

His body felt like it was crumbling, having no idea how long he'd been out cold for. Experience dictated that it would be a while before he could stand. He prayed he'd be fully coherent before the Termite became conscious.

The church tower stood above the rest of the high street as the first signs of sunrise dwindled from behind. Ryan had a brief flashback of the bell almost deafening him last time they were out. They emerged from the garden's assorted flora.

"Now or never." Mikey clicked the safety off on his weapon.

Moving quicker and turning right up along the church's graveyard, they reached the end of the side road, peering round the corner and checking in both directions.

"There." Mikey pointed left.

About fifty metres away, a single source of light silhouetted behind two cars.

"It's stationery," Ryan noticed. "We'll take the other side road that comes up nearer to it."

"Agreed," Mikey replied.

Their pulses pounded through their arms as they hurried behind the derelict restaurants, ready to shoot if necessary. The light shone from behind the next corner. Ryan peeked his head around and saw a body lying face down, a torch aimed at it from a few metres behind.

"Body," he whispered. "You check it, I'll keep an eye out."

"Okay." Mikey pushed Ryan in the shoulder and out into the road.

They swept their guns from left to right, checking the space around the body and windows of the buildings.

"Who's there?" Ryan called as they reached the body.

No answer.

He picked the torch up, turned it off and slid it into his pocket while keeping his finger on the trigger.

"It's one of them!" Mikey gasped.

"What?" Ryan resisted turning.

"It's one of the ones in rags."

"A slave?"

"Yes."

"Fuck!" Ryan paused, then asked, "Are they alive?"

Mikey checked for a pulse. "Yes."

We can get answers out of this guy, Ryan thought to himself. "Put him on your stretcher and tie him up. We'll take turns dragging him back—this guy could tell us what we need to know."

"Not carry him together?" Mikey asked, puzzled. "That would be quicker!"

Ryan thought hard; they could get back quicker, but neither would have a gun drawn. They'd be sitting ducks,

"One of us needs to have a gun up," he said. "These people are dangerous. Whether we get back with this guy or not, I'm not letting someone get a cheap shot at us."

Sacrifice pace for safety; it was the lesser of two evils.

"Okay," Mikey conceded, slipping the stretcher off and unfolding it. He rolled the dead weight body on top, tying the wrists and feet to the sidebars with zip wire from the medical bag. "Ready."

"Good, we'll have to take the main roads." Ryan kicked something hard as he stepped to the side. He didn't want to take his eyes away from his surroundings. "What's that by my feet?"

"A gun, big one. We have a couple of them at home." Mikey crawled closer to it.

Why is a slave armed? Ryan's brain raced, but he didn't have time to ask questions. "Strap it over my shoulder. I'll radio Sam when we get to the bridge," he said as Mikey shuffled back to the stretcher. "I'll cover you to the barricade. We'll switch there."

Ryan scanned behind every burnt-out car and up the side streets as Mikey dragged the body backwards, keeping an eye out for any activity from behind. The stretcher screeched against the road, cutting through the morning's silence.

"If anyone else is out, we're fucked about keeping ourselves quiet now."

———

Jake was fortunate that the voice called out from the other side of the car, and he recognised it as Ryan's. He had to hide. It was still dark enough that Jake wasn't spotted as he crawled underneath the car. They now had his weapon, the Termite, and he was on a burnout. It was futile to take them on; he'd likely be killed, or worse, captured. He waited until the two men had disappeared down the road with the Termite.

"We have a problem," he said into the radio.

"Do you have the other one?" Connor asked.

"No. He's in the vineyard's hands," he reluctantly reported. "They're taking him back now."

"How? Did you let him get to the vineyard?"

"No. Two of their men already in town."

"Why didn't you kill them?"

"They have my weapon," Jake said, holding back that he'd knocked himself out.

"Fuck sake Jake," Connor shouted.

"It's the same long-haired guy that tied Paul up." Jake made sure he diverted Connor's attention away from his failure.

"The cunt that killed Paul?"

"Yes, they're heading back now."

"We need to distract them," Connor said. Jake let out a sigh of relief and rolled out from under the car, reaching up the bonnet and agonisingly pulling himself up to his feet while feeling the pressure of his failure. Father demanded perfection from his soldiers.

"Get to the fucking sewage plant," Connor ordered. "Think you can do that without fucking up, you junkie cunt?"

"Yes." Jake's hands shook, the words piercing through him. To redeem himself, he would have to get that Termite back from the enemy by himself.

He sat on the bonnet and tried to take in as much oxygen as his body would allow. Pulling a lump of meat out from his side bag and taking a bite, he hoped his energy would return in time.

———

The first rays of sunshine brought their surroundings to life, revealing the derelict homes and beaten road, baring their scars. Trees wilted over garden fences; dark red leaves flared against a cloudless sky. Puddles glowed green with undisturbed algae.

Ryan groaned, pulling the stretcher at the foot end, the handles wanting to slip from his sweaty grip every few seconds. The journey took longer than they wanted. They gradually passed the train and petrol station before stopping under the footbridge.

"Switch." Ryan dropped the stretcher, pulling out the radio. "We're under the bridge, can you see us?"

"Yep," Sam replied instantly. "Who's on the stretcher?"

"A guest who'll hopefully give us answers," he huffed. "Get Jen to prepare the cellar-cage."

"On it."

Mikey grabbed the stretcher, his feet slipping against the morning dew as they reached the final stretch of road. Ryan carefully scanned the trees behind the sewage plant.

"We'll have to carry him through the maze," Mikey shouted. "We'll leave a trail if we drag him."

"Agreed." Ryan eyed the hilltop then the sewage plant, scanning every window.

Mikey looked around as they pulled level with the maze exterior. "Thank fuck."

He felt a splash on the right side of his face as if someone had thrown a water balloon at him. A high pitch whistle punched the floor beside his feet and a thunder-like crack tore across the sky. He looked down at the body on the stretcher. The Termites chest had exploded inwards.

"Sniper!" Ryan shouted, pulling Mikey by the shoulder and throwing him into the entrance at G10.

18

"Rogue Termite is down, Father," Aslan reported.

"I can see. You haven't shot like that since you killed the prime minister," Father replied over the radio.

The news of the Termite falling into enemy hands angered him originally, yet now he was happy. From his position, covered by the trees on top of the hill, Ryan and the other guy would accidentally show him the correct way through the structure around the vineyard.

———

"Where the fuck did that come from?" Ryan screamed.

"Behind us," Mikey trembled, wiping the blood off his face.

"Sam, Mikey says the shot came from behind us," Ryan shouted into the radio as he scanned the car park opposite.

"I see them, two guys heading out the train station." The sound of Sam's rifle bellowed from inside the grounds. "They've gone back towards the hill, but there's a group coming out the train station now. At least ten. They've all got spears, get inside now!"

Ryan's senses surged.

"Come on." He pulled Mikey to his feet. They jumped out of the maze and scanned the opposite direction of the carriageway.

"Clear north end," Ryan turned, noticing three spears arching over the sewage plant.

"Carparks clear," Mikey shouted.

"Mikey!"

The spears crashed unthreateningly onto the beaten road without the conviction and accuracy they were shown to have last time around.

"Sam," Ryan said, clicking on the radio. "We've got enemies opposite the road."

"I can't see them!" The anxiety in Sam's voice was apparent. "Get inside!" he shouted again, more panicked.

They can see us though. Ryan noticed the fear. *They want us to panic. They want us to show them the way inside, or we'd be dead already.* "Sam, focus on the group heading towards us. We'll find another way in," he ordered, putting his emergency plan into action.

"Another way?" Mikey asked while eyeing the sewage plant.

"There's someone watching. They're trying to panic us so we'll make a mistake," Ryan said calmly. "Head around the north side of the maze, then go round the back and hide in the woods. Take this radio with you."

"What are you going to do?" Mikey asked as he took the device.

"Draw their fire. Go now."

"I'm not leaving you here!"

"It wasn't a fucking request!" Ryan shouted, grabbing his arm.

Two more spears crashed behind them as Sam and Dominic opened fire on the incoming assault.

"Go, they're not trying to hit us, I'll be fine." Ryan looked back at the fallen spears some twenty metres up the road.

"Make sure you come back," Mikey said while tearing up. "We can't lose you too."

"I promise." Ryan clicked the safety off his G36C and slapped him on the shoulder. "Go!"

Mikey raised his own gun and headed for the northeast corner.

Ryan watched another spear arch unconvincingly over the sewage plant, bounce off the road, and roll off to the side.

"Is that all you've got, you fucking pussies?" he shouted above the gunfire.

At five hundred metres away, he could see the approaching group was shot down one at a time. One of the chargers took a hit to the leg, hearing them scream as they skidded on the ground.

"Come on! We're fucking killing you!" Ryan turned his attention to the sewage plant, hoping his gloating would bait one of the nearby ghosts into revealing themselves. He got his wish. The emergency exit burst open with two rag-clothed figures emerging. He was quicker to the trigger and caught both in the torso with a single shot each.

A third figure jumped out from the back of the building. Ryan adjusted his body to shoot while the spear flew towards him. Unlike the previous spears, it did not loop through the air with altitude, more so, it burst towards him like a missile at phenomenal speed. He dropped to the ground as it screamed over his head and ripped through the wall at G10. The experience left him dumbfounded that the human body could achieve that level of power.

The long-haired, addict-looking guy grinned back at him, rotted teeth behind his thin lips, and cold eyes pierced through his greasy, tangled hair. The man laughed hysterically, marched around the building into full view, and then disappeared into the fire exit.

Sam chambered another bullet and peered back through his sights. "Last one's down."

"Not yet," Fergie shouted from his position, clicking his fingers and pointing back to the footbridge. Sam followed with his scope. A group, double the size of the previous, poured out onto the road.

"Fuck." He picked up the radio. "Ryan, there's another group coming from the train station. At least twenty of them."

"It's Mikey."

"Mikey?"

"I'm round the back, in the woods. Ryan said we're being watched —he's diverting their attention."

Dominic fired a couple of shots at the newer group as Sam turned his gaze in front of the grounds, seeing Ryan with his gun raised and entering the sewage plant.

"If they send a third group from any direction, he's fucked," Sam explained.

"Okay." Mikey paused then said, "Locate their scout, asap."

"The sniper went back towards the hill."

"Search the hill then," Mikey huffed. "They can probably see everything from up there."

Dominic fired one more shot, pulsing its way across the derelict field and just missing one of the charging Termites.

"Okay," Sam replied.

"Get Doc upstairs with some binoculars or a scope. Fergie and Rich should get the families together in case we have to bail out. Understood?"

"Yes."

"This could be the real deal, Sam. If I say so, start releasing the animals and poison the water."

"Okay."

Dominic fired another shot; Fergie followed with another two.

"Get Jen to throw one of the big rifles over a part of the maze at the back. Understand?" Mikey ordered.

"Yes, I'll send her to Tıo." Sam dropped the radio and called, "Fergie!"

"Yeah?" Fergie looked away from the window.

"Did you hear all that?"

"Yeah."

"Good, take the rifle down to Jen, she needs to throw it over at Tıo," Sam ordered. "Get Doc back up here. He needs to help us find that sniper."

"On it!" Fergie placed his hunting rifle on the floor next to Dominic and headed into the weapons room. Sam turned his attention back to the advancing group.

"Two more down," Dominic shouted.

"Good stuff. You stay with the back of the pack, I'll fire at the front." Sam composed himself, pulling the butt of the rifle into his shoulder and fired. A second later, the front Termite's face exploded. "I'll kill all you cunts if I have to."

Ryan creaked the fire exit open, checked both sides of the processing room, and entered. It'd been years since he'd been in there.

The vast space opened three floors above to the dark grey ceiling, matching the walls in between the high-rise windows to his left. The ground floor had twelve large, open-water treatment vats, spread out in two rows of six and sinking two floors below. Each had two-bar rails encircling the top at ground level. A thick blanket of cobwebs covered the equipment, and the stale air weighed down on the lungs.

"You smell that?" a voice echoed from the far-right corner. "That smell will dominate here when we're done with you."

Ryan focused on the noise, ready to pull the trigger. "This place hasn't smelled in years. I'm guessing the odour is your friend decomposing in our walls," he taunted.

"You think you're funny."

"Not at all."

A metallic clunk thudded to his right. He spun and shot. An empty tin can bounced along the grated flooring.

Jake emerged from behind the furthest treatment vat ready to throw something large. Ryan saw just in time, throwing himself over the railing while managing to keep a grasp on the bars. He felt the spear cut through the air as it whistled over and slammed into the concrete wall.

The strap of the M16 got caught as Ryan flung himself back over. Trapped, he pulled out his pistol and swung around as footsteps thundered towards him.

Jake rammed shoulder-first under his outstretched arm, forcing the air from Ryan's lungs. He continued the momentum, picking up Ryan like a doll and hurtling towards the spear embedded in the wall. Ryan's right ear and cheek scraped along the length of the weapon. He'd ducked just in time. The concrete met Ryan's back like a sledgehammer. He leaned forward just enough to avoid the back of his head crashing into the wall.

Jake was not so fortunate. The top of his head, although slightly cushioned under Ryan's armpit, did meet the wall, knocking him unconscious.

Ryan's back and ribs screamed with a sickening agony as he fell on top of Jake's limp body. Blood dribbled down his chin with each gasping cough. His whole body was having a migraine. Each inhale had an involuntary groan, his lungs begging for more air.

Leaning to the right and kicking Jake off him, Ryan checked for a pulse. Though the top of his head was badly bleeding, he was still alive.

"Good," Ryan spluttered behind the metallic taste in his mouth.

"Have you seen Ryan?" Mikey loaded the cartridge into the rifle before laying it down.

"He's still in the water treatment room," Doc responded over the radio.

"Fuck." Mikey edged towards the southwest corner and peered over the muddy field. "I'm gonna crawl over to H10 and give you guys some support."

"Okay. Stay low—remember they have a sniper of their own."

"Got it." Mikey strapped the L96 to his back and began crawling elbow first along the maze's south side. Once he reached H10, he raised to his knee and slung the rifle round, holding it in firing position and zoomed in. After picking his target from the oncoming chargers, he gently squeezed the trigger.

The kickback nearly ripped his shoulder out of the socket, like someone had attacked the joint with an axe. The rifle fell out of his hands as he screamed under his breath. One more shot cannoned overhead from the restaurant windows.

Mikey winced as he pulled the radio up to his mouth. "Any sign of another wave?"

"No," Doc replied. "If possible, get over to Ryan, and make sure he's okay."

"Yeah, give me a minute." Mikey breathed through his teeth and checked for any dislocation. After hiding the L96 in H10, he shouldered the G36C. "Fuck it. Let's do it."

"Are you okay?" Doc asked, noticing the discomfort in his voice.

"I will be when I know Ryan is."

Ryan controlled his breath, carefully pushed himself back up, and leaned against the wall. Pain tore through his ribcage as he limped over to the rail, untangling the assault rifle with his left hand.

"Ryan!" Mikey's voice came from outside.

"What are you doing here?" Ryan's shout barely audible behind the gurgled blood.

"Sam and Dominic took care of a second wave. I got Jen to throw me over one of the big rifles, I've hidden it in H10." Mikey swung the door open, seeing Ryan's condition and the body on the floor. "What happened?"

"That prick threw that at me." Ryan pointed at the spear then spit more blood out. "We collided, and he knocked himself out against the wall."

"He's still alive?"

"Got a pulse."

"What do you want to do with him?"

"Get all the information we can and leverage him." Ryan leaned to the side. His broken rib ground loud enough for Mikey to hear it.

"That sounds serious."

"It sounds like agony!"

Mikey stood, clicking the radio. "Doc, what's the situation out there?"

"There's a third group forming on the southern platform."

"How many?"

"Can't tell yet. What's your situation?"

"I'm with Ryan and a hostage." Mikey held back from explaining his friend's condition. "Have you found their scout yet?"

"Not yet, but I've got an idea," Doc stated. "I need you guys to stay in there."

"What's the plan?"

"Set up temporary defence inside. We can cover you if they send another group."

"What else?"

"Be ready to run when I say so. Trust me with this."

"Understood." Mikey clipped the radio to his waist and tied Jakes hands with the remaining zip ties.

"I'll watch him, can you do a quick check of the floor?" Ryan asked, spitting again.

Mikey nodded, hurrying around the large room. "There's a door here." His voice echoed from the other side. "It opens to a corridor into the main building."

The sound of metal grinding against concrete pierced Ryan's ears. "What's that noise?"

Mikey appeared at the other end of the central walkway. "Just pulled a couple of metal shelvings across it." He rubbed his hands on his hoodie. "It's not much, but no one's getting through without us hearing."

"The only other way in is through them." Ryan turned to the windows, seeing Mikey pick something up in his peripheral vision. "What is it?"

"A small pouch. Looks like some kind of meat inside." Mikey threw the bag down the nearest vat.

"Anything else?"

"Another radio."

"Handy." Ryan turned his attention back to Jake. "I wonder if this prick took it on himself to kill me, or was that ordered?"

"When they thought I was going to show them the way in, they probably deemed you expendable."

"Makes sense. Well, we can show this guy the way in."

"What?" Mikey protested with dismay.

"Chill." Ryan nearly cried as his ribs grated again, and bloody drool dangled from his chin. "I won't let this guy leave alive."

———

That year had provided constantly unusual weather so far, and this winter's day with a crystal-clear, blue sky presented Doc with an opportunity that he had to take.

"It's half-past midday," Sam shouted from his window.

The sun was behind them now, beaming over the western slope of Maidhill. Doc raised the binoculars, searching for a flicker of light anywhere along the hillside; only a minute had passed before he found it.

"Got him," he said, trying to stay composed to not let his body language give away his motives. He gently lowered the binoculars and turned away, staying inconspicuous and not looking at anyone else.

"Where's the scout?" Sam asked, not taking his eyes away from the train station.

"Maidhill, where the treeline and meadow meet." Doc remembered everything down to the finest detail in the couple of seconds of spotting the scout. "There's a gap in the wire fence, two metres or so left of the public access gate. You'll see the sun's glint off their scope."

"I can make that shot," Sam said confidently.

"Good, I'll let them know." Doc picked up the radio. "One minute from now, be ready to run."

19

Father declined to tell Connor that Ryan had been isolated from his group, not wanting to risk losing his fiercest fighter to the gunfire. Undoubtedly, his soldier would kill the leader of their latest obstacle in the most violent way possible, but he would need Connor alive and safe for when they found a way in and invaded the vineyard.

Connor, Ben and Father hid in the safety of the western slope's thick pinewoods.

"How much patience do these bunch of cunts have?" Connor complained.

"I told you, they're more organised than the other groups we've found." Father chuckled from his own safe point and then asked, "Aslan, what are the shooters on the top floor doing?"

"Still aiming down the road, Father." Aslan was lying on the ground at the edge of the meadow, thirty metres to the left of them. "They're ready to fire at the train station."

"Send both waves at sundown, Connor," Father commanded. "Get someone through their entrance on the north side."

"Yes sir," Connor nodded. "Should we send a small group to—"

A sudden explosion cut him off, like someone had set off a grenade inside a watermelon followed by an air-bursting crack.

"Aslan's been shot!" Ben screamed.

"Get back!" Connor ducked, pointing towards the safety of the nettle pathways. Blood and bone sprayed across the trees.

"Send both teams to attack the sewage plant, now!" Father grabbed the radio. "Martyn, Parker. Do not join in the fight, they have too much firepower!"

"Affirmative, south team sent," Parker replied.

"North team sent," Martyn added.

———

"Run now!" Doc shouted seconds after a single rifle shot bellowed from back home.

Mikey hurtled out the fire exit and across the road, cutting the body free from the stretcher before folding it and sprinting back. Ryan placed his guns on it first, rolled Jake on top and tied him down.

"Your guns?" Mikey asked.

"I fucked up earlier when I said we both shouldn't carry it." Ryan bore against the pain while lifting. "I'm not making that mistake again."

They burst out into the car park. Sam and Dominic fired on the group at the train station. Ryan felt like his body would snap at any moment.

"Look!" Mikey pointed to their right. Two hundred metres up the road, another group was emerging from the base of the hill by the river.

"Keep going!"

They ploughed across the field with a couple of spears from the southern onslaught thudding into the soil behind them. They skidded in front of J10 as they swerved inside.

Ryan's ribs twisted. "Stop!" he yelled.

"Why?"

Ryan laid his side of the stretcher down on the floor. "Go, I need to help the top floor repel the assaults."

"But..."

"Where's the L96?"

"H10, in the wall on the left."

Another round of spears hit the ground ten metres outside of where they stood.

"Pass the radio," Ryan ordered as he spat a mouthful of blood. "Wait in J9. I'll get them to send someone out to help you."

Mikey tossed it over.

"Doc, send Fergie out to help Mikey bring in the hostage. He'll be waiting in J9," he said while wincing.

"What are you doing?" Doc responded.

"Get Sam to focus on the northern group," Ryan ignored the question. "There's only a few left of the southern barrage. I can finish them off myself."

"Are you sure?"

"Just get Fergie to J9! We can't leave stretcher trails through the maze."

"On it."

Ryan ran back outside and threw himself into H10, vomiting more blood over his feet. He located the rifle, flicked the bipod out, pulled himself into firing position, held his breath and prepared for the kickback.

Between the first nine shots, he'd successfully taken down four of the five remaining attackers. With the one bullet left, he aimed at the chest of the final Termite.

The gun clicked. Mikey had fired one shot earlier.

A maniacal laugh drew closer. There was a determination in the attacker's eyes, who was drooling like a rabid dog. Most noticeable was the knife held behind their head, ready to thrust down as they hurtled directly at him.

Ryan stood as sharply as the injury would allow, flipped the rifle around so he was holding the barrel, and swung it like a baseball bat. The butt of the gun met the Termite's face with a sickening crack, accompanied by the spray of bone and cartilage as they slumped backwards. Ryan pulled himself on top of the body with what strength he had left, kneeling on the shoulders and wrapping his hands around their throat.

The semi-conscious body tried to fight back, clawing at his arms and hands, but Ryan wasn't letting go. His eyes burned with rage, his pulse throbbing in his organs and ribs as he gripped tighter. A hatred for the people threatening his family boiled inside.

I'm going to paint this town with your blood.

Losing control, he released his right hand and drove his fist in the centre of their face, his ribs now numbed behind the veil of psychosis that engulfed him. Roaring in satisfaction with every strike, he pounded the Termite until no facial features were recognisable.

Kneeling over the body, he checked to make sure no one else had gotten close before realising the gunfire had stopped. A cold breeze pulled him out of his trance. The face looked back through its broken eye sockets, lifeless and yet relieved, free of the servitude they were forced to live.

The pain resurfaced as if a painkiller had worn off. Ryan lowered to his good side, trying to move as slowly as possible as he reached for the radio.

"Doc?" he wheezed.

"Sam and Dominic took care of the northern group. They didn't make it across the road."

"Did Fergie get to Mikey?" Ryan hyperventilated in agony, looking up at the clear sky.

"They've just come out of D1," Doc reported. "Rich has met them with the quad."

"Keep a gun on the prisoner at all times."

The pain was unbearable, but Mikey was safe. "Understood," Doc replied.

Exhaling cautiously and gently pulling himself up, he gingerly began hobbling into the opening of J10 with the empty rifle.

———

"How much fucking fire power have they got?" Connor punched the driver-side door of his van.

"Clearly enough to take down whatever barrage we throw their way." Father poured a double shot of scotch into a tumbler, hands shaking while swiftly downing it. "Has anyone heard from Jake?"

All his men shook their heads.

"We can't launch any attack until we know he's safe." Father did a quick headcount. "Parker, what's the Termites situation?"

"We lost fifty-six today, not including Aslan or the two runaways." Parker stood next to Connor's truck.

Father nodded and looked over his men.

"It's evident that taking the fight to them costs us more than it's worth." He drank another helping of scotch. "Sergeant?"

"Yes, sir?" Connor stood with his fists clenched.

"I need you to reinforce the front gates. Take Cody and Parker with you, build a couple of watch posts."

Connor nodded and took the younger men with him down the driveway.

"Everyone, we need the rest of the meat stored. Chris, get those freezers linked up to the generator. Pikey, keep guard on our west side in case they come up the hill. Everyone, keep the Termites active, understood?"

"Yes sir!" they all shouted in unison.

"In the meantime, I'll figure out what to do with Aslan's body." Father slammed the tumbler on the decking table.

———

Ryan had sat against the wall in J9 for hours, the sun setting with its familiar golden red and purple.

"What happened?" Sam kneeled beside him, taking the rifle out his hand and replacing the empty magazine.

Ryan's cheeks and mouth were now stained with his own dry blood, and his left eye had swollen shut.

"Cracked ribs, I think. That fucker hit me hard," he giggled immaturely.

Lyndon arrived with Rich.

"What are you doing here?" He glared at his nephew.

"Mikey asked me to stay here with you," Lyndon said.

"I'm fine."

"Your acting is worse than mine at college." Rich placed two water cans on the ground, both filled with lighter fluid. "Dominic and Doc have got the hill covered for any more scouts. We have enough sunlight for the next thirty minutes."

"Okay." Ryan limped out to Jio. He'd overlook the road while Sam and Rich were to set fire to the bodies.

"The road and footbridge are clear." Sam handed the rifle back.

"If I see anything, I'll fire an air shot." Ryan chambered a round. "Get straight back here in that case."

"Yes, Cuz." Sam took one of the cans from Rich before they both ran outside. Ryan dialled in on the footbridge and swept across to the sewage plant.

"Mikey gave me your pistol," Lyndon muttered behind him.

"Make sure you're ready to shoot then," Ryan said, not looking away from the scope.

20

S am lit the cafeteria's candles before turning off the basement's smallest generator. Ryan drew the meeting to a close as the overhead lights powered down, thanking everyone for following Sam's instructions and remaining calm.

"Is there anything you won't do?" Cassy frowned, approaching the podium.

"Yeah, die,"

"That's not funny" she scowled.

"It wasn't supposed to be." He tried to hug her.

"There's a fine line between your bravery and downright stupidity."

"I've known that my whole life."

"Today was too close."

"Which is why they need to be dealt with," Ryan groaned behind the pain. Even the small movement of lifting his arm hurt beyond belief. "It's hard enough that they took Cooper. Anyone could be next."

"Yet it always seems to be you in the line of fire."

"This is what I've been doing from the start." He pulled away. "Anyway, I'm not allowed outside until my ribs have healed or another fight starts,"

"Mikey's orders?"

"Yeah." Ryan rolled his eyes, trying not to laugh. "Even though he can barely hold a pencil now, fucking idiot."

"What did he do?" she chuckled, wiping away a relieved tear.

"Tried using one of the heavy rifles while kneeling." He looked around the room. "Where's Maisie?"

"Steph took her up to our room. I told her I'll be up in a bit,"

"Good." He kissed her and looked into her eyes. "I love you. The quicker I deal with them, the quicker I can go back to getting my dad of the century awards."

"Good luck with that," she smiled. "If the second kid is as mental as you."

"Hey, at least they can take an ass-kicking then!"

"Don't be long." She kissed Ryan and left.

Watching her head up the stairwell, he placed his hands on his hips and looked up. "If that was you looking out for me today, Cooper, thank you."

In the main basement, candles had been placed at the base of the four central foundations. A square table sat in the middle directly outside the jail door. Ryan limped out the stairwell to see that the chair at the nearest end was free. Mikey sat with his back to the cell. Doc was opposite him and Sam on the opposite side of Ryan.

Two candles in the table's centre lit their faces enough in the cold, dark surroundings. The three handheld radios they obtained laid face down at Ryan's end.

"Lyndon's on reception. Rich, Fergie and Jen are on outside patrol," Mikey said without looking up. "Sam and I will switch with them after a few hours' sleep. Dominic's already in bed ready for the changeover later."

"Perfect." Ryan sat, pulling his hoody off with a repressed scream.

"You have to rest until I say otherwise," Mikey finally looked at Ryan.

"I know, you've told me enough times." Ryan sat back and exhaled loudly. "Okay, what the fuck are we dealing with?"

There was a silent moment between the four, looking at each other in hope that someone had an explanation for the alien behaviour they had witnessed today. The unconscious body in the cell compiled the dark fear that coated them.

"They have numbers," Mikey spoke first.

"They're well-fed for those numbers too," Ryan added.

"They can also break Olympic distances with their throwing. They're fast and suicidal when attacking," Doc said, listing today's added knowledge.

"It's like they're on drugs," Sam said.

"Yeah, the one that got close to me outside was laughing like a fucking maniac." Ryan slowly leaned forward. "None of this is good for us."

He picked up the radio they found with Jake, pressed it to his forehead, and let a nervous breath, straining his aching ribs.

"What's on your mind?" Mikey asked, chewing the tip of his pen.

Ryan stood carefully, looking into the cage. "If there is half a thousand of them, and they're constantly this suicidal when attacking..." he huffed, "...it renders our traps obsolete. We could kill hundreds of them, but they'll eventually breakthrough in large numbers."

"I agree," Doc nodded.

"We're going to have to use our prisoner as a bargaining chip," Ryan continued. "Bring a stop to any attack that we're currently unprepared for and buy us some time."

"Do you think they're still nearby?" Sam looked up, twiddling his thumbs anxiously.

"Yeah." Ryan looked at the radio. "They planned to keep in contact with this guy."

"They're probably waiting for him to contact them," Doc chipped in. "You did say it looked like they were trying to panic you, or herd you."

"They were." Ryan kept his eyes on the cage. "We have to assume that when they find out they still don't know the way in, they'll barrage us. They have an army that's crazy and willing to do it."

"What about him?" Mikey pointed at Jake. "Did he seem as out of his mind?"

"No," Ryan shook his head. "Not psychotic, just enraged. That scrawny fucker picked me up and ran at full pelt."

They all looked into the cell. Jake's bandaged head began to turn red at the top.

"Do you think they'll accept a ceasefire?" Doc took his glasses off.

Ryan gingerly paced back and forth, trying not to stress his ribs.

"If they wanted Ben back, then I'd say yes," he rationalised. "There's also a false promise that Jake will remember the way in if we say we're going to hand him back."

"True." Doc put his glasses back on.

"Getting this ceasefire is our priority. If they send a full army through our walls anytime soon... we're fucked," Ryan said.

"And they could be preparing that right now," Doc added.

Mikey and Sam looked at each other before turning back to Ryan.

"Get our ceasefire." Mikey nodded and added. "Buy us time."

"I agree." Sam stood. "I'll start moving the bigger guns if this plan fails."

The hardening reality set in for the four of them. This was going to be a fight to the death. Nothing in any of their protocols prepared them for that. They stood in silence, knowing the next five minutes of conversation would decide their fate.

"Captain," Ryan said to the radio, trying to sound bolder than he really was.

The room caved in with a deafening silence. A week ago, they couldn't have pictured that they'd actually want to hear his voice.

"Ryan, I presume," Father answered coldly. "That was some impressive shooting earlier, holding off each attack and killing our sniper, but I've gotta admit, I'm fucking pissed off."

"Good." Ryan tried to force the confidence.

"You have Jake's radio."

"Correct."

"You have him hostage?"

"Yes." Ryan huffed between the pause. "We brought him in and gave him medical care."

He wanted to emphasize that part, giving Father false hope that one of his men knew the route from D1 to J10,

"Interesting." Father's smile was obvious as he spoke.

"What do you mean?"

"You've radioed to barter for his life, it's obvious."

"And?"

"Tell me what you want first, then I'll tell you why it's interesting."

Ryan's hand shook so hard he nearly dropped the radio as another slice of pain inside his chest caused him to fumble. Mikey led him back to the chair, gently lowering him to sit.

"A ceasefire, over winter." He repressed a groan.

"Hmm, this is interesting," Father chuckled softly. "I'd normally beg for one of my men's lives. But this I can't do."

Everyone's face dropped.

"Why?" Ryan pushed.

"He'll be dead before your proposed ceasefire ends."

"Dead?"

"Yes."

"How? We have a doctor, clean water and food. He'll be under constant surveillance so he can't kill himself."

"Your hospitality won't keep him alive..." Father paused then added, "... no matter how nice it is."

"What will kill him then?" Ryan tried not to sound desperate. "You've seen with Ben I'm not in the business of killing unarmed prisoners."

Doc signalled for him to calm down.

"Well, I thought you figured it out," Father replied. "But seeing as you were dumb enough to drag a stretcher one at a time instead of both of you carrying it, I can see why you missed it."

Ryan ignored the taunt, though his bad choice had been weighing on his mind. "What will kill Jake?"

Another haunting silence gripped the room. Father held all the cards, and they knew it.

"The infection."

The four of them looked at each other with their jaws open. *The man in the cell was infected?*

"The same disease your slaves have?"

"Termites."

"Whatever you call them." Ryan tried not to get angry.

"Yes."

Doc put his hand up to stop the conversation, leaning over to Ryan.

"Jake needs the antidote," he whispered. "We have to pretend we have it."

"A fucking antidote?" Ryan whispered back. "How can we convince him that we just so happen to actually have this antidote already? We don't even know what it is!"

"Father said the antidote was all around us," Doc pushed. "He said it's everywhere."

Mikey and Sam shrugged nervously. Ryan was going to have to play an ultimate bluff.

"What if I said we have the antidote already?" He cringed, knowing how ridiculous it sounded. "We may have made a mistake this morning with the stretcher, but we figured out the antidote. It's all around us as you said."

"You have the antidote?" Father laughed. "I doubt that."

"It's up to you whether you believe us, but we can keep, er, Jake, was it? We can keep him alive."

"You are telling me you have human meat for him?"

The basement cast into a terrifying darkness. A cannibal was in their house, a literal monster in the basement. They all stood, stunned in the silence.

Human meat is the fucking antidote?

"Yes," Ryan lied, trying to make his brain accelerate. "We kept some of the bodies of your dead from earlier, we burned the rest."

"How could you have possibly known to do that?" Father kept laughing, sensing the wool being pulled over his eyes.

Mikey bolted upright, looking at Jake before snatching the radio from Ryan. "Kuru," he blurted into the radio.

"Who is this?"

"A doctor, Mikey,"

"And why are you talking to me instead of the dreadlocked hippy?"

"Because I've seen the symptoms before," he lied. "Shaking, hyena-like laughing, loss of motor skills and communication. It's a human form of mad cow disease, Kuru, caused by cannibalism. That's how we figured out your antidote, you have a dependent strain of the disease."

The four of them hoped Mikey had just deceived Father into holding on to his cards.

"Very impressive. So, you figured that out, and you can keep Jake alive. That's only one problem solved for you though."

Ryan took the radio back, still not wanting to believe everything he'd just heard, but also wanting to stay on track. They needed this ceasefire.

"What do you mean, one problem?"

"You killed Aslan, my prized trophy. This I can't let slide."

We need this ceasefire. Think! "We'll give you our Muslims." Ryan shot his good hand out to silence the others. "We've seen that you look after them." Ryan had already accepted going to war against them, another lie couldn't hurt.

"Change of heart there?"

"If we get our ceasefire." Ryan stayed on point. "You get your man back, and you get our Muslims."

Doc, Mikey and Sam glared. Their eyes pierced him so hard it made his ribs twinge.

"I want to hear from Jake," Father deflected.

"Do we have a deal?"

"I want to speak to Jake."

"He's unconscious." Ryan pinched the bridge of his nose. "When he wakes up, you can talk to him every day. However, if I am to hand this guy back to you, I want a ceasefire, over the whole of winter. Your call."

The tension hung in the air like a bad smell.

"Deal."

Ryan exhaled in relief. "Okay, he stays alive. I'll contact you once he's awake."

He switched the radio off and tossed it on the table. Everyone remained glaring.

"We're not handing Rani and Sanjay over." Ryan tried to hold his hands up in defence. "Nor are we handing Jake back."

"What about your ceasefire deal?" Doc interjected.

"Jake's going to die anyway because I'm not feeding him human meat."

"I agree," Mikey said, once again chewing on his pen cap.

"Same." Sam brushed his thick, black hair. "We're going to have a fight either way."

Doc rapidly tapped the table with his fingers, his brain was in full flow. "I never thought the day would come where we would let an unarmed prisoner die," he claimed. "I also thought I'd never see the day when a good friend was murdered by cannibals."

There was no moral compass for this situation, and even Doc knew it.

"It's us or them." Ryan lit a cigarette with his good hand. "Think about how many people have tried to reason with them. Hamsa's family included."

"I know," Doc sighed. "It's the lesser of two evils."

"We haven't prevented the fight," Sam added. "We've just postponed it."

Everyone nodded, but a ceasefire was better than going in unprepared.

"These people are actually cannibals?" Mikey laughed in disbelief. It was all setting in. "Powerful cannibals."

"Mikey." Doc looked across the table. "How did you know about this 'Kiri?'"

"Kuru," Mikey corrected.

"How did you know?"

"There are very few diseases that show those symptoms." Mikey leaned forward in the chair. "When he said human meat, I knew enough about the disease to bluff him."

"Have you ever seen it?"

"Once," Mikey looked down. "During the early stages of the 2020 Covid lockdown. Police were called to a campsite in Horsham. Some psycho going mental with a shotgun, shooting at anything," Mikey continued. "They'd killed and eaten a someone, a Liberian refugee. Autopsies revealed Kuru, both of them."

"A cannibal disease?" Ryan still couldn't believe what he'd heard.

"Ever heard of Kuru giving people beyond human strength and speed?" Sam asked.

"No, it's transmitted through proteins in brain tissue. In most cases, it lays dormant."

"Is it viral?" Doc rubbed his temples.

"No, it can only be passed through consumption."

"How many people have they killed for it?" Ryan growled. His ribs twitched once more.

"At least we know their food source. Still no explanation for their superior strength and speed though." Mikey sparked a cigarette too.

"Keep him alive once he wakes up," Doc pointed at Jake. "He might give us some answers."

"Are you going to let him talk over the radio?" Sam asked. "He'll say we're not feeding him."

"No." Ryan stood and stroked his chin. "Was it Rich or Fergie who went to voice-acting classes?"

"Rich," Mikey said puzzled. "Why?"

"I want him in here as a guard so he can study Jake. We need someone who can impersonate his voice over the radio," Ryan explained. "In the meantime, we need to start planning. We're going to war because not only is Jake not leaving here alive, neither are those cannibal cunts."

Everyone nodded.

"Start reinforcing the maze interior tomorrow." Ryan stubbed the cigarette under his foot. "See if we can get Jake to tell us where his friends are hiding a fucking army."

"We'll need to get teams chopping trees out back." Mikey flicked through his pad. "Sam, can you organise the extra security shifts?"

"On it, Cuz."

"Doc, can you oversee the reinforcement of the walls?" Mikey brushed himself off. "Eastern and southern sides are the main priority."

"Yes."

"Hold a meeting tomorrow, get volunteers and the rota's drafted up," Ryan ordered.

They had a couple of months to make sure they were ready for the fight—one that would take place on their doorstep.

21

"**M**erry Christmas!"

Cassy entered the bedroom holding a dinner tray. Ryan looked back from the reflection in the bathroom mirror. Wiping the soap off his face, he surveyed the damage done by the women's leg razor: a small nick on the left cheek.

"Christmas?"

"Sam's been recording the sunrise and sunset times, today is the fourth day since the shortest day. He wants to make calendars. A little side project that's keeping him busy in his time off." She placed the tray on the desk opposite their bed.

"Fair enough." Sliding a black jumper over his head, he entered the bedroom. "What's for our first Christmas lunch in years?"

Their personal bedroom looked more homely than Ryan's night shift room. Dark red wallpaper decorated the interior walls, while the window side walls were a dark beige. A queen size bed with a black, leather backboard stuck out from the back wall, bedside tables were on both sides and a desk opposite the foot of the bed, and the windows looked out over the conservatory roof. A matching red carpet and black rug added to the room's comfort. The main door led into a small corridor, filing off into a room for Maisie and a clothes storage room.

This was typical of most family rooms, personally decorated and furnished with salvaged items.

"Raisin porridge, sourdough and thyme butter." She hugged him.

"Lovely." He kissed her on the cheek feeling the draught on his skin.

In the distance, trees getting cut down faintly made their way through the insulated walls.

"Has Doc got a projected date for the inner walls?" He stirred the porridge and blew as steam emerged from it.

"Couple of days at the rate everyone's been working." Cassy yawned, stretching her arms and revealing a tiny bump on the stomach of her green jumper.

"Won't be long before I can chip in with the manual graft." Ryan ate a mouthful. "Getting bored of only doing patrols and watching Jake in the cellar."

"Is he still getting more aggressive?"

"With each passing day. Rich has been imitating his voice over the radio," Ryan muffled through a mouth of porridge.

"I can't believe human meat can do that."

"Me neither." He stood, placing the bowl back on the tray. "That Father guy confirmed it though."

"How did they get like this?" she said in disbelief.

"We might find out if we ask the right questions." He moved the tray to his side of the bed and pulled back the duvet on her side. "Have a nap. I'll leave the rest of this for you."

"Thank you. I forgot how mundane it can be when bottling the grape water." She lay on the exposed bed.

"At least you're indoors." Ryan walked around and propped her pillows. "I'll bring Maisie with me after my shift, you don't have to worry about getting her."

"Thank you, baby." She leaned forward and kissed him. "Has the toilet been pumped?"

"Yes," Ryan laughed as he turned to the desk, unlocked the top left drawer and revealed his beloved Glock.

"Last time I nearly put my face in your pee during morning sickness," she said, snuggling her pillow.

"My bad, sorry." He giggled again, placing the gun in the back of his waistband. "I'll see you tonight. There's another candle in the bedside drawer and a couple of matches."

"Keeping the lighters for your cigarettes?" she shouted across the room.

"Yeah, stressful days at the moment!" Ryan closed the door behind him and began the walk to the basement.

Mikey met Ryan at the bottom of the stairwell with a concerned expression.

"He's foaming at the mouth and can barely make a fist. We can keep feeding him our food. It's like giving alcohol to a cokehead. It works, but it doesn't," Mikey said as the incoherent ramblings echoed around the basement. "What should we do?"

"Let it play out, see if it does kill him," Ryan replied coldly. "Thirty-seven day's we've had him. We need to know everything we can about them."

Rich sat at the table with Cooper's shotgun across his lap, not taking his eyes off the cell opposite.

"Never seen anyone like this." Rich's cleaned-shaved head glowed in the candlelight, his eyes looked tired.

"I got this shift for the next few hours, bud." Ryan pulled out the chair next to him. "Get your sleep in. I'll come and get you after I've got Maisie from school."

Rich smiled and said, "Hope it's drama lessons today."

"Unfortunately, it's geography. Learning about the earth and so on."

"Or what's left of it!" Jake laughed hysterically, interrupting their pleasant chat. "China, China, fucking China!"

"He's been shouting random shit like that all morning." Rich stood. "Have fun!"

"Thanks." Ryan lit a cigarette. "Still not smoking, Jake?"

"America's smoking, ha!" Jake stood with his back to them, twitching in his neck. "Big boom!"

"Whatever you say." Ryan took out his gun and placed his feet on the table, the five-year-old cigarette burning like a cigar in his lungs.

"China changed the war, they are the Nazis, they want the world,"

Mikey approached Ryan at the table. "I think if you want to find out more about the disease, you need to reset it."

"Reset what?" Ryan looked up.

"Antidote withdrawals." Mikey looked in the cage. "I don't like this idea, but I think we need to give him some meat. Human meat."

"Are you being fucking serious?" Ryan choked on the smoke as he inhaled again.

"If you want to see the real effects, yes."

"Red sky at night, China's delight!" Jake howled.

"Shut up!" Ryan shouted at the cell.

"Give him the food, then starve him," Mikey added.

"Is Doc cool with this?" Ryan asked with his eyebrows as high as they could go.

"Yes, even though it's something we'd never do. From a logical point of view, this is how we find out about the disease."

"'Logical'," Ryan smirked. "Puzzle boy."

"Innit," Mikey laughed.

"Big volcano!" Jake laughed viciously, slapping the walls with his hands and dragging his nails down the bare brick.

"I told you," Mikey whispered, both watching the blood smearing on the wall behind Jakes bent fingernails. "Human version of mad cow disease."

Ryan was left with no alternative. He took the radio far out of Jake's earshot and began the conversation. "Captain, you there?"

A minute passed before he got a reply.

"I'm here, how's Jake?"

"That's what I need to talk to you about. We've run out of meat," Ryan lied.

"How is he?"

"He's shaking a lot, self-mutilating, rambling on about china and some other random shit."

"We'll get you the meat!" Father hastily replied. "We'll leave it in the middle of the road."

Ryan was taken back with the immediate submission. "Okay, deal. Don't try anything."

"We won't. Just get Jake fed," Father pleaded.

"When can you drop off?"

"Midday, I assure you. Out."

Ryan looked at the radio in confusion before walking past the cell door. "Fuck me, Jake, they must have some serious love for you."

Ryan headed for the second reception where Fergie sat, reading a biology book. "Fergie, I need you to grab Mikey for me, please."

"Got it." Fergie flicked his blond hair and ran past Ryan towards the stairwell. "What shall I tell him?"

"Tell him I need to arrange pick-up for a delivery."

————

"We got the package, no trouble." Mikey emerged from the stairwell and approached the table. Doc followed with a box of latex gloves, "The lid was open. It's all clingfilmed into, like, portions,"

"No traps?" Ryan looked at it with a critical eye.

"No. They knew we were watching from the top floor," Doc said. "They took the lid off the box, showed us the contents, then ran into the woods behind the car park."

"Who delivered it?"

"Ben and a couple of the ragged ones," Doc reported.

"What if it's laced?" Mikey thought out loud.

"One way to find out." Ryan picked up the radio. "Is this going to make Jake go mental?"

"No," Father responded instantly. "Just get him fed, please."

Ryan tossed the radio back and looked at the pair, who stood in silence at the open cooling box. "What's up?"

They had both turned pale.

"That's, that's human meat," Mikey stuttered. "That's a fucking person."

Ryan peered into the box and felt nausea come over him. His weak stomach started bubbling.

Neatly rolled into individual clingfilmed balls, he saw dark red, diced meat. It could have been lamb for all anyone knew. Someone was butchered like cattle for what the result in front of them was.

22

The cafeteria's kitchen had never felt so dark, given it was the hub for the sustenance that everyone thrived on. The smell was like nothing Ryan had ever known in his twenty years of being a chef, even if his senses had all but forgotten what meat looked like. He'd just cooked the unholiest of Christmas meals.

He'd never felt so dirty.

"How do you think I feel?" Ryan spat out the last of his stomach content into the sink. "I've just cooked a fucking person."

"Don't think I'll ever forget that smell." Mikey handed over the sanitiser while covering his own mouth. "You covered your wounds and wore gloves—should be fine from any infection,"

"I know." Ryan turned the tap on and started scrubbing the inside of the sink.

"Better not tell Sandra you threw up in her kitchen, or that you cooked meat in here." Mikey pulled on a pair of disposable gloves and picked up the used soup pan. "Throw this out, too?"

"Yeah." Ryan rubbed his hands with an oven cloth. "And this."

"Alright." Mikey took the cloth and exited out the delivery doors, throwing the pan and cloth in a fire dumpster before quickly running back in. "Fuck me, that's rank."

They headed downstairs to find Doc with the empty bowl in the middle of the table.

"Less than a minute." Doc stared into the cage. "Less than a minute after finishing the food, he stopped shaking, rambling and started breathing normally."

"What does this mean?" Ryan sat next to Doc.

"It means, it's confirmed that human meat is said antidote for how they control their workers, or slaves, whatever you want to call them."

Ryan cracked his knuckles and leaned elbow first on the table. "We need to find out where they're keeping this army."

Mikey approached the cage door and placed a bottle of water on the floor while holding his pistol. "Have you finished your other drinks?"

Jake nodded and slowly reached to his side, pulling out an empty bottle and placing it next to the new one. "Thank you," he whispered with a wry smile.

"How's your headache?" Mikey kept the gun aimed at him.

"Completely gone."

"Good."

Doc nudged a notepad towards Ryan. On it was written: *We shouldn't interrogate him.*

"Why?" Ryan whispered.

Doc took the pad back and scribbled some more. He wrote: *We want to observe how the withdrawals affect them and added stress could taint the results.*

"How can you be sure?" Mikey pulled out the chair next to Doc. "He was rambling random shit last time. Fucking china, nukes, volcanoes and so on,"

"I don't think that was rambling," Doc said, thinking out loud. "Sounded too specific."

"And it stopped once he ate?" Ryan asked.

"Right away." Doc sat up straight, eyes wide. "That's why Father gave in too easy for the food. He's not given in to anything with ease. Yet, when you mentioned Jake was rambling, he offered it up straight away,"

"Maybe he just doesn't want Jake to die?" Mikey offered. "They've already lost one of their main guys and a lot of their workforce. Giving up on one of your men could breed resentment in your ranks?"

"Possibly. How exactly did the conversation go when he offered the meat?" Doc looked at Ryan, who scratched his head.

"Told him Jake was going batshit mental, talking about china. He offered the food there and then."

"He gave in too easy." Doc stood. "There's something going on. They're hiding something."

"What does this mean?" Ryan looked up.

"I don't know yet." Doc looked furiously through his notes. "But whatever it is, it might help us."

Ryan and Mikey shared a glance.

"I'll see you this time tomorrow." Doc pushed his glasses up before jogging towards the stairwell.

"Doc? What the fuck?" Ryan shouted.

"Give him time." Mikey put his arm across his best friend's chest. "He's onto something, but he'll need time."

"Why leave us hanging like this?"

"Calm. He'll have answers."

"Fuck sake," Ryan huffed.

———

"We should've fucking poisoned him!" Connor shouted across the large, round table. "He could be telling them everything!"

"We've already lost Paul. We can't lose another of our men." Martyn slammed his palms on the clothed surface.

"He's not a military man. He isn't one of us," Connor pointed out. "He's a fucking druggy who fucked up."

"Don't ever talk about Jake like that." Father stood, snarling through his teeth.

All eyes dropped on their commanding officer, the fierce leader who would destroy an enemy without hesitation and had an unnerving loyalty to anyone who served under him.

"He could be telling them everything right now." Connor stood up firmly. "Or are you fucking stupid?"

The table fell silent as Father paced around to stand toe to toe with Connor.

"You watch your fucking tone when you're speaking to me, soldier," Father glared.

"We should have poisoned him, captured this group, and started preparing for our defences back home." Connor refused to back down. "Admiral Caven needs our support."

"You don't give Father orders!" Ben interjected.

"You keep your mouth shut!" Connor's eyes turned to him. "I will break your other fucking arm in front of everyone here!"

Ben swallowed hard, having heard the rumours of what Connor had done to men, women, and children with his own hands.

"Sit down, sergeant," Father ordered, bending down and pressing his forehead against Connor's. "I said, sit the fuck back down."

The testosterone tension gripped the room. Though some of the men agreed with Connor, none of them wanted to intervene in an altercation between the two.

Maintaining eye contact, Connor lowered himself back into his chair.

"Good." Father grinned and looked around the room. "Anyone else think we should kill Jake and burst in with a botched plan against this well organised and heavily armoured group?"

"It's what Admiral would've done," Pikey muttered.

"Yes, he probably would've." Father walked back to his chair, looking around the dimly lit dining room. "But for the past three years, it's been us travelling south, finding new people, food and supplies. We've had nonservice people like Jake and Ben helping us along the way. So no, we are not going to abandon him, and that's my final fucking orders!"

Everyone, including a reluctant Connor, nodded.

"This situation hasn't been ideal, and these people have already taken enough from us."

"How do we know they won't just kill Jake?" Martyn asked,

"We don't, but either way, we came here to do something, and we're going to follow through on it." Father rubbed his hands together. "Admiral has given the green light for the reproduction program."

"The reproduction program?" Connor's eyes widened. "He said that was a barbaric last resort,"

"It is, sergeant." Father nodded ambiguously. "But right now, I need plans for how we deal with Ryan and his people—effective plans. They have a hell of a defence system."

"Why are you now so eager to attack them?" Connor quizzed.

Father grinned, pulling out one of the pairs of old handcuffs from his back pocket.

"First we get Jake back, then we attack." Tossing the restraints in the centre of the table. "Not just for food, but for our future children."

Every one of his men smiled at the news.

"Just because we haven't gone in guns blazing," Father said, "doesn't mean I won't do to them what we've done to everyone else. Now, I need plans for how to breach them, and it has to be effective. I can't afford to lose any of you."

"Or Jake," Ben added. Connor glared.

"So, come on." Father clapped his hands together. "Ideas."

———

"Ryan, hold up." Jen's unmistakable voice came from behind as he entered the cafeteria.

"What's up?" He greeted her with a hug.

"We just finished putting up the interior wall for the east side," she reported.

"All good to go?"

"Yeah, it's not bulletproof but should deter any projectiles."

"Good."

They walked to the hot counter. Ryan filled a bowl of risotto for himself, and Jen followed him to the table with a bowl of her own.

"Did I ever tell you my daddy was a doctor?" she asked.

"No." Ryan looked back in surprise.

"Yeah, trained in Dominican, then worked in St George's Hospital when he moved to England."

"Wow, Mikey and he would've had a lot to talk about."

"Well, that's just it, Mikey does talk a lot." She ate a mouthful.

"What you mean?"

"He talks in his sleep still."

She caught Ryan off guard. Having lived with him for years, he knew Mikey's sleep-based conversations revolved around what he had experienced during the day. Everything Mikey had recently experienced had been kept quiet from everyone else. No one else knew about the human meat other than Ryan, Doc, Mikey, Fergie and Sam.

"Okay. What's he said?" He put his spoon down.

"I thought it was a nightmare, but it's been three nights in a row." She looked down. "Ever since he picked up that package in the middle of the road."

"Fuck. We didn't tell anyone because we thought it was the right thing to do, nothing personal."

"Oh no, I'm not bothered about not being told." She looked back up. "But I have an idea when it comes to the infection."

"Oh, sorry." He cleared his throat and said, "Go ahead."

"If we need to take them out, we might not have to fire a single bullet. My daddy once said, the best way to beat certain illnesses, is to starve it," Jen explained. "If these people go mental without meat, starve them—they'll either die or kill each other."

"Destroy their food storage?" Ryan ran the idea through his brain, impressed by the simplicity. "That's good, logical. Doc'll like that. Nice work, Jen."

"Can I tell your best friend I'm smarter than him?" she smiled.

"He's your boyfriend. Do what you want with him!"

"Thanks!" She took a final mouthful of lunch before skipping over to the medical corridor.

Ryan began to chow down the lunch quicker so he could get back downstairs and explain the theory to Doc.

"It's probably the best idea in terms of preserving ammo," Doc said while scribbling on the notepad. "However, it might land us in a situation that could overwhelm us."

"What's the drawback?" Ryan frowned.

"We don't know if they'll turn on each other. They may just

advance towards us, out of their minds and hungry." Doc took a mouthful of bread. "If their numbers are as large a Father claims, it'll drain our ammo anyway."

"Fuck."

"I do like the idea. The longer I observe Jake, the more information I get about the side effects."

"How's Jake looking?"

"Already starting to twitch. Who came up with the food supply idea?"

"Jen. Mikey's been talking in his sleep. She put two and two together."

"That's still a cold idea, even for her. I know what she had to do to survive the first couple of winters after the war."

"She's been spending a lot of time with Cassy. I think the news of a baby is putting people's values into perspective." Ryan rubbed his bare arms. "Us or them."

"If this is the avenue we have to go down, we need to start planning." Doc rubbed his glasses on a cloth. "And you'll need to start planning something specific for yourself."

"What's that?"

"Start thinking about buildings in the area that could house their potential numbers and their food."

"Okay." Ryan picked up Mikey's notepad. Jake would never tell him where they were hiding. He'd have to bleed the information out of him another way. "Jake, you hungry?"

"Not for more of your rice shit, no," Jake murmured. "I need meat."

"Tell me the best way to store human meat." Ryan took the rolled-up maps from the table, then added, "And we'll get you some meat."

Jake sat cross-legged on the single mattress, his thumbs twiddling rapidly and head occasionally cocking to the right.

"Suit yourself." Ryan shrugged and turned for the exit.

"You can cure it, dry it out like jerky. Lasts a lot longer, has a better flavour, too," Jake chuckled. "The lactic acid and stress hormones give it an almost smoky flavour."

Doc dropped his pen and looked up as Jake went into detail about his diet.

"We stew it for mass feeding time, turn it into all into a watery soup, get more mileage out of a body that way. The bones hold their own gelatine. We can feed all of us for two days off five bodies."

"How many do you have to feed?" Doc asked, joining Ryan at the cell door.

"You heard what Father said."

"Half a thousand," Ryan whispered.

"One body feeds one hundred for two days." Doc calculated in his head. "They've gone through around a hundred bodies in the forty days we've had him."

"We dry the meat first. It can be stored in any condition that way. We keep some meat frozen or chilled in case we fancy a steak night." Jake roared in that familiar hyena-like laugh.

Doc and Ryan said nothing.

"Children taste the best." Jake looked up. "Like eating veal."

Ryan reached for his gun, realising he'd left it upstairs.

"The more he talks, the better." Doc stood in between Ryan and the iron bar door. "They won't be doing this to anyone anymore."

"Are you kidding?" Jake laughed. "You're all on the menu."

"Ignore what he says." Doc stayed firm. "Go upstairs and start putting this plan in motion."

"We're going to starve the cunts," Ryan whispered, not taking his eyes away from Jake.

23

J ake had revealed more than he probably wanted to over the following five days, returning to his random babbling and giving away the location of his friends.

The mansion on top of Maidhill.

He confirmed a converted hanging room, a fully restored walk-in fridge, and a wood fire oven for the dried meats. Additionally, he let slip that their recent supply of meat had been the vineyard's trading friends; the prison in Lewes. Mikey and Sam had to hold Ryan back after he found out, trapping him in his night shift room as Cassy spoke through the door, desperately trying to calm him down.

Whether they killed Jake now or let the disease take its toll, Ryan promised he'd be there for his death. Doc banned Ryan from going to the basement, forcing him to either stay with his daughter or finish putting the plan of attack in place. Meanwhile, Doc drafted up mass defence plans in case the whole army barraged them at once.

Ryan waited for Mikey in the upstairs kitchen, trying to finalise his plan as Doc explained what Jake had said about the infection and how it affected those who had contracted it.

"Latic acid and stress hormones."

"How does that create a super strength?" Ryan scratched his head, struggling to take in the details of the affliction.

"Apparently, they react with a protein in the brain—it causes an overload of cortisol." Doc stood arms folded with his back to the counter.

"Cortisol?"

"It's a steroid hormone." Doc remained still. "This manufactured strain of Kuru is dependent on it. It requires a constant supply of the protein found in human meat. If it doesn't get it, it rots the brain."

"And the lactic acid?"

"A preservative." Doc took his glasses off, "It helps the cortisol stay dormant in the muscles until it's released with adrenaline, causing the steroid-like running and throwing we've witnessed,"

"Fucking hell." Ryan rubbed his temples.

"Apparently the Russian/Islamic coalition found a way to keep enemy prisoners docile, giving them just enough meat to keep them alive but incapable of thinking for themselves." Doc pushed his glasses back. "When Father and his guys escaped from capture, along with Jake and few other civilians, they were already infected. They got back to their base in Hereford, killed the diplomatic officers, and started using the cannibal control thing on their prisoners."

"Jesus fucking Christ." Ryan wanted to believe something else. "How does it keep them docile? How can they not think for themselves?"

"Certain proteins and enzymes attack a part of the frontal lobe of the brain. It's called a 'something-or-other' cortex. It's the part of the brain that controls self-awareness."

"And his slaves are people who did the same to him?"

"Yes." Doc nodded. "And there's more I've learned. If Jake is telling the truth."

"About the disease?"

"No, about why Father gave up the meat so quickly. He didn't want Jake talking too much."

"Go on."

"There's a warrant for these guys. The European Allies want him trialled for treason."

"A warrant?" Ryan looked up, shocked that others out there knew of these monsters.

"Yes." Doc rolled out the map and placed it on the steel worktop. "It's something to do with China, but I haven't gotten that out of him yet."

"Okay. Thank you for keeping me away from him. I would've killed him before we found that out."

"It was necessary. You don't tend to do well around nasty people."

"Forced to eat human meat, then forcing others to do it." Ryan shook his head.

"Eye for an eye."

"Do you sympathise with him?"

"No." Doc held his hands up. "That's how he must see it. Father and his guys went through some horrific shit when captured."

"That doesn't justify them rounding up survivors and turning them into cattle!" Ryan shouted.

"I never said it did." Doc remained calm.

Ryan felt lightheaded and short of breath, his anger bubbling inside, and all because of a calm conversation with his friend,

"Sorry." He pulled himself back. "I don't know where that came from."

"We're dealing with some awful people." Doc handed him a pen. "That's where your anger came from."

"Sorry, can we get back to the food storage plan?"

"Of course."

They laid out all the notepads and waited for Mikey to come from downstairs.

"I'll destroy their food with fire." Ryan leant against the kitchen worktop. "The most simple and effective way."

"Set a fire without being seen?" Doc removed his glasses and rubbed his eyes.

"Anything that requires getting close to their food supply is a risk of being seen." Ryan stood up straight, stretching his arms out. "We need to make sure it's gone."

"How do you plan to get flammable liquids uphill?"

Mikey opened the galley door and entered with three bottles of grape water, then stood to Ryan's right.

"I don't." Ryan unscrewed one of the bottles and handed it to Doc. "I'll syphon it out of their vehicles."

"We don't even know if their fuel is flammable." Doc took the bottle.

"Doesn't have to be in the grand scheme of things, just as long as it burns," Mikey pointed out.

"And it only takes one person to set a fire." Ryan opened his bottle and took a sip.

Doc and Mikey shot each other a look. Even though Ryan already took on most of the solo missions with little regard for his safety, this was a new kind of stupid.

"You're not going on your own!" Mikey demanded.

"Yeah, I am. I'm only starting a fire."

"You can't go all the way up there on your own." Mikey tried to sound forceful, but it came across as begging. "Cassy's pregnant."

"I'm fucking aware of that." He placed his bottle on the counter, walked to the end of the kitchen, and pulled one of the assault rifles down from a shelf. "You can't come."

"Why not?"

"Because Cassy is pregnant, as you said." Ryan placed the gun on the bench. "If I die, yeah, it's horrible. If you die, my child might not survive."

"I actually agree," Doc said under his breath. "Thinking about it, it makes sense."

"You can't be fucking serious?" Mikey protested.

"It's logically the best call," Doc admitted. "Less people to get spotted, more chance of success."

"I fucking hate the pair of you." Mikey shook his head.

"Mikey, there are seventy-one people here. They need you." Ryan turned and glared at him. "I can be replaced, you can't."

"Fuck off with that shit, you've done stuff to keep people alive."

"Yeah, I gave orders to kill enemies, whereas you saved friends, like you did with Doc."

Both looked like they wanted to slap each other, not having a genuine fallout since they were at school. It felt almost alien that they didn't see eye to eye.

"Can we focus on the problems at hand," Doc interjected. "None of this, or the decisions we make, are going to be easy."

Ryan backed away and leaned on the counter. Mikey dropped his head and slammed his bottle down.

"Fine."

"Yeah," Ryan agreed.

Over the course of the next hour, Doc explained his contingency plan should they come under attack when the ceasefire ended. For all of the sickening thoughts that had crossed people's minds since the war and the fight for survival, the only method that Doc had for mass self-defence was once of the most calculated and disturbing things they had heard.

"I feel like I'm going to throw up," Ryan groaned.

"How can we do that?" Mikey added, pulling his hair.

Doc gave them time to absorb the information. Of all the plans he'd mustered up during the ceasefire, that one held the most effective outcome.

"I know it's inhumane."

"It's monstrous!" Mikey exclaimed.

"But remember who we're using it on," Doc pushed. "Father's men and his slave army. None of their hands are clean."

"Yeah, I hate you too now, Doc," Ryan chuckled in self-loathing.

"Why?"

"Because you're right." There was no point in denying it; he would have come up with the idea himself if he knew how to do it.

"I suppose if we're prepared to starve them, we're prepared to kill them," Mikey sighed. "However brutal it is."

"Are all three of us in agreement then?" Doc asked. Both of his companions nodded.

Listing off all the equipment and chemicals he'd need, the only protest he incurred was when explaining he'd have to prepare it himself, outside the maze walls at night. He quickly shot Ryan down by reminding him of his own proposed solo mission.

The sounds of bare feet slapping on tiles echoed up the stairwell before Rich burst through the kitchen door.

"Need you in the basement now," he stammered. "Fergie might have to shoot Jake."

They all hurried downstairs after Rich.

Ryan made sure he had his gun. The speed he was flying down the stairs was the fastest he'd moved over the last couple of months.

The clanging metal grew louder, each time more explosive. Fergie stood a few metres away from the cell door, pistol raised with a look of fear in his eyes.

"China's started the new war!" Jakes repulsive scream tore through the basement.

"Rich, shut the stairwell door. We don't need the kids hearing this," Ryan ordered.

"It's okay, we're here," Mikey reassured Fergie, pushing his gun downwards.

"The new United Kingdom begins now!" Jake thudded shoulder first into the barred door. Ryan looked the frame over; it was beginning to loosen from the hinge. *That's solid fucking iron!*

"Back away Jake, and we'll get you some meat," Doc lied.

"It's too late for you, the Russians have left!" He drooled. A sticky white substance hung from his chin.

"Left where?" Doc quizzed.

"Europe!" Jake laughed. "The country is ours to rebuild. Cattle farms will be built for the disobedient, and we'll rule this country like it should've been."

Ryan drew his pistol. Jake thudded into the door again, pushing it away from the hinge by a few centimetres. *He's going to take that fucking door off!*

"You had a chance to save yourselves!" Jake screamed with another thud, and the door was open a few inches. "Especially your daughter." He locked eyes with Ryan. "I watched you for weeks with that little girlfriend of yours. I wonder how they'll taste!"

Jake ran into the door with one final burst, only to be met with a bullet to the forehead, flying back as his brain burst across the wall. The door hung on by the bottom hinge. Blood dripped off the light-bulb, collecting into a pool on the mattress.

They had just stared in the face of the obscene power they were up against. Father and his people would run through metal doors to get to them.

"I don't care how we do it," Ryan said breaking the silence. "Melt these fuckers to the road if we have to. None of these people live."

He tucked the pistol into the back of his pants and left, leaving Mikey, Doc, Rich and Fergie stood in complete silence.

———

"Admirals men found five more groups of survivors," Connor announced, walking into the conservatory.

"Where?" Father looked over the mansion's back garden.

"Belfast, they're being transported to the second farm now."

"Anything regarding the Islamic coalition here?"

"There are a few pockets of resistance fighters holding the English/Scottish border, but other than that, they've retreated over to Scandinavia." Connor poured himself a coffee.

Keeping up to date with the current climate was crucial.

"Thank you, Connor."

"I'll keep you informed, Father." He saluted and left for the living room.

Connor had been cheery, even after the verbal confrontation the week before, and he was only ever happy when in battle or taking apart an enemy. The reproduction program gave him something, or some-one, to focus on.

———

"Daddy, did you know the earth is a ball?" Maisie asked from her room.

Ryan woke with a crushing headache and ringing ears. He reached for the bottle on the bedside table.

"Say again," he groaned, nearly falling out of bed.

"Teacher Dominic told us we live on a big, spinning ball." She rushed into the room and jumped on the bed.

"He's right." Ryan drank some water. "Although, there are dumb people who think the earth is flat."

"I'm telling mummy," she frowned.

"For what?"

"You said a swear."

"The word 'dumb' isn't a swear, it's just a word that only adults are allowed to use." He headed into the bathroom and switched the shower on. The water came through piping hot.

"You don't normally say that word in front of me." She jumped up and down on the bed.

"I know. I've got a headache, bit moody because of it."

"Because of the generator exploding yesterday?" she asked.

A flashback of Jake's body crumpling to the floor shot across Ryan's eyes, bringing another wave of pain.

"Yeah, generator exploding," he lied, undressing and stepping into the shower. The water instantly washed away the pain behind his eyes.

"Breakfast!" Cassy's voice sounded muffled behind the running water. Ryan turned to see her making the bed.

"What is it?"

"Fried egg sandwich. The chickens have been busy!"

Ryan gave his body a quick once over, dried himself off, and pulled on some jogging bottoms. "Hangover food, lovely!" He took the plate from the desk.

"You look like you have one." She hugged him from behind.

"Feel like it, too."

"Mummy, did you know the planet is a ball?" Maisie shouted from back in her room.

"Oh really, wow!"

"Yeah. Today, Teacher Dominic is going to tell us about other planets."

"That sounds exciting." She kissed Ryan's shoulder and walked into Maisie's room. "Maybe he can tell you about the planet Daddy's from."

Ryan laughed behind his food.

· · ·

Cassy returned after taking Maisie to school to find Ryan was doing pushups on the bedroom floor.

"I'm scared." She sat on the bed.

"I know." He continued exercising. "But this has to be done. After what that cunt downstairs said about you and Maisie."

"Is this our future?" she said sadly. Ryan noticed her tone and immediately pulled himself up to his knees. "We don't deserve any more shit."

"I know, I know," he held her. "We just have to get through this."

"I hate what this world has become."

"I know."

"Kill them all, please," she sobbed.

Seeing the mother of his two children this upset burned him inside. *Day after tomorrow, it's happening.*

———

"Father!" Ben rushed out the back doors into the garden.

"Yes?" He turned slowly.

"They've just left a message, no negotiation."

"Go on."

"We can have Jake. Two days, sunset, middle of the road."

"Any conditions?" Father smiled.

"No," Ben replied. "They just don't want to feed him anymore."

"Bunch of pussies," Connor spat, joining Father. "Can't even handle cooking meat."

"Weak stomachs," Father chuckled. "Connor, you've been planning for this."

"Yes."

"Once we get Jake back, you can initiate."

"Thank you, Father."

"It's a clever plan, I'll give you that." He chuckled. "I love it when you prey on people's weakness."

———

Saying goodbye to Cassy always hurt but seeing her reaction when she found out he was going alone broke his heart. In the long run, for the certainty of everyone's safety, it was what had to be done.

Not pulling off a mission always held its own individual fear, but this, if he failed, could cost everyone their lives. He had never felt this weight before.

Ryan remembered Cassy's tears as he kissed her goodbye. The final 'I love you' until he returned.

"I'm definitely fucking marrying her," he said out loud.

"What?" Doc whispered.

"Nothing."

They stood in the darkness, next to the very lamppost Doc had his head in a couple of months ago.

"Make sure you take the correct way back in," Ryan said, holding his hand out.

"Make sure you come back," Doc replied, straight to the point.

"Radio on at sunrise, yeah?"

"Yes mate." Doc shook Ryan's hand. "The backup plan is ready."

Doc's self-defence plan was only to be used in the worst-case scenario. Only Ryan, Mikey, Sam, Dominic, Fergie and Doc were aware of it. It had eaten at their methanol, sulphur, salt, magnesium, chlorine, ammonia and corn oil, along with six of the CO_2 fire extinguishers.

"If the screams get too loud," Ryan paused then suggested, "play whatever music in the cafeteria you can."

"I will, don't worry." Doc understood what Ryan was getting at. "It's our decision to do this. We shouldn't give everyone else nightmares for the rest of their lives."

24

R yan had visited the mansion only twice since the war ended. The inhabitants had never returned.

A public pathway was accessible from the back of the huge grounds, stretching down Maidhill's meadows to the hotel and train station. Pinewoods coated the hill's western face, once open to the public and converted to dirt tracks for mountain bike enthusiasts. Miles of trails, manmade jumps, and berms wormed their way through the groves. The river cut off the woodland to the north, forming a semi-circular moat around the northern side of the hill and sitting at the base of a hundred-metre drop.

Ryan began his journey before sunrise, using the dark side of the hill to his advantage while carefully treading the bike tracks. He made out footprints left in the mud while keeping his weapon in firing position.

Sam identified the assault rifle as a SIG716, once used by metropolitan-counter terrorist forces. It had an effective foregrip while also being one of the few guns they had with a suppressor attachment. All in all, this gun was ideal for a mission requiring stealth and accuracy.

Dressed in all-black, from trainers to gloves, and with some charcoal smudged across his face, he blended into the dark uncertainty around him. He borrowed Mikey's medical backpack. Sam had added four cartridges of 7.62mm ammunition and a spare clip for the pistol. In the side pocket, he put a thin plastic tube, rubber gloves, a lighter and some grape water.

During the tense ascension, his ears started playing tricks on him along with the thought of bumping into a morning patrol, adding to the growing anxiety.

A few metres from the summit, standing still and holding his breath, he let the silence take over. Nothing.

His palms began to sweat furiously. Instinct told him to test the situation. He crouched, finding a rock the size of a tennis ball, and threw it towards the border of the meadow before it thudded off a tree and dropped to the floor. No reaction.

At the hill's peak, the overgrown nettles still stood at least nine feet tall while wilting, like they weren't given permission to die like they should every year. The winter season still failed to truly show itself.

Two paths were cut into the nettles, leading inwards to the mansion's garden. Ryan quickly scanned inside the carved pathways before peaking over the southern slope's meadows, seeing a few disturbed patches in the overgrown grass.

Keeping the gun on poise, he trod over and investigated. *No fucking way.*

He had a view of the vineyard's whole grounds and the length of the carriageway, all the way up to the roundabout barricade outside town. The enemy could see more than his group had realised.

Henry roared his morning call once more, pulling Ryan out of his thoughts. The first beam of sunlight shone from behind the trees. "Fuck." He carefully paced northwards to the edge of the mansion's grounds where the border met the drop to the river below.

Though it was January, Ryan was comfortable enough in his minimal gear and probably would have sweated in a coat. Twiddling his thumbs, a morning cigarette crossed his mind as the sun sparkled off the windows and morning dew from across the road. Ryan pulled the binoculars up as one of the restaurant windows opened.

Mikey peeked out with a pair of his own, performing a sweep up the carriageway, tapping the top of his binoculars with his left index finger before pulling the window shut. The minor body movement was the signal that he'd spotted Ryan, one of the many codes they would be using today.

From that position, sitting against the mesh fence with a wall of stinging nettles behind, he had a clear view back across the hilltop. After making sure no one had exited the nettle pathways, he pulled the radio out of the bag and mentally repeated the sentence he needed to say, making sure he got all the wording correct.

"Captain, can you *confirm* that you'll be meeting us at sundown, tomorrow?"

"Yes," Father eventually responded.

"Good. Out."

He twiddled his thumbs again as the nicotine cravings surged, not caring for Father's answer but hoping that Doc had listened in on the brief interaction. Ryan had just sent his first code to the vineyard.

In the top floor restaurant, Doc sat at the table and out of view from the window. The two spare radios sat in the centre. One tuned into the frequency that Ryan would communicate with Father, and the other tuned into another signal for emergency communications.

"Ryan said 'confirm'," Doc announced, crossing the code word off his checklist. "They've been using the bike trails to travel down the western side, coming out behind the car park and sewage plant."

Mikey joined Doc at the table as Dominic took over at window duty. Sam continued his morning-long stock check of the ammunition in the galley kitchen. Grape water was dotted around the restaurant, and various breads and baked corn sat on another table, reducing the need to go downstairs.

· · ·

Mikey peered his head out and tapped the binoculars again, signalling that Doc had got the message.

"Thank fuck," Ryan whispered before clicking the radio. "What guarantees do I have this won't go *south?*"

"You don't," Father replied.

Ryan again didn't care for the response, since he'd just sent his next code.

"'South'," Doc said as he crossed off the codeword. "They have exit points on the south side of the hill, out of our line of sight."

"Explains how they got people to the train station without us spotting them," Mikey pointed out.

"That's good." Doc tapped the table. "If they approach from the south, they'll have to stay on the road or try and make it across the field. We can gun them down with the heavy guns if needed."

Mikey nodded.

"Let's see what Ryan say's next." Doc opened a bottle. "If they come from across the road, we only need one bullet."

Ryan's heart jumped into his mouth as the sound of boots became louder. Reverting to lying down and pressing up against the mesh fence, he covered himself with the assorted branches he picked up earlier, leaving a small parting to peer through.

"These exits are covered by the tree line. It gives us full cover all the way down to the bottom of the hill." It was a voice Ryan hadn't heard before.

"Understood," another voice replied, a thick midlands accent.

Two figures emerged from the nettle pathways. The shorter had a clean-shaven head and a monster shoulder frame. The taller had scruffy, chestnut-brown hair and a bushy beard to match. He was a lot slimmer in stature. Both wore the same attire as Father.

"We won't feed the Termites tonight," the shorter one said, pointing down the bike trails. "Have them on standby down there until we get Jake back."

They're ready for a fight, too.

"Yes, Connor." The larger guy rubbed his forehead. "I'll leave Parker in charge of organising the women and children. Should give you some clearer numbers for tomorrow."

"Good man."

Ryan waited for them to head back inside before warning everyone back home. Even with the hidden trick up their sleeve, it was better to know exactly what they were up against.

Back in the restaurant, the spare radio burst unexpectedly.

"This isn't a coded message," Ryan said, forcing the calmness. "They're ready for tomorrow, preparing an assault. They'll be coming down the hill."

Doc, Mikey, Sam and Dominic stopped what they were doing.

"They're separating the women and children from the men." He paused, then added, "I don't know how many they'll have for this attack as of yet. Stay safe."

Mikey swallowed hard; Doc remained silent. The confirmation that tomorrow was happening had sucked the air out of the room. It had just become real.

"Okay." Doc looked over the top of his glasses. "Any final preparations we can do?"

"Move the animals in." Mikey looked over the enclosures. "Bring a few days of their food and keep them out the crossfire."

Dominic and Sam nodded silently before moving back to their respective windows.

"Good," Doc agreed. "We'll do that after sunset."

———

A sharp breeze caught Ryan by surprise. The unordinary warmth took a cold turn with one sudden gust as the multi-coloured sunset painted across the sky. Fear buried in his stomach while looking back at the vineyard. It may be the last time he saw it.

"Fucking deal with it," he whispered, preparing to push inside the nettles and crawl into the mansion's grounds, avoiding any main pathways that Father and his men would use. Hopefully, he'd overhear some conversations during his stealth venture, giving him more information to relay back home so they could bolster the defence accordingly.

Balling his hands inside his sleeves and pulling the hood tightly over his head, he turned to view the vineyard one last time as he parted the first row of stingers.

Something flickered to the right, high in the sky and heading north. A singular red light, getting duller with each second. Behind his nervous breath and astonishment, he heard something for the first time in years. A helicopter.

25

C onnor whistled cheerfully, jumping off the marble porch to the driveway.

"I take it you've heard the news?" Father asked, sanding down a spear.

"Yes sir."

"What news?" Ben asked, dropping more spears onto a pile outside the main door.

"The European Alliance sent their first delegate to Milton Keynes to issue Admiral with his arrest warrant," Connor yawned with a cackle. "It wasn't exactly a return journey for them."

Father laughed at the comment, tossing the spear into the finished stack.

"What happened to them?" Ben asked.

"Medium rare, from what I heard," Connor sneered. Father laughed again.

Ben grinned before his face dropped. "If they're sending people to Admiral, won't they come for us?"

Father raised his hand to take over the conversation. "They were always going to come after us, and we need to be ready." Wrapping his arm around Ben and looking to the sunrise he said, "They're going to send troops our way, troops that have fought the same enemy as us. Not all of them are going to be opposed to what we do."

"Okay." Ben smiled. "I did the right thing joining you."

"Of course you did, son." Father patted his back. "Today you get to help kill Ryan and his friends. As a special gesture, I'll let you pick a breeding partner for yourself. You helped us get this far."

"Ryan's sister," Ben said without hesitation. "I met her once. She's a feisty bitch!"

"Good boy!" Father grinned. "Do me a favour, grab Connor and myself a coffee would you?"

"Yes, sir!" Ben stood sharp and saluted before running off.

"If he gets the sister, I get the girlfriend," Connor said.

"Patience. There is no favouritism." Father picked up another spear and blew on the tip. "We need to make tonight as quick as possible."

"What's on your mind?" Connor noticed the conflict in his eyes, like Father was preoccupied.

"We still have something to take care of."

"Aslan's son?"

"Yes. It's time."

Connor nodded before rushing inside. "Today's a good day, Father," he shouted back. "I'll have the blood defrosted in an hour."

"Indeed," Father whispered. "You did this to your son, Aslan. I have no guilt."

———

Ryan pushed relentlessly inch by inch, crawling agonisingly through the nettles throughout the whole night and early hours of the morning. His body seared by the horde of stings over his skin. He reached a circular clearing. The area was roughly an acre, surrounded by more nettle walls with pathways cut into them. A large, balding yew tree sat in the middle. Logs placed around like benches sat covered by a blanket of dead leaves.

Clicking the safety off the SIG, he pulled himself out the nettles and up to his knees, gripping the gun tightly to him. Surveying the area and quickly stretching, making sure his joints were flexible, he chose the part of the clearing where he would push into the nettles again.

The sky was slightly cloudier than the day before but clear enough for him to see the sun and realise it was only a couple of hours until midday. That forced him to step up the pace for the next phase of the mission.

Reaching into his bag, he pulled out the bottle of grape water and took two large gulps. The hydration felt like it was instantly soaking into his irritated body.

A rustling caught his attention, soft and distant at first. The shouting became audible, growing louder and more distinguishable. It was Father's voice, approaching through one of the pathways. Ryan tried to focus on where to aim, but then he heard the other voices.

"Yes Father," a crowd chanted, a wall of noise gradually closing in from all sides.

Ryan knew that diving hastily into the nettles would disturb them, and he didn't have the time to run all the way back out.

Looking at the tree, he slung his rifle around his back and pulled up onto the first branch.

"What do we do when we get to the sacrifice area?" Father's voice boomed. Ryan climbed faster than he'd ever had.

"We learn, Father," the crowd replied.

Rotating around the tree and reaching for the highest branch, Ryan's left foot slipped, and he landed chest first on the thick branch directly beneath. Gripping on for life thirty feet above, the crowd filled below with Father leading from the front, holding a child by the hand and stopping directly underneath Ryan.

He did his best to count the number of Termites that flowed into the clearing, but that was before the multiple spears they each carried drew his attention.

They're armed to the fucking teeth.

"Tonight, we get Jake back," Father shouted.

"Yes, Father."

"We avenge Paul!" He tied the child face down to one of the logs.

"Yes Father."

"And we avenge our lost trophy, Aslan." Father pulled a knife from his belt.

"Yes Father."

"Aslan started this war!" Ryan felt the hatred in Father's voice. "He let himself get killed so he wouldn't have to face his life of punishment."

"Yes Father."

"Aslan escaped justice, so his son will pay the price."

Without hesitation, he leaned down and grabbed the child by the hair, ripping the knife across his throat.

Ryan's heart stopped. The boy's brief scream turned into bone-chilling gurgling.

"Yes Father."

"Anyone who doesn't fight will be sacrificed and soaked in pig's blood!" Father waved for someone to approach. "Connor."

The bald, stocky guy walked over to the body, spat on it, and emptied a bucket. The whole child turned crimson.

"Little goat fucker!" Ryan heard Connor's whisper.

"Will you fight, or be damned to hell?"

"We'll fight for you, Father."

Father nodded, turning to another exit.

Ryan's body trembled. The army marched mindlessly underneath, following Father in the direction of his home with no one acknowledging the child's body.

Hours had passed, and Ryan's hands hadn't stopped shaking, the nettle stings had gone numb behind his thumping pulse. The eery silence interrupted by the child's brief scream, playing every few seconds inside his head. Cautiously stepping down a branch at a time, listening for any latecomers while silently meeting the cushioned ground, he pulled the gun into firing position.

"He didn't even call you by your name." Ryan's guilt surfaced, refusing to look at the child and avoiding the inevitable wave of tears.

You need to get moving. He clenched his fists and focused on the surroundings. *You can't let that happen to Maisie.*

The sun directly overhead told him it was midday. He'd lost a couple of vital hours while watching the army pour out underneath, meaning there wasn't enough time to crawl through the nettles. Now was the time to adapt.

"I'm sorry, I have to go now," he whimpered to the child. "I have to save my family."

He pushed inside the central pathway, more determined than ever to finish his mission. Determined to kill them all.

Unchallenged through the route, the army heading towards home had dominated his thoughts. He listened intently for any premature gunfire.

Focus.

It was easy for the paranoia to try and pull him off track. He itched to radio home and let them know the sheer size of the army that was approaching, but he knew that could blow his cover or distract him enough to be wounded or killed. Anyone could be round the corner of the green walls directing him through sharp bends.

Finding it ironic that the mansion was also protected by a thick wall of flora with routes weaving inwards to the grounds, he then froze, chills running all over. *What if they have defensive traps?*

Both his heart and stomach fluttered, and butterflies spread all the way up his throat. "Focus," he muttered through his teeth. Pins and needles took over, and his hands cramped up. "There are no traps, they just walked through here." Feeling both his breath and heart rate increase dramatically, he again said, "Focus."

He had to move on, but his body grounded itself to the path. "Move, or Maisie might end up like that kid!" he growled a little louder than he wanted, but it did the job. The weight evaporated though the heart rate continued to pound, forcing his feet to move and continue walking.

The pathway opened into the back end of the grounds. He quickly checked both sides before running to hide behind the fir tree closest to him. Ryan clocked the alarming amount of stumps. Most of the mansion's impressive array of trees had been cut down. *How did we not hear this?*

He noticed something else. A growing stench of unflushed or over-flown toilets. Pushing on tree after tree, ready to shoot anything he came across, Ryan found himself at the stables and edge of the main garden. The smell of faeces was overwhelming.

He used the scope to observe the surroundings; the southern edge of the garden was engulfed with more of the nettle walls. Ryan spotted two openings leading out to the south slope of Maidhill. He buried his nose into the hoodie's collar and swung left to observe the main garden, nearly slipping over in shock. Five new, wooden buildings took up the entire area, each was at least one storey tall and the length of a tennis court.

He checked for voices and slowly approached the nearest one. There was an open hatch to look through. Ryan's eyes widened. Two rows of built-in bunk beds, and three dinner tables ran up the centre with candles placed every few seats. Each build was the same on the inside. The bunk beds stacked four levels high, in two rows of ten.

These buildings can sleep eighty people each?

He was taken back by how cosy, strong and well-constructed the builds appeared. Cautiously running between the buildings, trying not to get caught in awe and making sure they were all deserted, he was unaware of the sun's disappearance behind the sudden formation of darkening clouds.

The conservatory was half a football pitch's length from him as he peeked around the central build. Drizzle started to patter down, and the clouds turned darker as he scanned the mansion's windows.

Reaching into his bag, he pulled out the radio and made sure it was set to the private frequency. "Uncoded message. I've reached the mansion. I think they've sent all forces your way."

"Okay," Doc answered, "We're ready."

"Understood."

Hearing the confirmation that home was prepared took a minor weight off, but the riskiest part of his mission was right in front of him.

. . .

The conservatory was in immaculate condition. Everything had been fully restored, dusted and organised like it was never exposed to lengthy post-war decay. Candles aided against the rapidly decreasing sunlight. Rain began to slam on the glass roofing, thundering through the silent surroundings as Ryan pushed into the large, open kitchen.

He knew the function room was through the door to the right. He bit his lip and used the barrel of the gun to creak the door open. The room bared no resemblance to the last time he had been there.

Three rows of wooden tables ran the length of the room, and a collection of butcher's equipment sat on each surface. A grid system was installed ten feet above, comprised of two large hooks hanging above each table.

Everything smelled sterilised, bleached and disinfected. The floor was covered in a sheet of plastic. The windows stood fifteen foot from floor to ceiling but offered little light with the storm brewing. There were no candles throughout the length of the room. Keeping below the windows and his gun aimed at the double doors on the other side, Ryan stopped. His brain got distracted. *There's no meat in here.*

The hooks, tables, hack saws, rubber mallets and butcher's knives all looked brand new. Completely clean and sanitised. *Are you fucking joking?* He hated it when reality punched him in the face. Father and his men were already prepared to butcher Ryan's people.

The first flash of lightning cracked through the windows followed by the slamming of thunder.

Ryan glanced out. His hate was in tunnel vision, and he had no idea how long he'd been staring at the nearest table.

"Ryan," a familiar voice called out. A southern American accent. "Ryan," it said again.

"Cooper?" His heart raced.

"You're not alone here."

Ryan jerked out of his angry haze, realising the thunder sound a few seconds before was actually the mansion's front doors slamming open.

"Love this weather!" a thick Birmingham accent shouted from the grand hall. Two laughs followed.

"Got a lighter?" The second voice was Ben's.

"Pikey would never offer a fag without a lighter!" a third voice laughed.

Ryan kept low with the gun pointed towards the end of the room, silently crouch-walking past the tables and pressing his ear to the door.

"That kind of stupidity is why you're on defence duty today, you little inbred," the one called Pikey retorted.

"I wish I was down there," Ben added.

"We all do, but someone has to stay behind. Gotta be ready to shift the bodies and women."

Ryan's eyes widened.

"Father let me pick one," Ben boasted.

"We heard," Pikey replied. "She special?"

"You know the main guy, Ryan?"

"Oh yeah, what about that cunt?"

"It's his sister. I'm gonna fuck her in front of him!" Ben cackled.

"Good lad!" The other two joined in.

Ryan's teeth nearly snapped as his teeth locked together.

"I think Connor's called dibs on his pretty little girlfriend," Pikey giggled. "He'll fucking destroy her!"

All three men laughed in unison once more.

Ryan felt like he was falling into the back of his head. The rage was all over him, each bellow of laughter setting his blood on fire. Without realising, he'd opened the door and surrendered to the lack of self-control. Everything turned dark; the grand hall's chandelier candles couldn't pierce his uncontrollable lust for blood. Out on the marble front porch, all three had their backs turned. Ben stood in the middle.

"They deserve it," Pikey laughed. "I call dibs on the black bitc—"

With two silenced shots, hidden more so behind the thumping rain, both of the larger guys' faces exploded outwards. Ben's laughter faded. The cigarette fell from his hand. Before he could turn, a sharp pinch erupted deep inside his knees, bursting out from the joints. Cartilage and blood sprayed as he fell sideways on top of Pikey, screaming in agonising terror. The air shot out from his lungs as his elbows exploded with the same pain, causing his body to spasm uncontrollably.

Ryan grabbed him by the collar, dragging the shaking dead weight into the hanging room, and threw him onto the nearest table.

I let you get away once.

"You led them to our friends in Lewes." He tossed the gun on the floor, picking up a wooden saw with his left hand and placing it across Ben's eyes, the cutting teeth down. "You want to make me watch while you rape my sister." Even behind the colossal hate, Ryan spoke perfectly calm, picking up a rubber mallet with his right hand.

"Please!" Ben cried. "I'm sorry!"

He held the saw in place and raised the mallet.

"Please! I won't kill again!"

Ryan ignored, crashing the mallet down onto the top of the saw, the blade bursting through the bridge of Ben's nose and into his eyes. He thumped down again, holding Ben still as the wails shook around the room—cries for help Ryan had never heard before, almost demonic.

Smashing down once more, the blade reached the temples. Ben thrashed wildly, his screams changing to airless shrieks. One final hammer forced the saw into the skull as far as the ears, and Ben's arms and legs limped off to the side.

This all because of you.

He launched the mallet across the room, crashing it into another table before staring at what remained of Ben's face. His mouth was still open like it was silently screaming. Blood dripped like a tap that had not been turned off fully, wind ripped through the open front doors, and the chandelier swayed violently like the world's worst windchimes. He flipped the table from underneath, tossing Ben to the floor like garbage.

"Ryan," Cooper's voice came back.

"What?" he shouted at nothing.

"Finish the job."

His breathing slowed as he pulled out of the darkened hate that clouded his vision.

"Finish the job."

Repeatedly clenching his fists to refocus, his motivation soared and discarded the horrifying act he had just committed. *It's them or us.* He picked up the SIG and prepared to search the whole building.

26

Since the animal's transition into the winery during the hours of the previous night, the cows and horses had made the reception their own. The chickens were locked in the spare storage rooms, deer were kept in the water purifying corridor, rabbits transported in their huts, and the cats roamed freely around the cafeteria. Everywhere would need a deep clean afterwards, should they survive the night.

Panic had yet to show itself, though fear squeezed the air within their main dining area.

"All entrances and fire exits have been boarded up, the only way in is through the basement's reception," Doc shouted up the stairs. "Last food is up if you want it!"

"Ryan's just radioed!" Mikey yelled back. "He's killed a few of Father's guys, including Ben."

Doc hurried back in. Sam and Dominic were glaring at the radio.

"Is he okay?"

"He's unharmed." Mikey picked up a rifle. "The place was empty apart from the three he killed."

"So, they've sent everyone else this way?"

"Yes." Mikey looked back. "Ryan found the hanging room, it's clean and ready for its next use. He heard Ben say that they're going to keep our women alive."

"They're dead!" Sam shouted, turning his attention to the window.

"Keep your heads in check." Doc exuded a calm tone, even in the gravity of the situation. "Don't let emotion affect your shots."

———

"There's one last thing," Ryan huffed into the radio as he sat against the wall, exhausted after moving all the mattresses to the dining room. "Father killed a kid. Slit his throat and covered the body with pig's blood. It was an example of what will happen if they don't fight."

"I hate these people." Mikey was seething. "Do they have many children?"

"I couldn't tell. Keep them away from the lampposts if you can."

"We'll do our best. We have to look out for ourselves first."

"I know. One more thing..."

"Go on."

"Their petrol is flammable. Make sure Doc makes a note of that. I'm starting the fire now."

"Okay," Mikey replied. "We'll be listening in. See you soon."

"Yeah, you will."

Placing the radio on the floor, he stood and tried to ignore the smell that clouded the dining room, a literal odour of marinated death.

The sheer effort it took to carry everything from the fridges, freezers and dry rooms without throwing up was a personal feat for Ryan. The stench stuck to his clothes and undoubtedly imprinted itself into his memory forever. Just the sight of it all would leave nightmares of the true evil they were facing.

A seven-foot pile of human meat sat in the middle of a ring of mattresses and assorted bedding; the number of human lives in the stack was impossible to tell. Removing his rubber gloves, he walked to the marble porch, picking up the two stockpots filled with fuel.

"You can rest now," he whispered, dousing the meat and ring of mattresses before lighting the end nearest to the grand hall.

The fire roared spectacularly, illuminating the room out of the gloomy darkness. The wallpaper peeled and bubbled after the flames shot up the curtains to the ceiling.

Ryan turned the radio dial to the original setting, paced towards the double doors, and knelt, picking up a packet of cigarettes from one of the bodies. The box was plain white with no identifying marks for which brand it was.

He lit one, noticing the lack of stale burning, like the packet was brand new.

"Don't have time to question that now." Ryan exhaled the smoke before clicking on the receiver. "You there, Captain?"

––––––––

Fergie joined Sam, Mikey and Dominic at the windows. Red lightning shot through the gloomy sky, the clouds tinted dark yellow and purple as the rain hammered down.

"I'm here," Father answered Ryan over the secondary radio. Everyone's blood boiled from just hearing the bastard speak.

"You ready for Jake?" Ryan asked.

"Of course."

"Who are you sending?"

"No one," Father laughed. "We've seen what your shooters can do. Impressive."

"You're cheery."

"I'm just looking forward to seeing Jake."

Mikey scanned the bottom of the hill furiously; no one was in sight.

"Can you see anyone?" he called out.

"No," came a unison of replies as a boom of thunder echoed over the downpour. The tension on the top floor was unbearable. The quiet before the violent storm.

"So, where is he?" Father quipped.

"Prepping him now. We're just taking all precautions."

"We're not going to shoot you," Father said, sounding impatient.

"You've tried before," Ryan rasped. He sounded out of breath.

Mikey looked out towards the southern slope, hoping to see Ryan coming over the verge at any moment.

"You sound like you're running," Father noted.

"So what?"

"Well, your pulse should be running, any time... Now."

The radio conversation couldn't have prepared them for what they saw next. All the hairs on Mikey's arms stood, and his mouth instantaneously dried. His heart felt like it had a lead weight attached at the bottom.

"Oh my god!" Sam gasped from his position.

A wall of Termites slowly emerged from behind the car park, side by side and unarmed.

"That's women and children!" Dominic shouted.

"Don't shoot!" Mikey ordered.

The approaching wall grew wider and deeper, stepping out into the road with no care that they were in the line of fire.

"You have one hell of a shooter, I'll admit," Father hailed. "Shame he wasn't quicker to the trigger when we killed your ginger yank."

"Fuck you!" Sam screamed, his face turning bright red.

"Stay focused, Sam," Mikey reassured.

"And I think he's now focused on the army gathering outside your grounds," Father taunted. "Shame."

Sam's face dropped; he had just been distracted. "Get down!"

A window to the right shattered, and a bullet tore through Fergie's shoulder and pierced the stairwell's exterior.

All four men dropped to the floor. Mikey crawled over on his elbows, pressing his hoodie on the entry wound. Fergie's eyes were wide with fear, blood sprayed up the right side of his face. His blond hair turned dark and matted to the side of his head. Crimson dripped over the beige carpet.

"Seems we were quicker to the trigger this time, Ryan," Father laughed before turning serious. "I want Jake, now."

"Sam, hold this!" Mikey ordered, pressing his hand down before crawling over to the radio. "Ryan, find their sniper!"

"Who's this?" Father barked.

"They shot Fergie," Mikey said, ignoring Father. "They're ready to attack."

"I'm coming now!" Ryan shouted back.

"It's women and children!" Mikey cried. "It's women and children! Find the sniper!"

———

Ryan nearly dropped the radio as he burst out the nettle pathway, coming out on the edge of the southern slopes.

Their firing team had been deterred by a sniper, while women and children were standing outside their walls as a human shield. The backup plan was either useless or inhumane.

Looking downhill, he saw two pathways cut into the meadow leading towards the train station.

Fists clenched and his head racing, Ryan pulled his gun up, staring at his two options.

Follow the trails to the sniper or come up behind the army of Termites.

———

The first two traps erupted within seconds of each other, screeching above the thunder, followed by another trap to the south. Mikey stood sharply, watching clouds of the acidic mix rising from within the maze.

"They're fucking breaching!" he yelled before the window shattered in front of his face, the bullet ripping through the frame and smashing through another on the left side of the room.

Dominic reached and yanked Mikey down. A fourth canister screeched, followed by blood-curdling screams. "We need to get downstairs now!" he shouted. "We're sitting ducks up here!"

Sam pulled Fergie up under his shoulder. Another bullet burst through, missing his head by inches. "Fuck!" He dropped to his knees.

"You two go help the defence downstairs," Mikey lay Fergie on his back. "I'll stay here with him."

A fifth canister exploded.

"Go! We don't know how much more time we have!" Mikey desperately tried to keep pressure on the wound.

"It's my fault!" Sam cried.

"Dominic, take Sam downstairs now!" Mikey ordered. "Get the machine guns ready. I'll bring Fergie down after!"

"Sam, let's go." Dominic pulled him by the shoulder.

"I'm sorry," Sam sobbed, looking at Fergie before crawling for the stairwell.

―――――

Ryan lost count of how many traps he heard in the distance as he sprinted along the hill. As he reached the verge, he saw the wall of Termites that stood outside the vineyard.

Rows of women and children standing in unison, men hiding behind them, waiting to burst through into the maze's multiple false entrances. One Termite ran back out, the flesh on their arms and face falling off as the mixture corroded into them. Another wave followed inwards, swarming like ants, setting off more traps and clearing safer pathways for the next barrage.

Ryan heard another canister go off, this time from behind the winery. The enemy had advanced around the whole perimeter. A sudden eruption of multiple traps cannoned around the grounds, all in the space of five seconds.

Ryan's eyes locked on a spear-wielding cannibal, charging down the driveway towards the winery's front doors. They were already inside the perimeter.

A group of Father's henchmen cheered as they marched out from behind the car park, all armed with M16's. Cannibals, child murderers and rapists, ready to take what they wanted. Ryan was left with no alternative, he had to initiate the backup plan. Women and children regardless.

A huge final wave crouched behind the human shield, hundreds of male Termites.

"I'm not a monster," Ryan pulled the gun up. "I'm not a monster!" The innocent child sacrificed this morning flashed in his brain. Cassy's smile; Massie's laugh.

A roar of gunfire erupted inside the vineyard. Those people were getting closer to his family. Ryan's face dropped. All emotion left his body. Everything went silent. Time stood still, and he accepted what he would become. "I am a monster."

Ryan aimed at the base of the furthest lamppost, firing multiple shots. The flash forced him to look away. He felt the fireball like he was sitting next to an open fire. The chain reaction set off the rest of the bombs in the two other rigged lampposts, the force knocking Ryan off his feet as the explosion tore through the air.

Women and children's wails of anguish bore into Ryan. The fiery figures hysterically crying as their skin bubbled from underneath, and their organs began to cook on the inside. He watched as a sea of people burned, their feet sticking to the bubbling tarmac.

"I'm sorry." Ryan shuddered, observing the nightmare scene he had just created.

Machine gun fire flashed by the winery's front doors. He fiddled with the radio, tuning into the private frequency. "Mikey, Doc, anyone? What's happening?" he begged. "Someone talk to me!" Ryan slipped as he ran towards home.

"Is that you up the hill?" Doc's voice replied. "Did you set the bombs off?"

"Yes, what's happening?" Ryan pushed, urgency coursing through his legs.

"We've bottlenecked the ones who breached, they can't get in," Doc answered. "Were the bombs effective?"

Effective? There was no correct term to describe the mass murder he'd just committed, no matter how you tried to gloss it. "Final wave, all dead. Human shield..." Ryan gasped sharply, "Dead too."

"Thank you," Doc said coldly. "I don't know if we could've held off many more. You just saved us."

I just killed a shitload of women and children.

A lone figure started firing shots from the top floor. Ryan couldn't make out who. "Who's in the restaurant?"

"Sam."

"What's he shooting at?"

"The sniper team that shot Fergie."

"Fergie." Ryan's pulse raced. "Is he alive?"

"Mikey's taken him to the medical corridor, he's doing all he can. Father really got to Sam earlier with that comment."

Ryan heard the sporadic rifle fire. Uncontrolled and ill-disciplined, nothing like Sam was renowned for. "Has he killed the sniper?"

"Hang on."

A mixture of severe guilt and relief overcome Ryan, knowing they had defended the winery. *At what cost though?*

"Move, they're coming your way. One of them is Father!"

Ryan dropped into the long grass, hiding himself from the pathway he had stumbled across earlier.

"Tell Sam to stop shooting!" Ryan whispered into the radio. "He might fucking shoot me!"

"He's screaming about Cooper and Fergie, he won't listen."

"Tell him to calm the fuck down. I can deliver him Father, but not if he fires a fucking stray bullet into me!" A few seconds later, the shooting stopped. "I'm going radio silent now." Ryan's heart thumped. "Wait for my signal."

"What the fuck was that? What the fuck was that?" A panicked voice approached Ryan, the footsteps pounding a few metres away.

"Some kind of acidic napalm. They're all fucking dead!" another voice cried from further behind.

"What the fuck?" The first voice halted abruptly. "Father, there's a fire coming from the mansion!"

"Goddamit!" Ryan recognised the third voice. His heart thumped. *Now, you die.*

The three sets of footsteps thundered past and up the hill.

"How the hell did that happen?" Father roared.

Ryan slowly rose out the grass, checking no one else was behind the three men. "I did it," he called out.

They all turned.

Ryan fired before they could raise their weapons. Parker and

Martyn dropped, receiving two bullets to the chest before Ryan aimed at Father, who raised his arms and let out a defeated laugh.

Ten metres separated the pair.

"You would've been a hell of a soldier for us."

"Stop talking," Ryan growled.

"You've just got your allegiances in the wrong place."

"I said stop talking."

Father smiled and mimicked zipping his lips.

"Walk that way." Ryan pointed his gun off the path and towards the top of the western slope. He kept his distance. Father could pounce with that phenomenal speed at any moment.

He remained calm, waiting for his prisoner to reach the peak that was in view of the vineyard.

"Stop."

Father halted.

The wind carried the odour of charred death up the hill while hammering drizzle fell harshly against them.

"Well, this is an anticlimactic showdown." Father lowered his arms. "You just going to shoot me?"

"Why not?"

"You never see any movie where the two main characters have a final standoff?" Father smiled, though his eyes turned serious. "Why don't we settle this like men?"

Above their heads, thunder roared.

"You're not a man." Ryan took his left palm away from the barrel and raised his thumb in the air. "I saw you kill that kid this morning."

"And you just killed more!" Father laughed maniacally. "You are a bigger monster than you claim I am. We're not so diff—"

Father's chest exploded open. Bone and internal organs dripped down behind a waterfall of blood, mulching into the soaked ground. Unaware of what hit him, he shot Ryan a look of bewilderment.

His right leg buckled first, crumbling to the side, and he fell shoulder first to the ground.

"Thank you," Sam whispered over the radio.

"You're welcome," he replied. "I'm coming back now, stay on guard in case there are any stragglers."

"Okay."

Ryan looked down at Father. The life had evaporated from his eyes with a final breath. There was no joy in seeing this man die. It was a necessity. He could not hurt anyone again. Turning his head to the road, the chemicals and smoke hung like a cloud over the ocean of bodies.

I'm a monster.

The vast amount of melted bodies he'd passed brought on wave after wave of vomit. He tried to remain focused as he passed through the maze. He buried his nose in his collar; the air was barely breathable. He kept his gun on point in case he bumped into a lost breacher.

The sun had set by the time he reached the front doors. Doc opened them slowly before laying the footbridge down. Bodies had been torn to shreds in the trench beneath, piled up in distorted poses, dismembered limbs scattered around and the blood running thick into the churned ground.

"How?" Ryan murmured. The ability to make a sentence escaped him. He didn't know if he was human anymore.

"We removed the footbridges and opened the second reception." Doc made sure the footbridge was secure for Ryan. "We baited them in there and bottlenecked them with two of the heavy guns."

"Safe?"

"They didn't get inside," Doc said, walking over and hugging him. He saw Ryan wasn't in a good way. The smell of broken bodies, death and gun powder permeated the air around them. "Dominic has started clearing the bodies into the trench, then we're locking up and dealing with it tomorrow."

"The traps?"

"We'll replace tomorrow." Doc pulled out the hug and looked into his eyes.

"Fergie?" Ryan asked, his stomach sinking.

"Mikey's got Lyndon to help him, they're doing all they can," Doc reassured. "Let's get you inside."

Stepping back over the bridge into the main reception, even the horse and cow droppings were powerless to overpower the vile stench that stuck in Ryan's nose. The horses were tied to a disability railing, and the plaster wall behind them was littered with hoof marks kicked deep into them.

"The animals were doing fine until the gunfire beneath." Doc kept his voice as calm as possible for Ryan's sake. "Then they panicked, as you could imagine. Luckily, none of the breachers thought about throwing a spear at the door."

Knowing it must've been hell for the animals, seeing them alive bought a great relief. They were family.

Family. "Where's Cassy?" Ryan blurted.

"In the cafeteria, safe."

He immediately dropped the gun and bag on the hay-covered floor, running into the cafeteria. All heads turned to him with looks of relief, all watching him run towards Cassy sitting at the far end.

"Oh my god," she yelped, covering her relieved smile and running towards him.

Their heads nearly collided, embracing hard, crying into each other's shoulders. Ryan never wanted to let go.

"I was so scared," she bawled.

"I know baby. I'm so sorry. I'll never leave you that long again." He kissed her cheek.

"I love you so much."

"I love you too," Ryan cried. Her basil shampoo beat the odour that engulfed him. Her love. This was why he did what he did. For her.

They kissed for what felt like an eternity, Ryan savouring the moment, painting over the horrors he had seen today.

"Where's Maisie?" He looked around.

"Steph took the children into the water room." Cassy wiped her nose. "The guns got really loud."

"Okay." Ryan hugged Cassy again. "I want to see her."

Cassy nodded in his arms.

"Doors are locked people. You can sleep tonight," Doc shouted as he exited the stairwell followed by Dominic. "Anyone who wants to stay on guard tonight or help with the clean up tomorrow, all are volunteers welcomed."

Everyone raised their hands.

Ryan held Cassy, leading her through the crowd of people towards the water corridor.

"Thank you." Multiple hands patted Ryan's shoulders as they passed.

"Thank you, Ryan."

They didn't know what he'd done to win the battle.

In the corner of his eye, Hamsa laid his hand on his shoulder. Ryan held it tight, looking back into his eyes and briefly letting go of Cassy's hand. Hamsa's left arm was still in a sling, residual damage from the torture that Father's people had inflicted on him. Since losing his family, he'd only known pain.

"The man who killed your family," Ryan said with a choke, "he's dead."

Hamsa's legs gave way, falling to his hands and knees, sobbing uncontrollably. "Thank you." He looked up, giving the best attempt of a smile he could muster as Sandra knelt to hug him.

Ryan nodded, taking Cassy's hand again, continuing to the water purifying corridor to see his little 'smelly bum'.

Maisie.

27

Seven Months Later

Ryan's feet pounded the tarmac. A soaring pain in the sides of his soles let him know there'd be blisters to deal with later. The sun blinded him as the sweat poured, and his dreadlocks were soaked through the back of his T-shirt.

He pushed harder, skidding at the finish line on the driveway.

"Twenty minutes and seven seconds!" Doc said, glancing up from the pocket watch. "One minute worse than last year. You're getting old."

"Fuck off!" Ryan laughed, wheezing hard and spitting on the tarmac.

Doc wiped his own forehead, looking up at the burning sun which had dried the surrounding grass into a dull brown. Fire extinguishers were left in stables as a precaution. The weather had alternated between scorching heatwaves to weeklong storms for the past few months. For all his intelligence, Doc couldn't find a viable answer for the diverse weather changes.

"Daddy!" Maisie ran over, a beaming smile to match her white shorts and polo-neck shirt.

"Hey smelly bum!"

"We grew this." She held her hand out.

"That's a plum," Doc informed her before turning back to Ryan. "I was going to tell you, but she insisted on telling you herself."

"Wow!" Taking the plum out of her hand, Ryan asked, "Did you grow this?"

"Me and Uncle Doc and Rich did." She smiled proudly.

"Well done smelly." Ryan rubbed Maisie's head. "Your turn to run, Doc."

"I'm not running today." Doc pointed at his casual attire. "You seen how much weight I've lost?"

"Still fatter than me."

"Whatever you say, old man. I'll see you at dinner."

"Alright, mate." Ryan turned to Maisie, "Shall we go see your brother?"

After January's battle, the maze's expended traps had to be replaced, nearly depleting the salt reserves while adding the painstaking and dangerous task of having to identify which ones were emptied.

Father, his two gunmen, and the bodies of the Termites who had successfully breached the walls were dragged to the train tracks and left to rot. Victims of the lamppost bombs had crumbled into ashes, disappearing with the wind, or washed down to the sewers from the downpour. The streetlights had split open, wilted and turned black. The melted road solidified like lava on a Hawaiian coastline.

At the mansion, the Termites' living quarters were studied, dismantled for timber, and used to reinforce the rest of the maze's interior walls. Barring the carriageway, any evidence of a battle was replaced, fixed, and cleaned. Everyone wanted to forget the three-month ordeal. No one had been outside the vineyard since the clean-up.

. . .

"Has Mummy given him a name yet?" Maisie skipped, holding Ryan's hand.

"Nope, and don't pester her for a name either. She's very tired," he warned, pushing the door open into the medical room.

Cassy lay asleep. Jen sat in the chair opposite, cradling his three-day-old son.

"This baby defo isn't yours, muppet," she whispered with a wry smile. "He's too cute."

Ryan grinned, resisting the urge to stick his middle finger up in front of his daughter, and kissed Cassy's forehead instead. Jen stood, gently passing over his son.

The baby had jet-black hair that was matted down and big hazel eyes with a slight green tint, highlighted more by the white towel he'd been wrapped in.

"Cassy asked when she can get back to work," Jen mumbled under her breath.

"What? It's only been three days!" Ryan exclaimed quietly.

"Don't shoot the messenger." She held her hands up.

There was a gentle knock on the door. Mikey opened it slightly with a concerned looked, waving for Ryan to join him outside.

"Jen, can you take my boy back, please?" Ryan asked.

"Sure."

The infant stirred briefly with a quiet groan before staring at whatever was nearest to him.

Ryan stepped into the yellow corridor, closing the door behind him.

"How are you feeling?" Mikey asked straight away.

Ryan pondered the question. Both Cassy and his son were healthy, Maisie was still the queen of the questions, and both the fruit and rice were coming in good. "Best I've felt all year," he smiled.

"Is there anything you're not telling me?"

"What do you mean?"

Mikey pulled him away from the door, out of earshot.

"As you know, Sam's woken up every night for four months, screaming and crying," Mikey stated.

"Yeah, so?"

"You've done the same the past three nights."

"How did you..."

"Maisie told me." Mikey's expression implicated that none of this was a joke.

"I've just become a biological dad," Ryan shrugged. "My brain is probably freaking out. We both know I can misjudge emotions."

"You'll come to me if you need help, won't you?"

Ryan nodded, not knowing what to say.

"Cassy should be ready to leave by tonight. Make sure you're there with her," Mikey said, changing the subject.

"Why wouldn't I be?"

"Just saying." Mikey pointed his finger at him. "Now, I gotta weigh your baby boy and run a couple of checks on him."

"Okay, I'll be out the back." Ryan rubbed his hands on the sweat-soaked T-shirt. "Doc says I'm getting old."

"You are," Mikey chuckled as he entered the room, leaving Ryan in the corridor.

"I'm only forty-one!"

He untied his dreadlocks and took his shirt off. The cramp began to build while he hobbled down the corridor to the largest medical room and out the fire exit. The wall of warmth hit before he trundled over the footbridge and towards the graves in the isolated northwest corner.

Hamsa had recently laid flowers on his family's graves at the far end of the row.

"Sorry I haven't been here a couple of days." Ryan twiddled his thumbs. "Got some good news, it's kept me occupied, to say the least."

Two of the cats had a minor scuffle in the vines to his left. The ginger one ran off to the winery.

"Cassy gave birth. We've got a healthy boy. Apart from my eyes, looks too much like her," he laughed. "She's already asked when she can go back to work. Her ethic is just like yours."

Ryan glanced at Cooper's grave before dropping his eyes again.

"I don't know if I can call myself a dad." Ryan bit his lip. He had been holding onto his guilt too long. With a groan, he dropped to his knees. "I'm a child killer. I'm a monster."

"Don't call yourself that!" Fergie shouted.

Ryan looked around, his heart skipping beats. No one. He looked to the grave on the left.

Fergie's.

Not even Mikey could save him from the gunshot wound, bleeding out not long after Ryan had returned that night.

"You wanna know why I'm a monster?" He wiped his nose. "I'd kill all those people again if it meant I could've saved you." Standing up, he accepted what he had just said, knowing it was all true.

"You wear that burden, so others can live." This time the voice came from his left in a thick Pakistani accent. Sanjay slowly approached; his ever-warming smile spread across his face. He wore a matching purple polo neck and shorts.

"You heard that?" Ryan tried to hide his face.

"We have already sacrificed enough." Sanjay nodded while pointing to the graves. "You don't have to sacrifice any more of yourself."

Ryan stood a foot taller than him. Sanjay was tubby, with black hair and a beard with greys starting to show at the sides. He had a slightly lighter skin complexion than Dominic, always displaying a charming smile, just like his wife, Rani.

"After they killed Mr Cooper, I blamed myself," Sanjay stated. "Mr Cooper died because they didn't get us."

"I wasn't going to hand you over."

"I know," Sanjay admitted. "But I didn't sleep for days. My wife told me you can't punish yourself for the sins of others. That is what you must realise, my friend."

"I killed hundreds of brainwashed people," Ryan said with disgust. "Some were women and children!"

"And you did not put them there," Sanjay interjected. "Without your actions, we would all be dead, and you would not have a son."

Ryan couldn't fathom that someone would appreciate his heinous actions.

"Fergie and Mr Cooper were very good men, and so are you." Sanjay put his hand on Ryan's shoulder. "Now, Mikey sent me to tell you to have a shower and be downstairs at sunset."

"Why?"

"He did not say."

"Okay." Ryan rubbed his eyes. "Sanjay, can you keep this conversation secret please?"

"Certainly."

Feeling the sun dry the sweat on his skin, a shower was a welcome idea.

"I have no idea what Mikey's up to," he sighed, staring solemnly at the graves. "I'll be back tomorrow, I promise."

———

"I think you should wear the green shoes." Maisie pointed to the middle pair in Ryan's collection.

"Why the green one's?" he asked.

"They match my brother's eyes." She walked out of the clothes room and sat on her parents' bed.

He held the illuminous pair up in the light. "His eyes don't glow in the dark!"

"They might do!" she giggled.

"Alright," he moaned, sitting next to her and slipping them on. The trainers stood out compared to his black jumper and shorts combo. Maisie remained in all white, hair tied back in a rough bun. He picked her up and locked the door as they headed downstairs.

Ryan gazed around the cafeteria. It was empty.

"Strange. Nearly dinner time," he thought out loud.

"No one's here to see Mummy?" Maisie whined.

"Oh no." Ryan shook his head with a repressed laugh. "I'm gonna kill him!"

"Who?"

"Uncle Mikey."

He spotted some heads hiding behind the hot counter before opening the doors into the medical corridor. Cassy sat in her wheelchair, cradling their son, and wearing her favourite baggy, tartan pants and blue hoody, her warm smile beaming.

"How are you feeling?" Ryan kissed her before kissing his son on the forehead and lowering Maisie to the floor.

"I'm good. I heard Mikey put all the baby clothes and bottles upstairs?" She smiled.

"Yeah, that was nice of him." Ryan rolled his eyes.

"What?" Cassy noticed his expression. Maisie played with her brother's fingers.

"Mikey's organised a lot of stuff it seems. Is our baby boy asleep?"

"Yes."

"Yeah... he won't be in a minute." He motioned for Maisie to join him behind the wheelchair.

"What do you mean?" Cassy looked back as he rolled the chair forward.

"Get ready." Ryan pushed the doors open, wheeling Cassy through.

The cheering knocked her back and made Maisie jump. The previously empty cafeteria was packed with every member, clapping and cheering. Cassy put her hand over her mouth and began to cry. Maisie jumped up and down excitedly.

"Want me to kill Mikey now or later?" Ryan whispered in her ear.

"Later," she chuckled, wiping her nose.

Ryan locked the wheels before holding Cassy's right hand, helping her stand.

Steph approached with two glasses of wine. "Hold these please." She handed them to Ryan before taking the baby out of Cassy's arms.

"We can't drink!" he shouted above the cheering.

"Tonight's your night," Steph winked. "Enjoy it."

Ryan looked at Cassy who stood with both hands over her mouth, still crying while smiling. He passed her one of the glasses and picked Maisie up with his left arm. They raised a toast to another loud cheer before Mikey plugged the MP3 player into the speakers.

"Better keep our son away from Sandra. We'll never get him back!" Ryan kissed her on the cheek before the flock of women engulfed her.

"Sam sends his best wishes." Dominic shook Ryan's hand.

"Is he on his own?" Ryan looked around the room for him.

"Don't worry about that boss. I'm not drinking, and neither is

Rich. We'll be joining Sam for night watch in a few minutes. This is a night of celebration, don't worry about us."

"Okay, thank you," Ryan smiled, gulping down a large mouthful of the wine. "It's been years since I drank."

The music thumped around the room. Ryan said goodnight to Dominic and Rich as they left for evening security shifts. Cassy was swarmed by everyone. She radiated with outstanding happiness as they congratulated her. Steph indulged in her aunty duties, reluctant to let go of her nephew, and Lyndon carried Maisie piggyback-style across the room, helping her get all her energy out.

Ryan sat on the podium, looking over the room of pure joy. People began dancing in front of the hot counter, everyone laughing and hugging. After the second glass, his head felt light, the sour grapes leaving a peculiar aftertaste.

"Last year's harvest wasn't the best," Mikey announced, handing him an open bottle.

"Don't think anyone's too fussed," Ryan pointed around the room before pouring himself another glass.

"Got a name yet?"

"Nope. We're taking this newborn parenting thing one step a time." He drank another mouthful.

"I'll take all the tips I can get." Mikey sat next to him.

"When the time comes, whatever you need."

"Soon then."

"Why soon?"

Mikey turned, gazing blankly back at him. Ryan's brain finally processed the information. "Oh my God, no fucking shit?" he slurred in surprise.

"Yeah."

"Mate." Ryan hugged him, almost slipping off the podium. "That's fucking great news, brilliant news, it's banging news!"

"Alright bro, calm down."

"Tell people." Ryan tried to stand. "Where's Jen? I gotta hug her."

"No, not today."

"Why?"

"Because this is for you." Mikey pointed around the room. "And it's because of you." His seriousness sobered Ryan briefly. "Whatever's eating you up isn't as important as all of this, remember that."

"Don't do that," Ryan frowned.

"I won't have to if you let it go. You're not a monster," Mikey said.

"Okay." He nodded before pouring another glass and handing the bottle back to Mikey. "Let me enjoy this toast then." They raised and chimed their glasses. "To secret Papa Mike!"

Mikey shook his head and chuckled before they downed their drinks.

"I could always out drink you!" Steph teased as Ryan leaned on the hot counter, downing a bottle of grape water.

"Yeah, but I'm the better-looking sibling!" he managed before letting out a vile burp.

The party had been going on for hours. Everyone was showing their lack of alcohol tolerance.

"I've got something to tell you." She stood next to him.

"Oh god, what now?"

"You can't get angry."

"I've just had my first wine in three years, no promises."

"I've been seeing Doc the past couple of months," she said bluntly.

That time he didn't need half a minute to process the information. They were the only family they had growing up, inseparable for the entirety of their childhoods. They had fought and defended each other through normal and post-war life. She had lost her husband shortly after Lyndon was born, raised him herself and helped Ryan with adopting Maisie.

"Are you happy?" he asked.

"Yes," she replied. A smile spread across her face. "We are."

Almost losing his footing again, he caught Steph by surprise and tightly hugged her. "That's all that matters then." He kissed her on the cheek and started walking backwards. "My old sous chef is banging my sister!"

"Shut up, you div!"

"Explains why he's lost weight."

"I will knock you out!"

"Where's my baby?" Ryan changed the subject, trying to remember where he was.

"Right behind you." Steph pointed, instead of punching him in the arm like she wanted.

Cassy stood with their son cradled in her arms. "I'm going to put him to bed," she smiled. "I'll be going to sleep, too."

"I'll come with you," he grinned.

"No, we both need to sleep, and you'll snore the place out. Stay down here with everyone."

"This is your celebration, too. You squeezed him out!" Ryan thought he was complimenting her.

"Night baby." She kissed him. "We'll see you later when you've sobered up."

He heard Steph cackling from behind.

"Told you I was a better drinker!"

———

The bedroom windows were left open, giving Henry the rooster a golden chance to pull Ryan out from his drunken slumber. Cassy groaned, turning to her side and checking on their son.

"Was I snoring?" His throat was dry, begging for some hydration.

"No," she mumbled before pulling the covers back up.

Ryan stood and closed the window, still fully clothed. Carefully leaving the room, he plodded down the corridor with a candle as the headache kicked in. "Fucking wine," he grumbled, descending the stairs into the basement, picking a room temperature grape water from one of the cages before opening the door into the second reception. He found Rich face deep in a medical book.

"Have a good night?" Rich asked, placing the book face down and glancing up in amusement. Ryan's eyes were red.

"I prefer being sober."

"Sam and Dominic just came in."

"Is Sam still not talking?"

"No." Rich rubbed the top of his bald head. "Are you going outside?"

"Just a quick smoke."

"Okay, I'll wait."

"Nice one." Ryan unbolted the door and stepped into the trench. The air was humid as the sun peaked. Henry added to Ryan's hangover once more. "Fucking chicken," he swore, lighting the cigarette. A few flashbacks from the previous night caused Ryan to cringe, reminding him why he never danced.

Another Henry morning call rang out, followed by another noise further in the distance.

Knowing his ears had played tricks on him previously, he dismissed it until it called out again, burrowing into his fears. The voices of Cooper and Fergie had acted like angels, pulling him from the dark, whereas this sound pushed him back towards it. Behind the hill, the hyena-like laugh of a Termite echoed.

28

T he first few weeks of newborn parenting had been significantly easier than Ryan expected, not taking for granted that he didn't have an employer or someone else's rota to abide by. Maisie had chosen the name Alfie for their son, named after her favourite horse from the small team they had. Mikey was satisfied with everything so far; Alfie had taken to breastfeeding without issue and showed an average growth rate.

Ryan had the morning off from security duty. He bought his son down to the medical corridor for his daily check-up.

"Thanks for coming down." Mikey wiped the thermometer at the foot of the cot.

"I wasn't gonna send Alfie down on his own!"

"He says he's your dad, but you look more like me, don't you?" Mikey played with Alfie's feet.

"You're boring him, that's why he's asleep." Ryan adjusted Alfie's black and white striped baby suit, pulling the cover over him.

"I need to talk to you." Mikey leaned forward, clasping his hands together as he sat.

"Okay." Ryan pulled a chair close. "What's up?"

"Sam says he heard one of the radios spring into life, just briefly."

"Was someone there?"

"He doesn't know," Mikey sighed. "It was like interference or something, no actual voices."

"Could be he's hearing things. I know what it's like," Ryan admitted.

"What do you mean?"

"Well..." Ryan exhaled, expecting to get a lecture for not saying anything sooner. "I've had a few moments of hearing things."

"And you didn't tell me this?" Mikey scowled.

"I thought it was nothing, just my brain being a cock."

"What have you heard?"

"Voices."

"What voices? When and how?"

"Up at the mansion. I found the hanging room. Cooper spoke to me and made me aware of Ben's presence."

Mikey sat back and processed the information. "Could be your subconscious? Made you aware of danger?" he rationalised. "What else?"

"Out at the graves. Fergie telling me I'm not a monster."

"Sounds like your brain is doing everything to keep you focused," Mikey summarized. "In my book, that's a good thing."

Ryan nodded, wanting to hold back on the next piece of information but realised there was no point. He didn't want mental health or anger issues anymore. It was best to be honest.

"Apart from the last thing. The morning after the party, I had a cigarette in the trench. I thought I heard a laugh, one of their laughs. That evil, psychotic laugh."

"How did that make you feel?"

"Terrified, like we were still at war, and like I'd have to do it all over again." Ryan rubbed his hands nervously.

"I can't find a reason for that one," Mikey admitted.

"How's the idea of being a dad?" Ryan tried to change the subject, getting tense at the thought of having to fight again.

"Jen can look after herself. She's told me not to worry unless she says so."

"Reminds me of my sister."

"I know," Mikey smirked. "My main points of focus are your little boy, Sam, and you."

"I'm a child killer, don't worry about me."

"Stop fucking saying that!" Mikey glared at him. "We didn't know they had women and children. You didn't put them out there."

"And you didn't melt them," Ryan protested.

Mikey put his finger over his mouth, silencing the conversation as Alfie stirred. "I won't lie to you. I can't imagine how you feel."

"So how can you tell me I'm not a monster?"

"Because I would have taken the shot myself if I could have."

"You would?" Ryan stared back in genuine shock.

"In a heartbeat. You're not a monster, and neither is anyone else here." Mikey stood, pulling down a book from the shelf behind him.

Ryan saw the title. 'PTSD: Coping with Trauma and Finding Resolution'.

"We'll take this one step at a time." Mikey tapped the book. "I'll study psychology."

"For me?"

"And Sam. Father's taunting set off a chain reaction in his head."

Ryan nodded and looked out the window. Sam was the only one who hadn't come out the same after the battle. "Neither Fergie nor Cooper's death was his fault." He rubbed his eyes. Knowing Sam put all the blame on himself was heartbreaking. He'd grown a full beard, hadn't cut his hair, and spent all awake time upstairs, rifle never leaving his side.

"Everyone knows that." Mikey held his hands atop his head. "But he sees himself as the reason our friends were killed."

"Is this an issue?"

"Long-lasting, maybe. He's not a danger to anyone and said he's not suicidal." Mikey stood and turned back to the sink. "Even Rich told him it's not his fault about his brother."

"How's Rich doing?"

"I've shown him a lot of basic`s, first aid and resuscitation." Mikey put the book back. "He's handled Fergie's death as well as he can—just wants to make his brother proud."

"He is."

"I know. Fergie would definitely be proud."

"Yeah." Ryan picked Alfie out the small medical cot. "Are we good to go?"

"Yes mate."

"Talk to me later about what you wanna do with therapy."

"Okay. When's good for you?" Mikey opened the door for Ryan.

"Thank you, er... dinner?"

"Sounds good, see you then."

"Perfect."

"And Ryan?"

"Yes, mate?"

"For whatever you feel about yourself, you're making an awesome dad."

The cafeteria bustled with activity. Doc sat opposite Ryan as everyone else finished their breakfasts.

"We're pressing more soap and bottling more water today. Ground team A is taking care of that," Doc said reading notes out loud. "Hamsa has taken over the toothpaste production. He's a workhorse."

He looked up. Ryan hadn't been paying attention to a single word as he fed Alfie while making goofy faces.

"Got any questions about today's shifts?" Ryan still ignored him. "Ryan, got any questions?"

"Want some breast milk?" Ryan offered him the bottle.

"No." Doc screwed his face, dropping the toast on the plate.

"Just gotta wipe your cheeks, little man, don't get grumpy." Alfie immediately ignored Ryan's plea and wailed at the top of his tiny voice.

"Here, I'll take him," Steph said, approaching.

"You're an absolute Godsend." He gently passed Alfie over, pulling a cigarette out of his pocket afterwards.

"I thought you gave up?" Steph said, sounding accusatory.

"I did until yesterday. Can you watch him for five minutes, please?"

"Sure, more time with my gorgeous nephew," she smiled, gently rocking as Alfie quietened down.

"Can have him the rest of the day if you want!" Ryan joked, hurrying towards the cafeteria kitchen.

Sandra was organising the dry store, unaware of his presence. Ryan stepped outside the delivery doors, observing Cassy and Jen heaving a large wheelbarrow of corn onto the driveway, making their way towards the main entrance.

No one had noticed. He could enjoy five minutes of peace.

"Perfect."

His smile was cut short as the all too familiar sound crackled across the grounds. A tripwire snapping back and a container of acidic salts spraying over the trespasser. Instant screams of the would-be intruder who was about to be slowly melted into a puddle of bubbling flesh and bone. Doc immediately came running out the front doors and drawing his handgun, shouting for the rest of the women and children to get inside. Ryan slammed the double doors behind him and sprinted round to the front.

"Any idea which trap that was?" Ryan shouted to the top floor.

"A10." Sam pointed his rifle out to the dual carriageway. "We're good on all other sides."

"You didn't see them approach?" he shouted back.

"Not a thing." Sam shook his head. "I'd guess they were hugging the walls outside since last night."

The enemy was back.

———

"There was one dead," Ryan explained in the emergency meeting. "We don't know if they're a straggler from the original group or a new threat. From now on, everyone who is weapon trained is always armed."

The tension could be cut with a butter knife.

"We can't go out until we know how many we're up against." Ryan scratched his head. "If it's a few stragglers, the traps themselves will finish them."

Rich raised his hand and asked, "What if there's a whole other army of them?"

All eyes rested on Ryan.

"Be ready to bring the animals in or put them down," Doc announced, joining him on the podium.

"Doc, Sam, Dominic and I will be on constant scout duty until we find out the full situation. Then, we'll finish them off." Ryan shuddered from inside, gritting his teeth silently and cutting the guilt out. "Whatever I have to do, I'll do."

29

S leep wanted to take over Ryan's body. He'd been in the prone
position for hours. The previous two days had been a slow
stakeout before the enemy began to show its ugly head.

From the lookout point where he hid with an L96 sniper rifle, a bag
of beetroot and three litres of grape water, he watched the Termites
dance around the top of Maidhill. They weren't even trying to hide
themselves in the treeline. The hyena-like laugh howled louder, like
they were ridiculing the last attempt at killing them off.

Ryan moved his eye away from the scope. A sharp gust of wind
punched him in the face. Taking his finger off the trigger, he reached
and pulled the last bottle out of the bag. It had been hours since he'd
drank anything. The activity in the distance had kept him occupied.

Hours passed; the laughter bellowed from the hilltop as the Termites
ran sporadically in circles.

"I think they're faking it," Doc said.

"Faking what?" Ryan kept his eye to the scope.

"Their behaviour."

"What do you mean?"

"Firstly, the laugh sounds forced. Secondly, even as sporadic as their movement looks, it's structured, disciplined. They're not doing anything outside of it."

"If they're not out of their minds, it means they've got food," Ryan groaned, realising the situation could be even uglier than anticipated.

"Which is why I think this behaviour is fake," Doc pointed out, biting into one of the beetroots. "It's too strategized for people losing their mind."

"They've got one of Father's men with them?"

"Most likely."

Ryan bit on his hand and let out a repressed scream.

"The good thing about this," Doc said after swallowing a large mouthful, "is this isn't an attack, it's revenge."

"How's that a good thing?"

"They'll get impatient and give something away. We can take them out from that."

"What makes you so sure?"

"The fact they're military, and we outsmarted them. Their brains have already succumbed to the disease. It's affected their decision making. Give it time, they'll mess up."

The wind picked up drastically like another storm was brewing.

"Ryan, Doc!" Dominic shouted from the restaurant window. "You'd better come up here."

Hurtling through the trench and into the basement, they sprinted upstairs.

All the restaurant windows, bar one on each side, had been boarded. Sam and Dominic sat in the far corner of the room.

"Have you spotted something?" Ryan wheezed.

Dominic shook his head.

Sam remained silent, leaning on the table with fists balled up by his mouth. The radio in the middle crackled, the only one they hadn't altered the frequency on.

"Sir, it's affirmative. Dartford tunnel is clear. No sign of Captain Jeffries here," a Scottish accent reported,

"Copy that private, set up a perimeter. All drones are recharging in Sheffield. We'll send them out tomorrow morning," a thick American accent replied.

Ryan's mouth dropped. Doc stared intently, his fingers tapping the table in rapid motion.

"Yes sir, won't be long before we crack open the whiskey!" the Scottish guy laughed.

"Easy private, we have to bring him in first. We'll convene at your point on the south side of the Dartford, 0500 hours," the American stayed professional.

"Yes sir. This fucker is gonna pay for what he's done."

"Affirmative."

Ryan snatched the radio. "Who is this?" he blurted.

"Sir!" the Scottish guy shouted. "We have an unknown communication coming through."

"Identify yourself!" The American demanded.

"My name's Ryan." The radio shook in his hand. Dominic held Sam to his chair as he started to have a panic attack.

"Are you military?" the American asked.

"No. Survivor, civilian, innocent."

"You are on a private, secure line. How is this possible?"

"We killed Father," Ryan stammered. "He attacked us. We killed him."

"Captain Morgan Jeffries?"

"Yes. He brought his people to mine, threatened to kill us." Ryan's palm began to drip.

"You killed him?"

"We had to. It was self-defence. They've sent some more to attack us. You need to get here!"

"Calm down. What's your full name?"

"Ryan Field."

"Okay Mr Field. Are you in the south?"

"If you are in Dartford, yes. We're off the Leatherhead M25 junction, dual carriageway, vineyard, Maidville."

There was a static pause. Ryan's lungs ached as the anxiety soared.

"Sir, we can get to them by tomorrow evening, latest," the Scottish guy chimed in.

"Affirmative. Mr Field, I need you to understand this. You cannot engage them. They are war criminals of the European alliance treaty, 2030, they need to be brought in for interrogation."

"What if they attack us?"

"The war is over Mr Field. Anything you do now will be considered a vigilante crime and obstruction of justice," the American voice said calmly.

"They came to kill us!" Sam shouted hysterically just as Ryan was about to reply.

"We understand what they've done to a lot of people, including our own brothers. But do not take this lightly. We will have to enforce law and order on you."

"What about the things we've already done?" Ryan panicked. "We killed some of them."

"You were defending yourself in a time of war without proper authority, and therefore, void of the treaty. However, any action from now will result in official consequences."

Ryan exhaled heavily. "Get to us as soon as possible please."

"We'll be in contact throughout the night Mr Field. Stay safe, your war is over."

The war is over?

Dominic stood and punched the air with both fists. Doc hugged Sam in his chair, who remained silent.

Ryan leaned back and looked to the ceiling. "May I ask your name?"

"Lieutenant Adam Harper," the American replied.

"Lieutenant, when you arrive, please don't enter our grounds without our guidance. I can't explain why, but I don't want to be trialled for manslaughter."

"Understood," Harper laughed. "We've seen some lengths people have gone to to defend themselves. We'll be in contact, stay safe."

The war is over!

Ryan screamed in ecstasy. Doc and Dominic joined him in a three-man hug. "We've gotta go tell everybody!"

"You guys go." Sam stood. Other than the teary eyes, he wore a blank face. "I'll stay on look out, just in case."

"Don't you want to celebrate this?" Ryan asked.

"I do." Sam picked up his rifle. "But it's not over until they get here."

"You heard him. You can't kill anyone."

"I won't." Sam smiled through his bushy, untamed beard. "Just some warning shots if needed."

"Okay." Ryan placed his hand on his shoulder. "One final shift, yeah?"

"Yeah." Sam looked away, resting the rifle on the windowsill, gazing over Maidhill. "I'll celebrate tomorrow. I know that's what Cooper and Fergie would want."

"You promise?"

"I promise. Tell everyone the good news."

"Okay," Ryan smiled. He, Doc and Dominic took off downstairs in a rush of excitement.

———

Connor stared at his naked reflection. The twisted skin spread out from the left shoulder, covering his face and chest. He was blinded in his left eye and had his genitals warped into an unrecognisable mess. The hair on his head would never grow back, eliminating the pointless effort of shaving it once a week.

Though he didn't believe in God, he had the feeling someone from above had been watching as the bombs exploded, sparing him from most of the blast's residue and launching him into the river. He had floated unconscious for hours as the acidic mix deformed his body.

Eventually washing up ten miles away on the outskirts of Guildford with a single firearm in hand, he returned to the mansion the next night only to find half the building burned to the ground. Pikey, Ben and Callum had been left for dead in the ruins, and no one else made it back.

A defeat of this magnitude was embarrassing. Admiral wouldn't let this slide, but they would have to form a formidable plan to defeat those people once he got back to Milton Keynes. Taking the only supply van that had not been drained of fuel, he began his arduous journey back to base as his skin solidified.

Radio chatter suggested that European alliances were sending more teams to bring in Admiral, forcing the eventual abandonment of Milton Keynes and transporting the human cattle to site B.

After making it home, Connor had been given two choices: stay and help with relocating, or head back south and kill the ungrateful, liberal scum. Admiral wasn't surprised with Connor's choice. Over the course of the spring and summer, he carefully planned an intricate way to bait that prick Ryan out of his safe zone and kill him with his own hands.

Now, with some food, chloroform and a group of Termites at his disposal, the plan was failing, and he would likely die before getting inside their grounds. The pathetic idea that Father could still be alive fell apart after the radio conversation he eavesdropped in on. Just hearing the hippy prick Ryan talk about it insulted him to within every cell in his body.

Connor hadn't seen his family since the turn of the war, doubting that they were even still alive, yet this spineless arsehole had been allowed to live in peace with a wife and children of his own? He had killed hundreds of Connor's soldiers, fellow comrades and deformed his entire body.

The European allies would be here soon, and Connor could not live with himself if Ryan was left to live happily ever after.

30

The maze wavered as the wind wrapped through it. In the restaurant window, Sam's eyes were stone cold, glaring at the spot where Cooper's killer had thrown the spear from. A shot he could hit ninety-nine times out of a hundred. He scrunched his fists, hating himself for the incompetence and pathetic awareness he had shown that day.

"Snap out of it." He slapped the side of his head, pulling away from the window and immediately seeing Fergie's bloodstain on the floor. "I fucked up, I fucked up, I fucked up." He threw his hands on his head, pulling at his hair.

"Mr Field?" The radio caused Sam to jump backwards. The voice was the Scottish guys. "Ryan?"

Sam picked up the radio and said, "He's not here now."

"Who is this?"

"Sam. I'm the lookout."

"Okay, Sam. I need you to report to Ryan. Tell him we're sending some drones your way, unarmed, but they have thermal imaging. We'll be able to locate the hostiles, so you'll know where to avoid."

"Okay," Sam stuttered.

"The drones are coming from Sheffield, so they will be an hour and half minimum. Out." The radio clicked silent.

He processed the information. That is how he could find redemption.

"No update yet," Sam lied, approaching Ryan by the hot counter.

"Okay mate. Who's upstairs now?"

"Dominic's covering for an hour, then I'm on night shift." Sam did his best to appear nonchalant. Ryan would probably knock him unconscious if he knew Sam was planning something.

"Get some food then. Maisie made some beetroot bread." Ryan gleamed proudly. "It's banging!"

"Yeah, okay, I will." Sam laughed nervously and placed two rolls on a plate, despite the fact his stomach was in knots.

After taking over the night shift, Sam switched the radio back on and sat at the table with Cooper's shotgun. He dismantled it, cleaned the parts, and put it back together.

The sky gleamed through the un-boarded windows, leaving Sam to play the waiting game while watching the sunset.

———

Breakfast boomed in the cafeteria as everyone woke up earlier than usual, ready to welcome their first day of liberation. Every face expressed a smile while tucking into the raisin porridge, theorising what answers they would get about the war.

On the table nearest the hot counter, Ryan sat opposite Hamsa as they broke bread.

"Now, my friend, we have closure."

"I always feel like I brought this problem to you." Hamsa's thick Arabian accent radiated remorse.

"Don't be stupid." Ryan tore into the bread with his teeth. "You were never the cause of the situation. Ben was."

"In Islam, we're taught to forgive our enemies."

"Can you?"

"I don't think so," Hamsa sighed. "Though Allah blessed me with finding you, it was the devil who took my family."

"The devil took a lot of people, and today is their reckoning," Ryan added. "Let's remember that."

"I will." Hamsa forced a smile. "Thank you for everything you've done, for my family."

"I was never going to turn you away. I haven't lost faith in humanity," Ryan joked.

"The war brought out the worst in people," Hamsa agreed.

"Not just the war," Ryan snorted as he stood. "Remember the 2020 lockdown and all those idiots went shopping for pasta and toilet rolls?"

"I remember," Hamsa laughed.

"Nearly punched my TV every time I saw it."

Ryan tiptoed behind Sandra as he entered the kitchen. She didn't notice him till he reached the pot wash section.

"Trying to sneak up on me?" she accused.

"Yes." Ryan put his hands in the air in surrender. "Was gonna make you jump."

"Please, I had enough of that from Sam this morning."

"Sam?"

"Sped right past me as I came downstairs. That boy can run fast, even with the extra kilogram of hair hanging from his face," Sandra chuckled.

"When was this?" Ryan asked.

"Just after sunrise."

"Where did he go?"

"Towards his room. Poor lad could do with every ounce of sleep he can get," she sympathised. "He's punished himself enough."

"Yeah, he has..." Ryan trailed off before heading to the stairwell and running to the top floor. His brain was bugging him again.

Dominic sat at the eastern window, hunting rifle in hand. "What's up, boss?" He greeted Ryan with a smile, the mid-morning sun glowed orange against his dark skin.

"Your wife said Sam bolted past her this morning, was just seeing everything was okay up here?"

"Everything's cool, he left his gun up here." Dominic pointed to the far corner where Sam's rifle rested against the wall.

"Anymore contact from the lieutenant?" Ryan asked, breathing a sigh of relief.

"Not since I've been up here, boss."

"Please, stop calling me that," Ryan begged.

"I only do it to wind you up now."

"It's working."

Footsteps echoed from the stairwell before Doc entered. "Anymore contact?" he asked.

"No, Sam didn't report anything." Ryan shook his head and approached the table; the radio was still switched on.

"Where is Sam?" Doc asked. "He isn't in his room, I just passed it. The door's wide open."

"He isn't in the cafeteria either," Ryan muttered, remembering Sam seemed more off than usual the night before with the nervous laugh and stuttering. He snatched the radio from the table.

"Lieutenant, are you there?" Static. "Lieutenant? Are you there?" No response. Ryan frowned before checking the radio's dial.

"You've gotta be fucking kidding me!"

It was set to a different frequency. The handset screeched as Ryan retuned it.

"Sam, Ryan? Answer immediately. Who left your grounds?" Lieutenant Harper sounded impatient.

"This is Ryan."

"Why has someone left your grounds?" Harper yelled. "You're supposed to be inside."

"Fuck!" Ryan screamed. "What's going on?"

"Sam hasn't forwarded the message?"

"Forwarded what? What message?"

"We found the location of the hostiles, and our drone has spotted someone leaving your grounds heading in that direction."

Ryan, Dominic and Doc glanced urgently at each other.

"Where is it?"

"There's a building southeast to you, just outside the town centre. It could be a school."

Ryan punched the table. "It's a hotel, we're going after him."

"Ryan, I order you not to!"

"Until you get here, I don't fucking take orders from you." Ryan tossed the radio, grabbing his dreadlocks and pulling them up so tightly that the sweat dripped between his fingers. His heart tightened with each second. The promise of today's liberation now had a rescue mission in the way.

"I had... I had no idea he sneaked out," Dominic stuttered. "He knocked on my door to cover his shift earlier than normal."

"It's not your fault." Ryan ran into the weapons room. "Doc, we need to get him back now. He left his fucking rifle here."

"We'll be straight back, I promise." Ryan kissed Cassy on the lips as she cried.

"Please, I love you so much."

"I love you too." He hugged her tightly before kissing Alfie's forehead. Not wanting to let go after smelling her hair and feeling her body against his, he resisted the urge to cry. "Maisie, look after Mummy and your brother while I'm gone."

"I will Daddy!" She smiled in the innocence of not knowing what was really happening.

Not looking back, he met Doc by the front entrance and handed him a G36C.

"Let me go with you." Mikey grabbed Ryan's arm from behind.

"You need to be here for Jen." Ryan shook his arm away. "Lock the doors, keep everyone in the cafeteria, and arm anyone who's had training."

"Don't get caught," Mikey said, welling up.

Doc slammed the door shut and waited for someone to bolt the interior locks.

"I always hate going out," Ryan whispered, picturing his family on the other side.

"This is the first time I've been out since I've been with Steph," Doc added.

"Not returning isn't a fucking option then," Ryan said just before turning for the run-up to D1.

As they passed the rows of spinach, a noise bought their feet to a skidding halt. It bounced off the hills and buildings, tearing into both of their souls. From over a mile away, Sam's screaming for mercy buried into their ears from before suddenly cutting short, leaving Ryan with only the sound of his heart thumping in his temples.

31

The plume of smoke became visible as Ryan and Doc crouched through the car barricade, unchallenged for the first length of their mission. They held their guns tightly, pacing along the main road and checking the overgrown gardens. The space to the left opened, exposing the hotel's gravel carpark. Ryan's pulse thundered.

Sam sat tied to a chair outside the revolving doors. Behind him stood a shorter man, bald and heavily built. Ryan recognised him; the guy who poured blood over the child's body. *Connor*.

His skin was warped horrifically, the whole of his left arm twisted like crumpled paper, and his left eye was nearly welded shut behind the scarring across his face. Holding a gun to the back of Sam's head, he wagged his left index finger at Ryan and Doc.

"If I die, he dies," the raspy voice shouted out. "It's your choice to save him."

Doc pointed to the balcony above the front entrance. Twenty or more Termites stood armed with spears, all aiming at Sam.

"Lower your weapons, and I'll give you a chance to save him." A sadistic grin spread across Connor's mutilated face.

Slowly edging into the driveway, Sam's injuries became more apparent. Both eye sockets were busted, a mixture of saliva and blood hung from his beard, and his breaths were short and laboured.

"I thought you'd be bringing more," Connor said, looking up the road.

"How'd you know we were coming?" Doc asked.

"Radio." He gently pulled the device from his back pocket. "Put your guns on the ground."

"No fucking way," Ryan growled.

"I haven't got time for this shit," Connor laughed. "I'm very aware the army is coming. So, lower your weapons, and I will give you a chance to let your man live. If not, I'll kill him, or they will." He nodded to the balcony behind him.

"He's got nothing to lose. This is our only way," Doc whispered.

Ryan's brain raced; his fingers began to cramp. "How do we know you won't kill us?" he shouted.

Connor rolled his eyes, then let out a childish groan and unloaded the clip from his pistol. The magazine was empty, and the only bullet he had was in the chamber.

"I've seen you guys shoot," Connor said. "You're not bad for amateurs. I'll even let you keep your guns by your feet, as a sign of goodwill."

"Don't do it," Sam spat the sentence behind a wince. He'd suffered a chest injury too. Ryan realised they'd have to get him back to Mikey urgently.

"Okay." He raised his hands. "Guns by our feet."

"Guns by your feet," Connor agreed before turning to the hotel. "Hey, bring out some chairs for our guests!"

The revolving door turned with two Termites pouring out, carrying two beaten armchairs and placing them behind Ryan and Doc.

"Please." Connor motioned for them to sit. "Termites! Lower your weapons."

"Yes, Connor," they all answered in unison.

Ryan hesitated. *Think!* He could easily reach down, shoot Connor, and take out most of the Termites once they'd stood at ease. He sat in the chair, trying to disguise his intention. "Okay, how can we take Sam back with us?"

"I'll tell you, now I've got you where I need you," Connor flashed a wink with his better right eye.

As Ryan felt the urge to dive forward, he heard the burst of gas next to him, the water balloon tatters shot across his eyes before the sweet smell of chloroform invaded his nose, and everything faded to black.

———

"Wake up!" Connor's fingers clicked in Ryan's face.

The headache so was so severe that his vision blurred with every minor movement.

"I was planning to use the chloroform once I was inside your place," Connor explained. "But with your man leading you here, I had to improvise."

Ryan turned his head left. Doc was bound and unconscious in his chair.

"Hey!" Connor grabbed Ryan's jaw, turning his head forward. "I know I can't outrun the army. They've got fucking thermal drones."

Ryan noticed the fire in front of him. *How long have I been out?*

Two dismembered arms sat over the open fire, roasting on a mesh fencing.

"I promised I'd give you a chance to save this guy, you also have a chance to save that specky dork beside you." Connor pointed the gun between Doc and Sam. "I don't know if you'll want to save them though. I mean, one-armed cripples on a vineyard, what good are they?"

Ryan slowly absorbed every word as his head span wildly, like a hallucination.

"One-armed cripples?" he whispered, shaking his head, continuously blinking to try and force his visual clarity to return. With his brain clearing, his eyes met a sight that killed him inside. An unconscious Sam, left arm missing from halfway up the humerus. He had a rough tourniquet attempting to keep the blood in as it puddled around the base of the chair. Ryan flung his head left. Blood spread out under Doc, where his left arm would've been.

Gravity pulled down on his stomach, feeling like his throat would cave in at the unbearable sight of his amputated friends. Hatred surfaced behind the nausea. Ryan attempted to stand, only to discover he was tied down at the wrists and ankles.

"They screamed like schoolgirls," Connor chuckled, poking one of the charred arms. "Taking off a limb normally isn't that slow, but you burned all my butcher's stuff back at the mansion."

"You're going to fucking die!" Ryan roared, staring straight into his eyes.

"Maybe, but first you have to make a choice," Connor said calmly. "Like when you chose to not hand your mud rats over, and when you chose to set all of us on fire."

There was nothing that Ryan could say to turn the tables. All the desperation in the world could not alter the fact that he was not in control, and he knew it.

"But now I get to kill you." Connor smiled with his distorted mouth. "Or your two friends. Choose."

The words stunned Ryan. He was now staring at death's door. He would never sacrifice a friend for himself—the choice was easy.

"Well?" Connor raised his gun. "Who's it gonna be? You, or your two friends? I doubt they'll taste as good as your girl."

Cassy's bright eyes flashed in his mind, her perfect smile and laughter, and the way she held both children at once. She was the brightness in Ryan's darkness. The thought of this man touching her skin caused his adrenaline to surge inside his wrath.

"You fucking touch her and I'll rip your soul out your throat, you child-killing, cannibal, arsehole cunt!" Ryan bellowed from every molecule in his body. Saliva drooled off his chin, gripping the armrests with so much hate that his fingernails nearly split open.

"Well, for you to do that," Connor said smiling and aiming his gun at the side of Sam's head, "you'd have to be alive. I guess you've made your choice."

Ryan realised what he'd just done.

"No! Me!"

"Sorry, we'll have to accept your first answer," Connor winked, pulling the trigger.

"No!" Ryan watched, paralysed.

The right side of Sam's head exploded outwards, his body flinging violently out of the chair before thudding to the bloody gravel. His head twisted underneath his shoulder, facing away and exposing the gaping exit wound on the side of his skull.

Spears soared from the balcony, piercing the air in slow motion before sinking into Doc's chest. Shattering ribs echoed in Ryan's ears. The chair toppled backwards, impaling Doc to the driveway.

In an instant, with no chance to plea or any last words, Ryan's world had two more beloved people taken away. The silence enveloped him. Whether he'd put them in danger or not, it was Ryan's angry outburst that had killed them.

"I didn't choose this!" Ryan screamed, burying his head by his knees. "I didn't choose them!"

"Yeah, you did." Connor calmly patted him on the back before removing a spear from Doc's body. "Now you have to live with it."

32

Tears, snot and vomit hung from Ryan's lips as he desperately tried to convince himself that none of it was real. That the scene in front was a nightmare. Hours blurred into a never-ending stretch of horror. Doc and Sam had been hacked to pieces and thrown on the fire to cook as the blood pooled around Ryan's feet.

Connor knelt in front of him, a bowl of meat in his right hand. "They told me the way in through your emergency exit," he smiled. "I did say they screamed like schoolgirls."

"This isn't real." Ryan shook his head, begging himself to wake up.

"Oh, it's very real," Connor chuckled. "Set the canister off where you tied Paul up, then it's every first left and second right isn't it?"

Ryan shot his head up. *They do know the way in.*

"That's an expression I won't forget!" Connor slapped his thigh in amusement. "That's the beauty of being human—emotion."

This can't be happening... "Strange isn't it?" Connor looked back at the cannibal barbeque. "We all have faces and personalities, yet when we're treated like livestock, we look no different to beef."

The Termites tore ruthlessly into whole limbs, pulling flesh away from the bone like a pack of wolves fighting over the biggest piece.

Ryan couldn't tell who's leg it was. Doc and Sam's bodies were now unrecognisable while they were devoured.

"You see, I was planning on feeding them to you to let you experience what we feel," Connor leered into his face. "Having realised you're too much of a good boy, you'd kill yourself before having to hunt another human, wouldn't you?"

Ryan vomited into his lap.

"You found out about the disease, didn't you?" Connor asked, chewing with an open mouth. "Did Jake tell you?"

The ability to speak was void.

"I don't care." Connor shrugged dismissively. "Having the extra physical power from the reaction isn't the highlight of this affliction." He stuck the bowl under Ryan's nose. "It's the taste beneath that makes this all worth it. All those extra fear hormones, the lactic acid—it's like a seasoning."

Ryan inhaled the odour, bringing another retching fit.

"You have a weak stomach, don't you?" Connor looked at him with a fake pity. "Don't be disgusted, your man with the glasses, he doesn't taste half bad. Nice twang to him, like citrus."

The Termites finished the eight limbs in succession before tossing the bones on the floor like they were chicken wing scraps.

"I hear you lot are vegetarians? Ironic way to die."

Ryan didn't have the strength to say anything. His world had exploded from the inside.

"You can sit there and cry." Connor tipped the bowl in his mouth, chewing briefly before swallowing the lot down. "Either way, I want you awake for this. To hear what I do to your people, including your girl and children."

Ryan twitched, trying to release his wrist grip. Connor's hand thrust forward, grabbing his chin tightly. "This is all your doing, you fucking prick. Now I'm going to take what's yours."

Standing and clicking his fingers, all the Termites stood to attention before he called them. "This is our last battle. You fight with me, you will be rewarded in the afterlife by Allah!"

The tranquil state faded from the Termites' faces. Simultaneously, they snarled through their teeth; flesh and blood still stuck in their mouths. Their eyes were so wide that it was hard to make out anything other than the white, clouded out by the synthetic power they felt. Muscles tensed, veins bulged, and fists clenched as they marched past Ryan and onto the road.

Connor strode behind them, picking up a shotgun from where Sam had been sitting. It was Cooper's shotgun.

"Nice piece of hardware," he said examining it. "I'll use this for your family." Ryan stared back, dead inside. Connor held his hands out innocently. "All is fair in love and war."

The first gas canister exploded in the distance, followed by the recognisable gunfire from Dominic's hunting rifle. Ryan's clothes stuck to him, matted down with sweat, blood and vomit. The smoke billowed around, burning his eyes. Panic gripped all over as he tried furiously to release his bound legs.

"Come on!" he screamed, inhaling the ashes, breathing in his friends' remains. His body weakened, overcome by the fear that coursed through each artery.

"Cassy!"

With a defiant last attempt to kick his leg free, the chair fell backwards, landing with a hard thud. His throat filled with phlegm and saliva; tears ran down the side of his cheeks. Struggling for breath and bound to the chair, the smoke strangled his lungs. Every surge of raw emotion ate at his energy. He began to slip away from the world. One final breath and everything faded to black again.

———

"Sir!" The Scottish accent rang like a bell in Ryan's ears. He felt two fingers on the side of his neck. "We got a live civilian!"

"Get him off that chair!"

"Yes, sir!"

Ryan's arms and legs dropped free before someone rolled him onto his side. He coughed up blackened mucus.

"What's your name?" an American voice asked.

"Ryan," he sputtered.

"Ryan Field?"

Only able to nod in return, he forced his eyes open to look at the soldier that stood above him.

"Help him to his feet, private."

"Yes, sir."

A strong hand picked him up by the left arm before resting him over their shoulder.

"Help my family!" Ryan coughed. "Please help my people."

His vision started to unblur. The American before him had a clean, ginger buzzcut, wore grey coveralls and khaki boots. The man was a couple of inches shorter than himself.

"How many were there?" Lieutenant Harper asked.

"Twenty." Ryan spat out a large ball of black saliva. "At least."

Two loud gunshots rang out. He saw a plume of smoke coming from his home's direction.

"NO!" Ryan dropped to the ground by the chair looking for his G36C.

"Private, secure that weapon." Harper dragged Ryan away.

"Yes, sir!"

"Ryan, follow me." The lieutenant led him to the road before lifting him onto something hard. His feet dangling down as he sat upright, watching the hotel starting to move away. The private jumped onto the platform and sat to Ryan's left, making sure the G36C was out of his reach.

"Sir, barricade ahead," a voice shouted from behind.

Lieutenant Harper grabbed Ryan's right arm. "How do we get through Ryan?"

"There's a blue Ford Escort and two red Nissan Micra's. They can be pushed back, brakes are cut," Ryan mumbled while looking around, establishing he was in the back of a military troop carrier.

Harper nodded for the Scottish private to move the mentioned vehicles.

Ryan saw his G36C strapped to the interior wall, tightened above two pistols on a rack. He'd never reach his weapon before the lieutenant prevented it.

The truck edged forward before turning right, the Scottish private joining them in the back again.

"Can we speed up?" Ryan slammed his palm on the metal surface.

"We're gonna get them and save your family Ryan, I promise you. Where's Sam?" Harper asked.

Ryan's head dropped, remembering his body flying to the side, the blood and skull tainting the air.

"Fuck, I'm sorry," The lieutenant banged his fist on the metal partition behind them. "Corporal, let's move!"

"Yes, sir."

The vehicle picked up speed along with Ryan's heart rate, his hands seizing up. Both soldiers checked their weapons. The gunfire grew louder as they passed the petrol station.

"Twenty seconds!" the voice in front shouted.

"Roger that."

The vehicle slowed outside the sewage plant before coming to a standstill.

"How do we get it in?" Harper asked.

"I'll have to show you."

"Okay. Private, cover our rear,"

"Yes, sir."

"Ryan, with me," Harper jumped down, motioning for Ryan to follow him.

He nodded, waiting for the private to circle behind the vehicle, then shot his left arm behind and grabbed for a pistol. *Got it.*

An array of bodies littered the road. Ryan counted twelve. Dominic and whoever else on the top floor had done part of a job for now. Part of another Termite's body melted inside C10, sacrificing themselves to set the trap off.

Connor's body had yet to be seen on the panicked run through the emergency route. The smoke emerging from inside adding to the urgency.

"Left here," Ryan huffed, running between the two soldiers as they emerged out of D1.

Both soldiers stood either side, sweeping left to right along the east border before they started moving down the driveway. The horses' barn was on fire. Ryan saw Mikey and Jen desperately trying to put it out. Rich watched from behind them, checking all directions with an assault rifle sweeping the area around them.

Ryan ran faster down the driveway, nearly tripping over a body. It was Hamsa. "Oh, no, no, no."

An open wound to Hamsa's midriff exposed the intestines. His eyes were wide and lifeless, blood spattered against his tanned skin. "I'm sorry, so sorry, so sorry."

Mikey chucked buckets of water over the barn as Jen started opening the doors, helping the horses get outside.

"Ryan!" Dominic shouted from the restaurant window. "There's one more, dressed like a henchman!"

Connor.

"Where?" Ryan wiped his face, trying to conceal his last-minute plan.

Dominic pointed his rifle to the vegetable patch right next to where they stood.

Harper faced the wall of corn, raising his weapon.

"This is Lieutenant Harper of the European alliance division 14. We have orders to take you in alive. Come out, surrender yourself, and you won't be shot."

"Well, that's no fun!" Connor's voice croaked straight away, emerging from the tall crops.

"Hands on your head!" Harper barked.

"You're supposed to shoot me!"

"We're not out of our brain like you, you fucking ham doughnut!" the Scottish guy taunted.

"You won't take me alive!"

"I agree." Ryan stormed forward, pulling the stolen pistol out of his joggers and pressing the barrel to Connor's forehead.

The yelling in the background faded. Ryan fell into the back of his head again, the same feeling when he killed Ben. The visions blinded him from the world.

He saw Connor eating Doc, licking the juices off his fingers. Cooper's smile shattered into thousands of pieces. Fergie drowning in a pool of blood, and Sam failing to save him as he reached out in despair. He remembered Hamsa's recovery, only to see him shot down by the vile animal who stood before him, laughing in his face.

The anger begged to kill this man. The final piece of Father's puzzle, invading their safety and happiness, dousing his world in a cloud of fear.

"Don't do it, Ryan," Mikey's voice pleaded through the hate. Everyone had come outside, standing behind and witnessing this final standoff.

The corners of Ryan's eyes turned black; his mouth dropped as the realisation came over him. He'd sacrifice his freedom to kill this man. *I'm a monster.*

"Ryan, drop your weapon!" Harper commanded.

A soft wailing caught his attention; an infant. His child. He was a dad to two beautiful children, and yet to ask Cassy to marry him.

You're not a monster to them. Some light returned to his vision.

"Do it," Connor smirked with his twisted lips, looking over the crowd that had formed behind Ryan. "I'll tell them how your friends died."

"What? No!" Steph cried.

Ryan felt the anger return into his body, pressing the gun so hard to Connor that he voluntarily dropped to his knees, eyes wide, welcoming death.

"Don't do it!" Mikey begged.

Is this all I'm good at? Torn between avenging everything that happened and being the man he wanted to be, his trigger finger tensed. *The pain won't go away. Everyone'll be safer with you still here.*

Connor's evil smile beamed, taunting Ryan that he'd killed two of his friends and would've happily killed everyone here.

Steph will need you.

"Do it!" Connor roared.

Your family needs you.

"Fuck you," Ryan whispered, closing his eyes. He raised the gun, battling every instinct and turned away, tossing it to the ground.

Connor immediately bolted for him. Harper was quicker to the trigger, catching him with a quick burst to the thigh, sending him flailing to the ground. Both soldiers pinned him down, handcuffing him from behind.

"You all deserve to be livestock, you're swine like the Muslims!" he roared. "This isn't over!"

Ryan shut out the noise, hurrying over to Steph who crumpled to the ground. "I'm sorry." His eyes welled up. "I'm so fucking sorry." He hugged her close as she bawled into his shoulder.

"There's more pain coming for the rest of you, I promise you that, you fucking fairies!" Connor laughed before being struck in the side of the head by Harper's gun.

Ryan held onto his sister; her grip so tight that the nails dug through his jumper. Kissing the top of her head, repeatedly, he told himself it was better to be grieving with her than leave her on her own.

I'm sorry Doc! He felt all her pain, still resisting the gun calling out to end Connor's life, though his soul screamed at him to do so.

33

The nightmares became Ryan's alarm clock for the next month. He woke up screaming, soaked in sweat and sometimes his own urine, fuelled by the imaginary smell of burning flesh. He'd shower furiously to get rid of the stench, scrubbing so hard that it would draw blood, leaving scratch marks all over his malnourished body.

Cassy would take Maisie and Alfie into his night shift bedroom, preventing them from hearing their father claw at his skin in self-loathing. Once the crying stopped, he would then fake taking breakfast back upstairs before throwing it in the bin. Several more weeks would pass before his appetite returned and the nightmares finally started to calm down.

He brought food to Steph every lunchtime, who had buried herself into Doc's work, holding onto anything that reminded her of him. Absent from most conversation, she became so distant that Lyndon started performing night watches to give her space.

Ryan retrieved the small amount of Doc and Sam's remains on his own, not letting anyone see the true horror of what had happened at the hotel. The few of their bones that remained, and Hamsa, had been buried in the northwest corner with the other graves.

Rich had crafted a large, wooden headstone, running along the head end of the eight graves, dedicated to everyone who was lost since the Termites arrived.

The horses survived the stable fire. It had started when a ricochet from Connor's shooting had exploded a fire extinguisher and ignited the dry grass. Mikey repaired the roofing, ordering Jen not to come outside until she had given birth, which she ignored and helped with repainting instead.

Night shifts were all performed from the top floor, and until Lieutenant Harper returned and the area was rescanned by drones, no one was to leave the grounds.

———

Sam's pocket watch glowed in Ryan's hand as he sat on the bed, patiently counting down the minutes until midday.

Everyone had mourned while trying to get back to their normal lives. Now they wanted answers for what was happening in the world, and more importantly, if they were still in danger.

"They're here, baby," Cassy announced through the bedroom door.

"Okay." Ryan ran the towel through his hair and pulled on a black vest and blue jogging bottoms. "Are you going to bring little man to meet them?" He looked in the cot. Alfie lay fast asleep in a bright blue onesie.

"Get our answers first. That's what we all need." She held Masie's hand as she entered the room. They were both dressed in blue jeans and white jumpers, their hair tied back. Apart from their hair and eyes, they looked identical.

"I'll get all the answers I can." Ryan wiped a tear, still grateful that he had them.

Today was needed. He couldn't bear any more days of fear suffocating his family and friends.

. . .

"This is an astonishing set-up," Harper complimented, gazing around the cafeteria.

"Thank you," Ryan replied, offering him a seat.

"Running water?"

"Running water, electricity, soap, washing powder, toothpaste."

"Very impressive."

Mikey emerged from the medical corridor with the Scottish soldier. He was smaller like Mikey, though much more chiselled. He sported black spiked hair and a scraggly beard. A pair of aviators hid his eyes. "Sir, this place is fucking unreal!" he shouted loudly.

Mikey sat next to Ryan, and the private sat next to his commanding officer.

"What's happened with Connor?" Ryan said, getting straight to the point.

"I'll tell you what I can from a classified perspective." Harper brushed his ginger hair back. "He's being interrogated in Rennes. He's not cooperating, so we've reduced his food rations."

"Started to lose his mind?" Mikey asked.

"Everyone under Admiral is a fruit loop!" the Scottish guy exclaimed. "And this bald guy's a few nuggets short of a fucking happy meal!"

Ryan stared back, unamused.

"We haven't been formally introduced." The private stuck his hand out. "Private Chris Drinker."

"Ryan." He shook Drinker's hand. "Who's Admiral?"

"The big man, Captain Jeffries's boss," Harper answered.

"Father wasn't the top guy?"

"No, Admiral was his commanding officer."

"Are there more Termites?"

"Yes, but not here, and that's the information that Connor is holding back on."

Mikey rubbed his forehead, and Ryan tensed up. This wasn't the news they wanted, but knowing the threat wasn't close by was better than nothing.

"How did Father have access to fuel and fresh cigarettes?" Ryan asked.

Harper and Drinker shot each other a look of apprehension. "I can't answer those until Connor talks because we don't have definitive answers ourselves. Once we know, and it's not a breach of classification, I'll tell you."

"Is our area secure?" Mikey interjected.

"There's potential wildlife threats, including packs of feral dogs and some wild cats. Looks like they escaped from a zoo," Harper reported. "From what we could see on the drones sweep, the Kent/Sussex/Surrey area is void of human life."

Ryan and Mikey both exhaled in relief.

"What about the war?"

"I'll tell you what I can," Harper started. "China and the Russian/Islamic coalition are now at war with each other. It was something to do with a disagreement about other biological weapons."

"There's more man-made diseases?"

"From what we've heard," Harper nodded. "China evacuated its personnel from America, flooded Yellowstone Park, and detonated two nukes either side of it. It killed ninety percent of the Russian/Islamic coalition who were stationed there during the occupation."

"Jesus fucking Christ," Mikey gasped.

"The blast was so loud that border forces heard it in Panama."

"What's Yellowstone?" Ryan asked, oblivious to what this all meant.

"A volcano in Wyoming, closer to Canada than Mexico," Harper answered. "Largest magma chamber on the planet."

"The whole of the central states are buried under ash, rock and other material," Drinker explained.

"Jesus," Ryan said, shaking his head.

"The eruption, or explosion, whichever you want to call it, cooled the planet's climate, apart from west Europe, which is still receiving excess heat over the Atlantic," Harper replied. "Our scientists say this is what's been causing the severe weather changes."

"And the sunsets?"

"That too, unfortunately, we haven't got full data on how it's affected the rest of the globe."

Ryan and Mikey nodded, at least they had an answer for the weather.

"Russia and the Islamic coalition withdrew their soldiers from the European front, calling for a ceasefire and peace deal with us. In the meantime, they're diverting all their forces to attack China from over the eastern European borders," Harper continued. "Our own forces have pushed out as far as central Poland and northern Italy, hoping to secure a new European border."

"That means you can start rebuilding in Europe?" Ryan asked. "And here?"

"Yes, now that we know Admiral isn't on the British mainland," Harper nodded. "We know the size of their group. None of our satellites are picking up thermal images for a populace of that size."

"They've left the country?" Mikey's eyes widened with hope.

"Yes, they knew we were coming and have gone into hiding. We think they made it over to Ireland, or maybe even Iceland."

"Please confirm for my people," Ryan begged. His fingers tapped the table rapidly like Doc's used to. "We're safe from any war or danger?"

"Yes."

"Oh my God." Ryan leaned forward and laughed in ecstatic relief. Mikey hugged him. "I've gotta organise a meeting. You can break the news!"

"We'll supply the news if you supply the wine!" Harper stood and shook hands with both Ryan and Mikey.

"Deal!"

"Free wine and a meet and greet? Sign me up, sir!" Drinker joked, slapping the table with enthusiasm.

"We have some spare rooms made up for you two and your other men. Your vehicle will be safe across the road." Ryan led them to the hot counter, offering them a bottle of water.

"Thank you," Harper smiled. "When do you want to hold this meeting?"

"As soon as possible," Mikey said, running outside to gather all the crop pickers from their afternoon shift.

———

Ryan was standing at the graves when he heard the cheer erupt from inside the winery. The news of the war ending was just broken to everyone. He looked up to the sky and smiled, tears of joy streaming down his face.

"We're free, we're free now." It hurt to look at the names of everyone who'd been murdered over the past year. "I wish you could've been here for this."

"You saved everyone," Doc spoke to Ryan's left.

He felt the tug of war between his happiness and guilt, knowing the voice wasn't real.

"I'm so sorry," he cried.

It broke his heart, not just losing his friends, but the fact that he hadn't given his sister closure. Whether it was the right choice or not, it killed him.

"You're not a monster."

Ryan tried to figure out who's voice that was until he realised it sounded like his own. He'd said it out loud. *I'm not a monster.*

"I don't have to be that person anymore," he whispered, looking at the graves and feeling everyone smiling down on him from above. They all knew he'd done more than enough to keep everyone safe.

There was no more war, no more threat, no more reasons to give into anger. The weight he'd felt constantly for six years was lifted off his shoulders. *I don't have to fight anymore.*

Ryan wiped the tears away and jogged back to the winery, eager to see his family and celebrate the end of their war, and the war within himself. Though the nightmares would never leave, the darkness was expelled.

"I'm coming Cassy." He laughed then added, "And you're fucking marrying me!"

ACKNOWLEDGMENTS

Wow, where do I start? It's been such a long and winding journey to get to this stage.

I'll start from the beginning. A massive thank you to all the first stage beta readers who volunteered to read the very first draft. That in itself was a massive steppingstone for me and gave me the confidence to finish this book.

Nastassia Carroll and Lucy Cordery, the lovelies to my lovelies! Your continued feedback and notes have proven invaluable. I'm not just grateful to know you both personally, but to have you involved in future projects is an absolute Godsend. I can't wait for our next wine and video chat night!

The editors involved during the process. Ericka S. Baldwin, CJ, and Abby Hale. For someone with my lack of understanding and education in literature, to have your support and knowledge throughout the self-publishing route has been beyond vital. (Though you're probably cringing while reading this part as i haven't ran it past anybody!). I've learned so much about storytelling and how to express it in a correct manner. I still have a long way to go, but I'll get better with each step, and I look forward to working with you all again.

The artist! The man who magically once healed my busted ankle by scoring our charity teams' first ever goal, Dean Gaida. Like Nas and Lucy, knowing you is a personal gift, and having you on board is an absolute bonus. Your incredible, artistic talent is only matched by your vision. Buddy, I'm so grateful to work with you on this, future novels, and our cheeky, secret venture (wink.)

Michael Lewis Cunningham. Bro, I think I would've finished this book eventually, but this mindset you've given me has helped take it to a level that I doubt anyone thought possible. We're definitely having a free kick session when I'm over stateside.

Ryan Hunter. If it wasn't for that extremely disturbing conversation on a dead night in the kitchen, I never would have thought up the ending to this book. It gave me the vision and determination to finish this. I owe you.

Michael Morris, my gobshite little brother. Having you for the photoshoots and bringing characters to life is something I never would've pictured us doing, and I'll never forget it. Also thank you for those early morning calls during lockdown, our chats always put stuff into perspective.

My close family and friends who have supported my idea since the get-go. Always by my side, always keeping me in check and guiding me to the right path. We've survived a lot to get here, and this is just the start of it. When looking back at the black cloud that dominated all my adult life, I can proudly say, we won.

Anyone who's followed this journey via Facebook or Instagram, whether you liked a post or commented, showing any form of interest in what i was doing, truly, thank you.

And finally, Edita. When we first met, we said we wanted a relationship that encourages each other, to grow as people. I don't know how much more of that we could've done. We came into each other's lives at the right time, and we've done what we said we would. Your encouragement, your belief in me, and your willingness to push yourself outside your comfort zone for me and what I was doing, i've never known a love like it. All your photo work, help exporting and downloading stuff that my brain still struggles to understand and the extra finances when i had a tight month. I wouldn't be writing this page right now, with the broad smile and confidence on my face if it wasn't for you. Thank you Mooplesnoot.

To everyone who got this far reading the book. Thank you. I hope you enjoyed it, and I can't wait to release more to you over the years.

DANIEL MUNRO

This is normally where you find out about the author. What they do in their spare time, where they live, and so on.

I've got a unique moment to help people here, so I'm going to take it.

If you're someone who is struggling mentally, or you know someone who is struggling, I just want you to know that you're not alone and things can get better.

This book that you're holding, was the beginning of my fight back against the mental health issues that I've had since the late 90's. I've been fortunate enough to come out the other side stronger, though it has taken over two decades to fight these voices, I still won. You can too.

There is help out there, and many people who care.

At times it can feel lonely, like the whole world is against you, and I get that. I just want you to know that you're stronger than you know, and I believe in you.

This book is my proof of that. If you had said to me in 2017 when i started this project, that I would've gotten this far... no way I would have believed you.

If you want to know more about my journey, or you want to reach out, you can on my Instagram.

Thank you for taking the time to read this, take care.

Daniel Munro

 instagram.com/author_danielmunro